AXES
& O'S

Also by Kayla Grosse

Praise for

AXES & O'S

"Kayla gets it! *Axes & O's* has everything I crave in a good MMF: blazing hot spice, beautifully complex characters, and kink that's both hot and heartfelt. And can't forget that broody lumberjack. I ATE this one up."

—Sara Cate, *USA Today* bestselling author of *Praise*

"Sweet, seductive, and hella kinky. Kayla knows exactly how to make readers swoon endlessly and blush profusely, with an extra helping of lumbersnack contained within these pages to devour. *Axes & O's* is an adventure in the woods not to be missed."   —Elliott Rose, author of *Chasing the Wild*

"Steamy, snowed-in, and deeply tender—*Axes & O's* isn't just about the heat (though there's plenty of that). Kayla has a way of blending raw emotion with irresistible spice, and this one is no exception."

—Bailey Hannah, *USA Today* bestselling
author of *Change of Hart*

"Surrounded by snow and undeniable desire, Kayla crafts a thrilling tale where every moment is heated, intense, and full of emotion. With sizzling chemistry, a touch of humor, and a unique hero to keep things interesting, this book delivers all the thrills of an unforgettable winter romance."

—M.A. Wardell, author of *Teacher of the Year*

AXES
& O'S

KAYLA GROSSE

FOREVER

New York Boston

Forever
Hachette Book Group
1290 Avenue of the Americas, New York, NY 10104
read-forever.com
@readforeverpub

Originally published by Kayla Grosse in 2024

First Forever Trade Paperback Edition: January 2026

Forever is an imprint of Grand Central Publishing. The Forever name and logo are registered trademarks of Hachette Book Group, Inc.

The publisher is not responsible for websites (or their content) that are not owned by the publisher.

The Hachette Speakers Bureau provides a wide range of authors for speaking events. To find out more, go to hachettespeakersbureau.com or email HachetteSpeakers@hbgusa.com.

Forever books may be purchased in bulk for business, educational, or promotional use. For information, please contact your local bookseller or the Hachette Book Group Special Markets Department at special.markets@hbgusa.com.

Library of Congress Cataloging-in-Publication Data has been applied for.

ISBNs: 9781538780589 (Trade Paperback); 9781538780596 (Ebook)

Printed in the United States of America

LSC-C

Printing 1, 2025

This book is dedicated to anyone who's ever looked at a person in flannel holding an axe and said, "Yeah, I'd let them split me in half."

Author's Note

This book is a high heat, MMF, vanilla businessman meets "lumbersnacks" snowed-in holiday romance that's meant to be a fun escape from reality. If that's all you need to know, skip this note, and go to Chapter One. If you'd like to know more about what's in store for you, here's what you can expect inside these pages:

- Toy play

- SO much oral

- Dominance/submission

- Bondage/rough sex

- Polyamorous relationships

- Primal play

- Fisting

- Sword crossing

- Humiliation/derogatory language

- Light discussion of the foster care system and PTSD

If you'd like a full list of tropes and content warnings, please visit my website http://www.kaylagrosse.com.

Now, if you're still here, please enjoy my Fox, Little Lamb, and their Wolf.

Xoxo,
Kayla

Morgan's Mulled Wine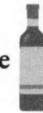

Ingredients:

1 bottle of red wine (750ml, something fruity like Merlot or Zinfandel)
1 orange, sliced
2 tablespoons of honey or sugar (adjust to taste)
3 whole cloves
2 cinnamon sticks
2 star anise
1/4 cup brandy (optional add for an extra zing)
1 teaspoon of whole allspice berries (optional)
1/2 teaspoon of whole black peppercorns (optional)
1/4 teaspoon of grated nutmeg (optional)
Additional orange slices, cinnamon sticks, or star anise for garnish

Instructions:

Pour the bottle of red wine into a large pot or saucepan and add the sliced orange, honey or sugar, cloves, cinnamon sticks, star anise, and any optional spices (allspice, peppercorns, nutmeg) to the wine. Warm the mixture over low to medium heat. Stir occasionally to dissolve the honey or sugar. Be careful not to let the wine boil, as this will cook off the alcohol and can create a bitter taste.

Once the wine is warm and fragrant, reduce the heat to low, and let it simmer for at least 15–20 minutes. The longer it simmers, the more the flavors will meld together. You can let it simmer for up to an hour for a richer flavor.

If using, stir in the brandy just before serving, then strain the mulled wine to remove the spices and orange slices. Pour into mugs or heatproof glasses, then garnish with additional orange slices and cinnamon sticks. If you want to get fancy, use dried orange slices! Serve warm.

♫ Axes & O's Unhinged Playlist ♫

"Animals" Maroon 5
"Lithium" Nirvana
"Fuck You" CeeLo Green
"White Christmas" Frank Sinatra
"Christmas Eve/Sarajevo 12/24" Trans-Siberian Orchestra
"Meet Your Master" Nine Inch Nails
"Mount Everest" Labrinth
"Such a Whore (Stellular Remix)" JVLA
"Pillowtalk" ZAYN
"Hungry Eyes" Eric Carmen
"Closer" Nine Inch Nails
"The Happiest Christmas Tree" Nat King Cole
"Addicted" JON VINYL
"Play with Me" Rendezvous At Two
"Inside Out" Eve 6
"At Last" Etta James
"Reunited" Peaches & Herb
"Surrender" Shelly Peled
"Have Yourself A Merry Little Christmas" Sam Smith
"The Bad Touch" Bloodhound Gang

AXES
& O'S

CHAPTER ONE

The Hunter

I LICK MY CHAPPED lips, the bite of frigid winter air freezing the fresh saliva as my heart thuds in my chest. The night is eerily quiet, the newly fallen snow dampening the sounds of Mother Nature, requiring me to call upon every ounce of training ingrained in my body so I have an element of surprise when I catch my prize.

Snap!

The heated blood pumping through my veins rushes straight to my cock, and the corners of my mouth tug up.

Gotcha, little lamb.

I lighten my footsteps and even out my breathing, turning my head languidly toward the origin of the sound. She'd been doing so well until that little mess up. Now she's caught my attention, and it will not waver.

I'm a predator, a cunning fox ready to devour his meal, and she doesn't stand a chance.

Chapter Two

Nathan

"Nathan, did you get my email?"

My head pops up to meet the blank stare of my manager, Kathy. She's got on an oversized white sweater that blends in with her pale skin. If she was standing against a white wall, you'd miss her. Scratch that. You'd see her red lipstick and that's it. Just red lips. Big, giant, bright-red lips that, when opened, micromanage the shit out of me.

"Which one?" The snide question is out of my mouth before I can stop it. Those stained red lips press together, and I swear the pronounced blue vein on her forehead pulses like a worm.

"The one about the Newman presentation. I need the entire slide deck proofed again. It has typos on it."

My jaw ticks. There aren't any typos on that fucking slide deck. I've proofed it near a million times. "I've gone over it, Kathy. I promise, it's good to go."

"You didn't open my last email from four p.m."

An exasperated sigh catches in my chest as I stare at the woman I'm certain is the devil in disguise. Her muddy-brown eyes are narrowed, and she doesn't blink as she waits for my answer. Come to think of it, I don't think I've ever seen her blink. Maybe she's a robot.

"You sent a different email this morning about the deck," I reiterate. "I looked it over. I promise—it's good to go."

Her lips press together so tightly, all I can see is a thin red line. The action only makes the vein in her forehead pulse harder. I understand my pushback could get me fired or at least warrant a warning. But I'm beyond caring. I'm tired, I'm overworked, and I should be on Christmas vacation by now. But no—instead, I'm still here, stuck with Kathy the Grinch until she lets me leave.

She crosses her arms over her chest. "But you never emailed it back to me for a final proof. That's what the email was about, and I want to see it. The slide deck needs to be perfect, and you know that only *I* can find double spaces. You had two the last time I checked."

My hand clenches around my mouse. I'm convinced this woman puts in double spaces just so she can chastise me. I was born after typewriter conventions were a thing, so I don't put double spaces after periods. Not to mention, I told her verbally in passing that the deck was proofed and ready to go. But apparently she wasn't listening. Or she was, and she's just doing this to be a jerk.

"I swear, Kathy. The slide deck is perfect. I did my job. It's done."

Her high heel taps on the floor like a petulant child, and I think I can see steam coming out of her head. "I'm your manager, Nathan," she huffs. "You do what I ask. Please send me the current deck so I can look it over. You know I need to approve the changes."

I lower my gaze from her heated one and glance at my watch. It's after six and three days before Christmas. I had wanted to get on the road early to avoid holiday traffic, but clearly that's not happening.

Kathy's still standing near my desk with her arms crossed and an expectant look on her face. For a split second, I debate whether I should keep antagonizing her or not, but I'd rather get the hell out of here before she finds something else for me to do. I exhale a breath and open my email, finding the one she sent at four p.m. among a slew of other emails from people asking me for stupid things that they 100 percent could do on their own.

With a few more clicks, I attach the deck and send it to her. "Okay, you have it."

Kathy doesn't say thank you. Instead, she stalks back to her office without another word. I grit my teeth and take out my phone to text my older sister, Lindsey.

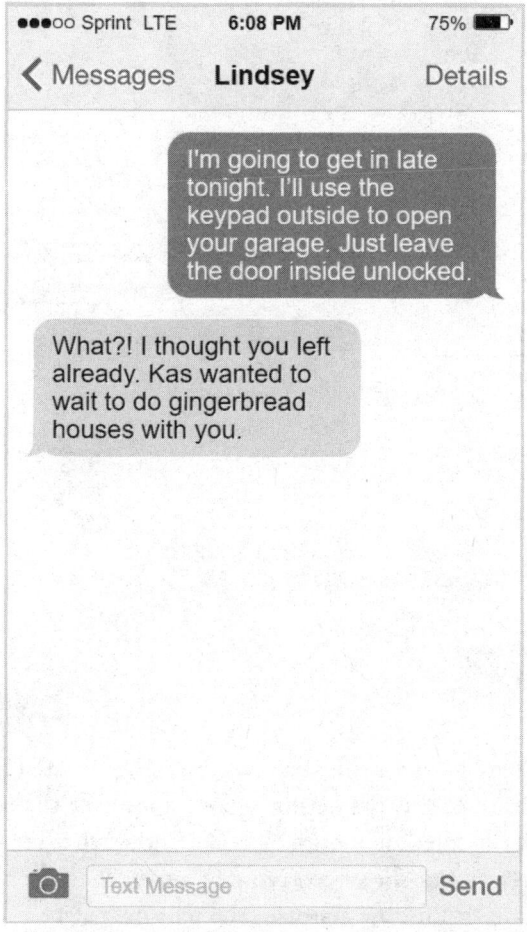

I sigh, even more upset that I'm now going to disappoint my six-year-old niece because of my jerk of a manager.

I read my sister's last text a few times. I've debated quitting my position at this marketing agency a lot over the last year, especially in the last month. I don't know what crawled up Kathy's butt, but she's been more of a twat than usual. Every time I talk to Lindsey about it, she tells me to get a new job.

But the money is good, I get great benefits, and the job makes my mom happy. I've also been working my way up the ladder the last couple of years to snag a director position and eventually be the boss of people instead of them being the boss of me.

My email pings, taking me out of my thoughts. Of course, it's from Kathy. Nobody's left in the office except for us, so she could have just told me what she had to say.

With an eye roll, I open the email to see she says I missed another space. I swear to god, this woman gets off on being this way. There's no way that was there when I sent it to her. It truly makes me wonder if she's doing it just to keep me here. Maybe she's lonely and wants company. But I'm not going to try to psychoanalyze my manager when all I want to do is leave.

I delete the space she's highlighted, then save and send the doc back to her. Once I'm sure the email is fully sent, I begin to shut down my computer. I can answer the rest of the emails from my sister's if need be, but the office is closed all next week for the holidays, and everyone is gone. I want to be gone, too. Kathy can deal with it.

I reach for the messenger bag I have tucked near the side of my desk and then take my suit coat off the back of my chair, standing to put it on. My stomach growls as I pack up, reminding me I haven't eaten since this morning. I'll have to hit up a drive-through on my way to Starlight Haven. If I don't, I won't be eating until I get to my sister's since everything in her remote California mountain town closes early.

"Where do you think you're going?"

My head turns to find Kathy stalking toward me with gusto in her step. I should just not answer and walk out, but I'm too nice for that.

I place my bag over my shoulder and grab my travel mug from my desk. "Home," I lie, not wanting to divulge any of my personal life to this madwoman.

"I have something else I need you to look at."

"No."

Kathy's eyes bug out of her head, and to be honest, I think mine do, too. But I've had it, and I don't regret saying no. I should've been doing it for a long time now. But as Lindsey would say, I'm allergic to that word. I'm a people pleaser, especially with a dad who expected us to never say no and always follow the rules. I even had an ex call me a golden retriever once, always aiming to please. Which I'm not saying is a bad thing—I do like to please—but sometimes I wish I could be a pit bull. Maybe it's time I started trying to act like one.

"Nathan," Kathy says, that stupid vein on her forehead pulsing again. "We aren't done working yet. I need you to stay until seven."

I hike my bag farther up my shoulder, my fist clenching around my mug as my sister's voice enters my head: *You should quit that soul-sucking job.*

"I'll have to tell Mr. Brentmoor about this if you leave now," Kathy adds.

Our boss, Mr. Brentmoor—who isn't a bad boss, per se— probably wouldn't care that I left. But I don't trust Kathy to tell the truth. Knowing her, she'd make it seem as if I were being hostile or not doing my job. When in actuality, I do too much. And it's not like I get paid overtime for all the evenings I've stayed late or mornings I've come in early; I'm salaried.

I take a step back as Kathy watches me carefully. Even though the exit is toward her, I don't want her to find my behavior threatening. I may not be a very large guy at five-foot-nine, but I do work out, and she's a tiny human. I've often questioned if she eats more than just protein shakes and bars.

"I need you to stay, Nathan."

I take another couple of steps back, then walk toward the exit, giving her a wide berth. When our bodies are parallel, I pause to meet her confused glare.

"I'm not staying, Kathy."

"But—"

"I quit."

Her mouth drops open, and I don't wait for her to respond. I hasten my steps so I don't lose my nerve and try to take it back, pushing open the office doors as Kathy's eyes watch me leave. The cooler air from the hallway hits me, and I suck in a calming breath, taking another step, then another, until I'm at the elevator that will take me to the parking garage.

It isn't until the heavy doors slide shut that I let out a loud laugh. The noise springs free from my chest and bounces off the metal walls, echoing back in my ears. The joyful sound is foreign, but it feels good. Really good. Before I know it, I'm laughing in earnest. Cackling, even. I can't believe I just did that. I can't believe I quit my job.

Holy. Shit. I quit my job.

I quit my job.

Fuck. Fucking fuck.

I quit my job.

Chapter Three

The Prey

My sly fox heard me. I knew the moment that twig snapped that he was on to me, and now I have no choice but to run again.

My head darts to the left and then right, snow muddling my vision. It's coming down like crazy, but I love it. The cold flakes melt on my heated cheeks and collect on my lashes, only adding to the beauty and thrill of the moment.

I take off as quietly as I can through the fresh snow as I pump my arms and lift my legs high so I don't trip. I know our property like the back of my hand, but so does the one hunting me. Even if I could mute the sound of me running and clear my footprints in the snow, he'd be able to track and find me. He always does.

I come to an abrupt stop when I reach a fork in the powder-covered trail. I debate my options, wondering which way I should go. I could go right and head to the old hunting cabin, but with the snow coming down, I'm not sure I'd make it that far. And if I'm being honest, I don't think I want to make it that far.

"I can hear you thinking, little lamb."

The hair on the back of my neck rises, and my nipples automatically tighten at the timbre of my hunter's deep and taunting voice. I have no idea how he snuck up behind me—I didn't hear him running after me. But that's what makes him my cunning fox. And why I know I'll always lose this game.

I take a step forward, finally hearing the snow crunch behind me.

"If you run again, know I'll show you no mercy when I catch you," he warns.

Hot arousal pools between my legs, and despite his taunt, I know him. I know he wants me to run. The corners of my lips pull up as images of what will occur when he catches me pop behind my frozen eyelids.

I inhale the scent of winter: damp earth, pine, and burning wood, soaking in the scenery for just a moment. The way the world has gone quiet from the falling snow makes what my fox and I are about to do far too dirty for such a pristine and beautiful setting. But that's part of the fun.

I slowly turn my head over my shoulder, my long blond-and-black-streaked hair wet from snow and sweat. My hazel eyes connect with my hunter's cool blue ones, and in the dark evening light, they look like two pools of haunting black.

"Who says you'll catch me?" I taunt.

He flashes me his white teeth, but I don't wait for his sly and mischievous smile to fully seat itself. I burst forward and take off to the left, weaving my way through incense-cedar trees and pines while his amused and throaty chuckle follows behind me, telling me he'll make good on his threat.

Which is exactly what I want.

CHAPTER FOUR

Nathan

MY SISTER WASN'T KIDDING when she said it was snowing. When I left the office for the four-hour drive to Starlight Haven, it was just about forty-five degrees and raining. But as I started my ascent into the mountains, pure-white flurries danced in the air and have only gotten heavier with every increase in altitude.

The wipers frantically cut back and forth across my sedan's windshield. I should've gotten a Jeep or something better, but when I bought my car, my sister and mom hadn't yet moved to Starlight Haven, so I didn't foresee winter driving in the mountains in my future. It's also an El Niño year in California, so everything has been wetter, meaning we're set to get a lot of rain and snow this winter season.

Good for people who love to hit the slopes, bad for people like me who only go into the mountains to see their family. And by the way this snow is coming down, I have a feeling I'm going to be at my sister's for more than a week like I had originally planned. Not that I mind. Now that I have no job, it's not like I have anything to do but work out, maybe surf, drink a few beers with my friends, and of course, start looking for a new job. I have a good amount in savings to live off for now, but it's not enough to last more than six months without an income.

I express an audible sigh. I turned twenty-eight this year, and as I think about it now, my life is a little boring, though by my own design. I've always been a focused person, someone who's worked hard and achieved the goals I set out for myself. I like the routine of a nine-to-five, the predictability of it. I like waking up, going to CrossFit, heading to work, then going home to my meal prep or to the bar to meet up with my friends—and sometimes, though it's rare these days, taking a woman home for the night.

That last thought creates a crap ton of new rabbit holes in my head. As soon as I hit my mid-twenties, my mom and sister started constantly asking about my dating life. They want to know when I'm going to settle down, get married, and have a family. But there's this little problem I have...

Every relationship I start ends.

Not because of anything the women have done wrong. I've dated quite a few amazing ones, but something has always been missing. On the outside, everything would be fine and look like a healthy, thriving relationship, but inside...

I dated one woman in particular, Sasha, for a year after college. I think she thought I was her forever, and there was a part of me that wanted to give myself to her. She was smart, funny, and beautiful, and we had a lot of the same interests. We even surfed together. But as our relationship went on, I realized if I proposed to her, I'd doom her to a life with a man who loved her but would always feel like something was missing. Like something wasn't right. And I didn't want that for her. So we broke up, and now she's married to a wealthy guy in Maine and has two kids. Which is exactly the life I knew she wanted and deserved.

And Sasha isn't the only woman in my past with a similar story, which is why I eventually stopped dating for a partnership and now mostly just date for fun.

If one can even call it that, because I have a similar problem there. Even with sex, I feel as if something is missing. It's nice, sometimes great, but it lacks. Again, it's not anything to do with the women; I know it's a me thing.

Since I was raised to do things with every ounce of my

effort—to be the best at it or not do it at all—in the last couple of years, I've invested most of my time and energy into work. Which has gotten me absolutely nowhere.

Okay, maybe not nowhere.

If I hadn't quit tonight, I probably would've gotten a promotion after the new year or at least a good raise. And minus not being in a long-term relationship, I live a nice life. A life my dad told me he was proud of before he died two years back from a sudden stroke. A life Mom tells me she's proud of every time I talk to her.

I grind my teeth, wondering what Dad would say if he was still alive and I told him I quit my good-paying job because I didn't like my manager. I already know Mom is going to be disappointed. At least Lindsey will be happy, but I'm still fighting myself over my decision. I'm the first person in our family tree to go to college and get a corporate job. And now—

"Fuck!" I slam my hands against the steering wheel, frustration and anger boiling over—at myself and the situation I'm stuck in. But the tantrum was a stupid move, because the force causes my car to swerve on the wet, icy road. I release another curse as I grip the wheel, managing to steady my car before I scold myself for being reckless. The last thing I want to do is get seriously injured or die, especially right before Christmas.

With my heart beating fast in my chest, I take a relaxing breath and focus. I consider pulling off to the side of the road to check the weather, but I have a feeling that even a few minutes' delay will only make things worse. The snow is coming down even harder now, to the point where it's difficult to see. The white flakes are more like sheets as the harsh wind whips against my windows.

I dare a quick glance at the phone mounted on my dash. I still have about an hour left to go until I reach my sister's place. It's past eleven now—my arrival was further delayed after I stopped to grab a burger and because I'm driving at a snail's pace to avoid an accident.

"Keep it together, Nathan." My words bounce through the cab of my car alongside the smooth tones of Frank Sinatra singing "White Christmas" over the radio. Very appropriate. And now that I think of it, this will be my first white Christmas. My family never came up to the mountains, though they aren't that far from us, always opting to stay in town and drive to the beach if the weather was warm enough. I have fond memories of Lindsey, Dad, and me making snowmen out of sand while Mom took pictures and laid out a picnic lunch.

My chest tightens with emotion. This will be our second Christmas without Dad and the first we'll be spending together in Lindsey's new home.

From what she's told me, she never pictured herself in Starlight Haven. But after a bad divorce, she decided she needed a change for her and Kas. They'd taken a weekend trip to this charming lake town and fell in love with it. That was shocking by itself, since Lindsey was always a city-loving girl who dreamed of moving to Los Angeles one day. But then Mom decided to sell our childhood home and move in with her, which was even more of a surprise.

It had to have been hard for Mom to live in the little three-bedroom without Dad, so I understood. Now, the only bad part is that every time I want to see my family, I have to make this drive.

Frank Sinatra's voice fades out, and the radio station's host comes on. As soon as I hear something about snow, I take my hand off the wheel and quickly turn up the volume.

"A white Christmas is indeed happening for the people of Starlight Haven," a female voice says. "Looks like the snow is going to keep coming down for the next few days. The county has issued a warning urging residents not to leave their homes, and the roads at the bottom of the mountain have been closed off. If you're currently traveling, stay vigilant, and find a place to shelter if you can. It's getting wild out there!"

Fucking Kathy. Had she let me go home when everyone else

left the office, I would already be safe and warm with my family, not battling a winter storm.

I lick my already chapped lips, easing my foot from the gas to go even slower. I didn't think it was possible, but the snow is coming down heavier now. The flakes are thick and fluffy as they hit my windshield and then disappear against the heat of my vehicle before being replaced by dozens more. If I wasn't shitting myself, I'd think it was beautiful. And it *is* beautiful, but I'd rather be observing it from inside my sister's cozy A-frame home with a cup of Mom's hot chocolate in my hands.

"Carol of the Bells" comes through the speakers, and as the music builds, so does my anxiety. I'm climbing higher up the mountain now, and according to my GPS, I'm going to reach the peak soon, which means I'm on the outskirts of Starlight Haven. Unfortunately, my sister's place is on the other side of town. While I'm glad I'm getting closer to civilization, I'm not out of the woods yet.

I huff at my choice of thought. I'm definitely in the woods, thick forest flanking the road on both sides. Right now, it looks black, but I remember the pines from my previous drives up here. I wonder if I've passed Starlight Lumber & Logging yet, a sign I see every time I almost get to this point. I smile, remembering that Lindsey mentioned they host the Lumberjack Games every year, which has axe throwing, speed pole climbing, and other events. The idea made me laugh when she told me, and I know the only reason she's excited to go next summer is that she hopes to meet a single guy who likes kids and can "throw her around." I grimace. My sister tends to overshare, though it's part of her charm.

But honestly, I want a good man for her. She deserves it after her divorce, and my niece deserves a constant male presence in her life like me and my sister had. In the past few months, I've wondered if I should actively try to come here more weekends, but Lindsey always assures me they're fine, that they don't expect me to make the drive often, and that video calls are enough. It was their choice to move up here, after all, but it still bothers me that I can't be here all the time.

My decision to quit comes to the forefront of my mind once more. Maybe leaving my job has more benefits than just getting out from under Kathy's thumb. I don't think I want or could move here permanently since this town doesn't have the type of firms I'd be looking to work for, but if I found a hybrid company that would allow a work-from-home option, I could visit more—and not during hellish winter storms.

I automatically tighten my grip on the wheel as another Christmas song plays, and I press my foot on the gas to accelerate up an incline. I quickly glance at the directions on my phone again, only to realize it's died.

"Dammit."

Panic in my stomach swells as I try to inhale. I know this road will take me to the center of Starlight Haven, but once I get there, I won't know where I'm going, especially with the current whiteout. It's late, so nothing will be open, meaning I'll need to pull over and plug in my phone. I should've done that earlier, but I wasn't thinking, too eager to get on the road. I also had enough juice, or at least I thought I did, to make it to my sister's, so the charger that plugs into my adapter is in my bag on the passenger seat.

I look to the left and right and debate if this is a good spot to pull over, but then I realize I haven't seen another soul on the road since I started my ascent into Starlight Haven. Which isn't a good thing. It's better to keep going until I get to town and *then* pull over. At least if I get stuck there, I'll be in civilization instead of surrounded by forests.

I press the gas pedal down, picking up a tiny bit of speed. With the action comes a grinding noise, and my shoulders instantly tense. My car vibrates, and then a loud snapping followed by more grinding has me gripping my wheel on instinct.

Everything happens in slow motion. My car swerves, and then I'm spinning out, my body being thrashed around while

I'm too stunned to even scream. A loud thud sounds as my car slams into something, and everything jerks to a stop in a jarring instant.

For several minutes, or maybe it's just seconds, I sit frozen while "Jingle Bells" plays cheerfully over my speakers and my chest heaves with short breaths. My vision spots, and I close my eyes, my hands white-knuckling the wheel so tightly they hurt. When my brain finally reaches the conclusion that I'm not dead, I exhale unsteadily, loosen my grip just a bit, and drop my chin to my chest.

Holy shit.

After another minute, when I'm sure I won't pass out from lack of oxygen or shock, I shakily unbuckle my seat belt. I have no idea what happened, but the airbags didn't deploy, and my car is still running, which I take as a good sign.

I press on the gas, but all I hear is more sputtering and grinding. *Fuck.* Now I have to get out and see what's going on or at least try to see what caused me to spin out. Given the conditions, I'm hoping my car will still drive.

I suck in another breath, and then another, before I grab the heavy winter coat I ordered online last week from my back seat. I put it on, bracing myself for the weather I'm about to face. Even though the heat is still blasting, I think the temperature in the cab has dropped several degrees already. If I had another option, I wouldn't get out of my car, but unfortunately, I don't.

I zip up my jacket, turn on my emergency flashers, then push open the door with the engine still running. The freezing wind whips in, wet flakes of snow hitting my heated skin and melting. I was not made for the cold, but I try to push that thought out of my head as I shove my door open further and stand. My headlights are still shining, but the relentless weather covers the beams, so it's still hard to see.

I walk around my car, and when I get to the back, I see the culprit. The back chains I had put on my tires snapped and are now completely useless. But what's worse is that I'm very clearly stuck in a snowbank.

"Fuck!" I kick at some of the snow around my tires and immediately regret it as the white powder enters my shoe and begins to soak my sock. I'm still in my work clothes, and my shoes are a nice pair of loafers not meant for the snow.

I attempt to ignore the bite of cold on my ankles as I crouch and dig some of the snow away from my tires, but my hands instantly freeze. My new gloves I ordered are packed in my suitcase, which isn't helpful right now.

When I realize digging is futile, I know I need to try to get some help. There's no way I'm going to be able to dig myself out of this. I go to stand, but as I do, spots fill my vision, and I sway. I mutter a curse and press both hands on the cold bumper of my car, squeezing my eyes shut. When something thicker and wetter than snow drips down my forehead, I bring a hand to my skin and feel a tacky substance on my fingertips. I swipe it away and open my bleary eyes to see blood staining my fingers.

Did I hit my head when I spun out?

With my hands still on my car, I attempt to take a step toward the heated cab to find my charger and call for help before shit gets worse for me, but when I do, the world starts to spin. All the adrenaline from the accident has left my body, and now my head is throbbing.

"Come on, Nathan," I urge myself. *Get into the car.* I try to blink away my blurry vision and release the bumper to take another step, which turns out to be a huge mistake. It feels as if someone has pulled a rug out from under my feet, and I fall backward. My ears ring, my eyes fall shut, and then I'm hitting something soft and pillowy. But it's not a bed, because the pillows are cool like satin but cold and wet like ice. Water droplets hit my face, and I don't know if it's snow or maybe the blood I felt trickling from the wound in my head.

It feels harder than it should, but I manage to pry my eyes open to watch the endless white fluttering down from the dark skies. I'm not sure how long I do that, but as my vision blurs again, my mind drifts to everything and nothing at all. I think of my mom and sister, of my niece, of my dumb job, of my failed relationships, of surfing on my favorite beach, of tacos in the summertime with Lindsey, and of course, Dad. I guess it's true—your life really does flash before your eyes when you're about to die.

Is that what's happening right now?

A tear—or at least, I think it's a tear—streaks down my face, and my eyes fall shut, heavy with sleep. My heartbeat slows, and I hear a voice in the back of my head telling me to stay awake. I know I should try for that voice, but I'm so tired, and this bed is so cold. No…not bed. Snowbank. I'm in a snowbank.

More time passes, and my body is numb, yet everything hurts to the point I can't move. My lungs feel frozen, my toes are cold, and my head is aching, but I'm still alive. In the distance, I think I hear a noise. A twig breaking or trees rustling. A spark lights in my chest that maybe help is coming, but then I remember I crashed in a place surrounded by trees. It's probably just an animal. Maybe I'll get eaten by a bear. *Ouch.* Though maybe that's better than slowly freezing to death like I am right now. If that *is* what's happening. Is it?

I chuckle to myself, my thoughts fuzzy and my body heavy. In my mind's eye, I imagine myself on a beach somewhere hearing the sound of the waves crashing and kids laughing. There's a warm touch on my cheek that lights my body up as if it's on fire. I think it's sunshine, or at least, that's what it feels like. Warm, beautiful, euphoric sunshine.

"What are you doing out here?"

I turn to my sister, who's on the beach with me now. "I'm surfing."

Lindsey's hands grasp my shoulders and gently shake me. "Stay with me," she says. But it's not her voice that comes out. It's a huskier one, a commanding one.

"I am staying," I say.

"That's good to hear," a male voice says. Is that my dad?

I don't have time to wonder, though, because the beach begins to fade, and my body goes cold again. For a brief moment, the warm sunshine returns to my cheek, and I force my heavy eyes open. When I do, I'm not met with sunshine but the round face of an angel. She looks sad—or at least, I think she does.

"I'm here to help you," she says.

"To die?" My words come out scratchy and soft, but she's heard them.

"Not if we have anything to say about it."

We. Who's we?

That's the last thought I have before everything goes dark, my body falling into cold oblivion as the void welcomes me with open arms.

CHAPTER FIVE

Nathan

I'M WARM. NO, NOT just warm—sweltering. Wasn't I cold before? No. I was at the beach with Lindsey. Wait. No, I wasn't. I was driving. Then I was cold. Really cold.

My eyes pop open, and I groan. Wherever I am, the lighting is dim, but that doesn't stop the ache I feel in my temple. I attempt to bring my hand up to check the spot, but it's trapped. Panic bubbles in my gut as the events leading up to this moment come back to me.

The chains on my tires broke.

I spun out.

I went to check on my car, and I passed out in the snow.

I was cold and thought I was dying.

But then there was an angel? No…

I press my eyes shut again and shift, fabric sticking to my overheated skin. Wait, fabric? I look down and see I'm cocooned in blankets, as if I've been swaddled, which explains why my hands are trapped. I shift again and wiggle my hands free, noticing that my body feels like I got hit by a truck. I didn't get hit, but when I spun out, I might have gotten whiplash. Then there's the fact I was freezing in a snowbank, and my head—

I lift my now free hand up and press it against my forehead. There's a bandage over it, and not a very big one. Which means it must not be too terrible. There doesn't seem to be a bump, either, but I won't know for sure until I see it in a mirror. I drop my hand back down to the bed.

Wait, bed?

I sit up too fast for a man who was just unconscious, and I squeeze my eyes shut again for a moment before opening them.

Where the hell am I?

My gaze drifts around the room. The main overhead light is off, but there's a small lamp on the rustic wooden bedside table with a red lampshade that emits a warm glow among the space as well as a fire blazing at the front of the room inside a brick fireplace. It must have been tended to recently, because the logs haven't turned to ash and the heat it's giving off explains why I started to sweat through the evergreen-colored sheets and blankets piled on top of me.

The room itself isn't that large, but it's nice and woodsy. The walls are dark-stained logs, and the ceiling is vaulted with exposed beams. Besides the lamp and bedside table, there's only one piece of decor, and that's a large painting of a fox hunting a lamb. It's oddly beautiful yet a little strange and kind of frightening. My body naturally leans forward to take a closer look, and I think I see another figure or animal in the distance.

Snap!

I jolt in the bed, sheets dropping down to my waist as I bring a startled hand to my chest. Wait…am I? I look down at my body, pulling away the blankets to find no clothes covering me. Jesus. I'm naked. Not even the briefs I slipped on this morning are on my body.

I survey the room, looking for any sign of my clothes, but I don't see them. I think about calling out, but I have no idea where I am or who picked me up. This place seems nice, but who the hell knows? I was literally in the middle of nowhere, surrounded by forests. Who would've found me out there? And how the hell did they get me back here?

I run my tongue against the roof of my dry mouth and turn my head to the bedside table to find a cup of water along with a washcloth that still looks wet. I wonder for a second if the water could be drugged.

Wait, why am I assuming they're murderers or crazed woods people? Especially if they took the time and effort to rescue me from the storm. I think I've listened to one too many true crime podcasts recently, which I can thank my sister for.

I pick up the glass and sip from it. It's cool, the outside of it sweating from the heat of the space. Which again leads me to believe whoever brought me here was recently in this room, probably making sure I was okay.

I set the water back down once I've almost drained it, then decide I should try to find some clothes. The pain in my head is still there but lessening with each moment I'm awake. The water helped, too. I'm taking the fact that I don't want to go to sleep again and I'm not dizzy or nauseous as a good sign that maybe I don't have a concussion. If my sister were here, she'd be able to tell me. She's an ER nurse, and a damn good one.

Oh shit. Lindsey!

I push the blankets back and stand, not caring anymore that I'm as naked as the day I was born and that my body aches. I figure it'll pass the more I move around, so I start searching the room for my pants or my jacket, hoping I put my phone inside a pocket or whoever brought me here thought to grab it. I need to call my family and let them know I'm fine.

Eventually, I find a folded pair of red-and-green flannel pajama pants with a drawstring and step into them, not caring that I'll probably look like Buddy the Elf wearing them. They may not be mine, but at least they're something. I quickly pull them up and tie the string, surprised to find they fit pretty well on my lithe form.

When I'm certain my phone and clothes aren't in here, I decide to venture out of the room. I have no idea who I'm going to find, but if they were kind enough to rescue me in a snowstorm, they must be nice, right? Though I'm confused as to why I was completely stripped down. I get my clothes were probably wet from the snow, but my underwear, too? The thought of a complete stranger or strangers undressing me is weird, one I have to push to the back of my mind as I walk to the bedroom door.

It's not completely closed. Whoever put me in here has left it ajar, and when I open it, I'm faced with a hallway. The lights are off, but enough ambient light filters in that when I turn my head to the left, I can see three more doors lining the logged corridor, one of them cracked open at the end. It's not a very long hallway, and just like my room, it lacks decor. Though the stained wooden logs are expertly placed and look almost crafted.

I take a step forward and glance to the right. Light floods from an open space, and I notice then that shadows flicker on the walls from what I assume is another roaring fire coming from a living space. Though the door at the end of the hallway is cracked, I decide the safer option is venturing toward the living room. Hopefully, whoever got me here is there, and I won't have to awkwardly figure out what to do next.

I stretch my neck from side to side and roll my shoulders, loosening up my muscles and taking a deep breath. My feet move from the plush cream carpet of the bedroom to the cool wood of the hallway. The change in temperature causes a shiver to run up my spine, and I wish I'd found found a shirt alongside these pants.

Swallowing, I take another step, and then another, until I reach the main room only a few feet away. I glance around the large open living area with cathedral ceilings, more exposed beams, and unfortunately for me, not a soul in sight. Just a giant flat-screen TV and a large, plush red couch with a matching recliner and a love seat.

The light of the fire dances across my skin as some of the wood pops and crackles from water trapped within. I study the brick fireplace, noticing the design is similar to the one in my room, but this one has an ornate wooden mantel with more foxes and lambs carved into it. I run my tongue along the back of my teeth as my eyes settle on the two green-and-red velvet stockings hanging from it. Had those not been there, I wouldn't think whoever was here celebrated Christmas, as there are no lights, no tree…just the two stockings.

Two.

Did a couple find me?

I think back to the moment and remember hearing a woman's voice, but I can't remember if I heard two. I let out a soft sigh. It doesn't matter who found me—I need to see if I can find my phone. Or any phone. And Jesus, my car! If someone finds it on the side of the road without me in it, my family will think the worst.

Rubbing the back of my neck, I circle the room. Eventually, I find my coat on a hook near the door, and my heart speeds up in my chest. I hurry over to it and search the pockets but come up empty save my car keys. Doesn't help me, though—not what I was looking for. I spin around and keep walking.

The kitchen is nice and looks newly renovated with stainless steel appliances. It's just a normal kitchen. But as I turn to head back toward the hallway, a picture on the fridge stops me. A magnet that says "I Pine For You" is holding a snapshot of a beautiful, voluptuous woman.

But that's not what caught my eye. It's the fact that said beautiful woman is completely nude and straddling a giant tree trunk. Her arm covers her large breasts, though the soft skin spills over—and I think I see the crest of her dark nipples. Her other hand is covering the V between her legs, and her smile is contagious. Light blond hair streaked with black sections blows in the breeze behind her. The summer sun scatters beams of light on her skin, a lot of it decorated with tattoos of varying colors, shapes, and sizes.

Is this who rescued me? It has to be. I start to reach for the photo, feeling a little like a perv for even thinking of studying it closer, but I can't stop myself.

Just as my fingers touch the outer edge of the print, a loud cry pierces the air. I turn toward the noise, the hair on my arms standing on end. While it did come from behind me, it didn't come from this room. It came from down at the end of the hallway.

Another cry, followed by the sound of what I can only describe as a slap, reaches my ears. Before I can really comprehend what I'm doing, I'm walking back to the hallway.

The fire is still going strong in the living area, casting my shadow on the floor as I eat up the ground, getting closer to my room. In my gut, I know I should stop. I should go to sleep or wait for whoever is here to come find me, but instead, I step past the open door of the room I was in, then past the door across from mine, then past the other.

Another shout rings out, the cries becoming louder and more frequent. The sound is most definitely feminine. I tell myself the only reason I'm seeking the noise out is because I'm concerned, but I'm smart enough to know that those cries and noises aren't ones to necessarily be concerned about.

I lighten my steps as much as I can and ease my way to the door. The crack is wide enough that I can clearly see into the room yet keep my body hidden.

My eyes first find the massive fire that lights the room, flickering and sending warm light across the floor like the other two fires that have been lit and stoked throughout the cabin. On the ground in front of it lies a bearskin rug strewn with several articles of clothing, including a lacy red bra and what looks to be a matching thong. I blink rapidly at what I notice next, not quite understanding what I'm seeing.

Not only is there a ball gag on the floor that's shining as if it was just used, but there's something I can only describe as a stockade or a strange type of massage table. It has a place for someone's legs, stomach, and arms, even their face. But that's not the most bizarre part. At the back of it sits a low stand with a large silicone cock protruding from it. My eyes widen, and

I forget that my head is still hurting and my body is aching. I forget everything entirely. My head shifts to the left as another loud cry resounds, my gaze now focused on the two people fucking on the large king bed.

If my eyes hadn't popped out of my head from the contraption on the floor, I think they're about to. The woman from the photograph is kneeling on the bed, her plush body facing toward me as what I can only describe as a beast of a man pounds into her from behind, making every part of her jiggle from the force.

The man is kneeling as well, his torso pressed to her back, one of his tattooed arms between her breasts so his hand can grasp her throat. His other inked arm is between her legs, long fingers circling her clit as she moans.

Like any man in this situation, or maybe something is just wrong with me, blood rushes south, and my dick begins to fill, throbbing inside my loose flannel pajamas. Disgust with myself itches at the back of my throat, telling me to walk away, telling me I should at least close the door and pretend I never saw them like this. But I keep watching, my eyes glued to the debauched scene before me.

"Fox," the woman says in a husky tone, another cry following her one uttered word.

The man I assume is called Fox squeezes her throat, and her swollen lips part as a silent gasp escapes her. "Do you need me to gag you again? You said you could be quiet."

The woman bites her lip hard, her head falling back against the broad shoulder of her partner before I think she utters a quiet "no." He says something I can't hear in her ear, and then he's shoving her forward onto the bed and pressing her head into the end of the mattress. Her cheek is now flattened against the pine-colored comforter as the man lies on top of her, his hips slapping in a measured cadence against the curve of her plump ass, drawing out more feminine moans.

My hands turn into fists at my sides, a trickle of sweat

caused from the fire and the rising heat of my own body dripping from my brow and dropping onto my foot where it's curled against the wood floor.

"You're such a needy whore tonight, little lamb." *Thrust. Thrust. Thrust.* "I like it."

My eyes draw from the woman being thoroughly used to the man doing the using. To the man who just said such vile words that I should be disgusted or step in to ask if she needs help.

The notion is silly, though, because it's clear she's very much enjoying it, enjoying the words he's saying and wanting more, because she whines something I can't understand. Whatever she says makes him chuckle, makes him drive into her harder and use her body like a toy for his pleasure, abusing it, owning it.

I've never seen anything like it. It's raw, dirty, and so unhinged.

"Your cunt is squeezing me," he nearly whispers. "Tell me how it feels."

"Like your dick is splitting me in two."

He pulls off her body in a swift motion, his cock still inside her, and he moves one hand to the soft pouch of her generous stomach and the other to her outer hip. With the light of the fire now shining on him, I can clearly see the beast who's been having his way with his beauty.

It's not just his arms and hands that are covered in tattoos—it's nearly every inch of him. Black and gray designs swirl and cut across his body's canvas, from his ankles up his tree-trunk thighs to his soft yet muscled torso and painted up his thick neck and even under his chin. I've seen heavily tattooed men before, but never like this. And like the woman writhing under him, his hair is long and blond. Though his is a golden-blond color with no black.

If I didn't know any better, I'd say this man is a living god, as if a tattooed version of Thor jumped from the pages of myth and legend. But he looks like the traditional Thor, thick and muscular yet soft and pliant, not like the ones in movies with an eight-pack of abs. Even more interesting than that, though he's a massive man, he moves with an ease and grace you'd not expect someone built like him to have. He's beau—

My cock swells and aches as I watch him, study him. Without thinking, I bring my hand to my crotch, palming the aching flesh to get some sort of relief. As soon as I squeeze, a zap of electricity sluices up my spine, and I realize what I'm doing. My stomach falls in on itself, and I feel strange.

Did I just get turned on by him? The warm air around me becomes stifling as I shake my head and pull my hand away from my dick as if it's been burned. No. This is like watching porn. The act has me turned on, the way he's thrusting into her with swift precision, his cock gliding in and out of her wet pussy, the way their bodies come together so violently yet so perfectly. It's the moment, the depravity, the way she's looking at me—

My thoughts stop. *The way she's looking at me.*

I blink. Then blink again. Hazel eyes stare at me from beneath dark lashes that kiss pink cheeks, and she smiles. The man's tattooed hand is now back on the side of her head, pushing her forcefully into the mattress as he pumps into her. The bed shakes from the force and squeaks as if it will collapse beneath them.

I blink again. She sees me. She knows I'm watching. The smile on her lips widens, and instead of acting like a person who has just been caught having sex by a stranger in their home—jumping up and trying to cover herself, maybe, or screaming at me to leave at the very least—she doesn't do anything. Her eyes remain on me while the man behind her grunts and shatters. She squeezes her eyes shut as her orgasm is triggered by his brutal release, stifling her cry by planting her face into the mattress. She fists the sheets as the man, still thrusting, rides her through their mutual orgasms.

Embarrassed and flustered, I do the only thing I can think of: I turn and walk away, determined to get out of here before they can get their clothes on.

CHAPTER SIX

Morgan

"HE'S GOING TO TRY to leave," Fox rasps.

I expel a breath. "I told you he'd wake up."

"You also told me you'd be quiet if I took your gag out." He chuckles against the shell of my ear. "It's not my fault you can't follow directions."

That has me smirking. "Yeah, but I'm not the one who left the door cracked open."

I can't see Fox's face from this position, which irks me because I want to study him, try to figure out why he left the door open. I think he wanted our rescue pup to hear us, to come find us. I think he wanted to know what he would do. If he would—

No, I can't think about that right now. I swallow against the pain of past rejection that springs into my throat, threatening to choke me.

Fox exhales, then swiftly extricates himself from me, softening cock and the mess of us exiting my body. I close my eyes for a moment, allowing the adrenaline from the night and our playtime to melt away and the pleasure of my orgasm to ground me.

My peaceful moment only lasts for a second before Fox is gently rolling me onto my back. My tired body protests. It's been a long night, and all it wants to do is curl up in bed and fall asleep with Fox's steady heartbeat in my ear. But we have a man we rescued in our home who's probably going to try to leave during the worst winter storm I've seen in years, maybe ever. Which won't end well for him.

One of Fox's inked fingers smooths out the furrow in my brow.

"Did I go too hard on you?" he asks with a sly smile on his lips and a glimmer of sadism in his blue eyes.

"You could've gone harder."

He chuckles, moving from his kneeling position to lay his heavy body over mine, pressing me into the mattress. I groan when I feel his length hardening against my belly. If we were alone, I'd let him take me again, not caring that my vagina would probably cry mercy. Yet knowing my husband, he'd use my mouth or my ass—and I'd allow it. Especially since our little Christmas tradition got derailed.

The sound of something falling over has our heads turning toward the source of the noise: the man in our second bedroom.

"We need to stop him before he hurts himself."

"He'll figure it out," Fox replies.

I huff. I love my husband, but sometimes he's an idiot. "Be nice."

"I am nice. I carried him back here, didn't I?"

He did, and despite his attitude now, I know he cares for that stranger's life. Fox likes to pretend he's a big ole grump who doesn't care about people, but he's one of the kindest and most caring people I know. He's had a hard life, so I understand his desire to protect himself, to protect his heart and me. Which is why I'm even more curious as to why he left the door cracked. He could have easily locked it, preventing our house guest from watching us fuck. And watch, he did.

"Let me up. We have another few minutes before we end up chasing him through the snow."

"And that's a bad thing?"

I roll my eyes. "Get off me, will you?"

"Yes, ma'am."

That earns him a punch to the shoulder, and he grunts playfully before relenting and letting me up. I can feel his lazy gaze on me as I stand, his release spilling down my leg. I smile to myself, the depraved part of my soul enjoying that I'll be convincing our stranger to stay while my husband's spend drips from me. I know

Fox likes it, too, enough that it will drive him so crazy he'll fuck me into the mattress again when we get back to bed.

Heavy footsteps moving down the hallway make me pick up speed, and I grab a red silk robe and a simple pair of cotton underwear. I take a couple of tissues from the oak dresser and wipe my thighs and legs, then slip on my clothes. Fox has gotten off the bed, too, his long hair now tied in a bun and a pair of briefs on his legs.

I throw him a shirt, and Fox balks at it, but this guy we saved is going to be skittish. And despite the fact that he walked off when he found out I saw him watching, I noted the way he was looking at Fox. The way he was looking at us. It's better if we at least have most of our bodies covered.

Once I'm dressed, I exit the bedroom with Fox on my heels. My long legs eat up the ground, and I expect to find our new friend halfway out the door. Instead, he's sitting at the kitchen table Fox made by hand for me, bundled in his winter coat and an old pair of flannel pants he found, ones I didn't know were still in that room. I push down the emotion that came up earlier and try to make my features as normal and welcoming as possible. For a split second, I debate what to say; then I go with the first thing that comes to mind.

"Hi."

The man snaps his head up at the same time Fox stands beside me. Our guest's dark-brown eyes move from mine to my husband's, and his cheeks turn a ruddy red color— I should've told Fox to stay behind. He's a very large man, tattooed from head to toe and scary as hell. I think our guest finds him attractive—at least, that's the impression I got. Not to mention, said guest also just witnessed us having rough sex and probably saw Fox's favorite new toy near the fireplace. I flush a little but not with embarrassment—with arousal.

"We're snowed in," he says, his tone matter-of-fact, yet the warm timbre of his voice turns my nipples to peaks and sends a shiver racing up my spine.

Fox moves, and I don't miss the way the man at our table jumps as if he thinks my husband is going to lunge for his throat like a fox capturing his prey.

"He's just checking," I say, trying to calm him.

"I'm not lying," the man retorts.

My lips tip up in a gentle smile. "He doesn't think that. He just wants to see for himself what kind of weather we're dealing with."

Fox opens our front door, the muscles of his broad shoulders bunching beneath his navy Henley. Shit, the white wall he reveals looks like the snow I've seen in movies about snow days—it's piled almost the entire height of the door. Some of it falls in, and cold wind along with snowflakes whip through the space left open at the top.

"I told you," the stranger snarks.

I ignore his comment and cross my arms over my chest as Fox closes the door. My husband turns toward me, and unsurprisingly, he doesn't look worried, but his face is hard. That's the way he looks when he's about to talk about a new reforestation operation or a seasonal harvest. He's got his chest puffed out, and the moment his bearded jaw clenches, I know he's about to go into military mode and begin barking out commands.

I hold up my hand before he can speak. "The generator is working fine, and you know we're prepared. Let's sit and talk to our guest."

Fox's mouth presses into a hard line, and I know he wants to argue, to shovel snow or whatever else he wants to do to keep me safe, but he also knows I'm right. The man we saved needs the gaps in his night filled in. And while Fox probably enjoys watching him squirm to a certain extent, if their positions were reversed, I know my husband would've dug his way out of here until he either made it back to his car or froze to death.

"I'll make us some coffee," he grunts, walking behind our guest to the kitchen area.

I nod and take a seat across from the man who's back to fiddling with his keys.

"Do you have my phone?" His brown eyes meet mine, and my stomach twists. By the light above us, I can see the worry etched in them. In the whirlwind of rescuing him in the storm, I didn't even stop to think he might've been heading to someone and that they're probably worried for him.

"I'm sorry, we didn't see one. We were concerned for your life, so I turned off your car and grabbed your keys."

"I need to reach my sister, let her know I'm not dead."

"Does she live in Starlight Haven?"

He tips his chin, pushing some of his tousled brown hair from his forehead. "Yes. About thirty minutes north of the town center."

"Unfortunately, even without the storm, we have shoddy reception, and right now, none at all. The power and internet are also out, and we've got the generator going. But I can have Fox radio the sheriff, and they can get word to her. We have to let them know about your car, anyway, and that you're safe, but we were going to wait till a decent hour." I look at the Scandinavian-style clock on the wall and see that it's already approaching four in the morning. I guess that's decent enough.

When my eyes connect with his, he's looking at me funny, confusion riddling his handsome features. "Radio?" he asks.

"We're used to remote life up here. Sometimes old-school works best." I could explain to him that the ham radio comes in handy with the type of work we do, especially when we're on jobs in the middle of nowhere. We usually have a satellite phone, but we were in the process of getting a new one. Neither of us expected the weather would get this bad.

"Please, can you radio the sheriff now?" His voice is so pained, it stabs at my heart. I feel bad about how he found us and wish we had closed the door. In the heat of the moment, it was a little thrilling, but this poor man is scared—and I know I would be, too.

I reach out to try to comfort him, but Fox steps up to the table before I can touch him and plunks down two mugs full of steaming coffee. The man jumps a bit at the motion, but then I watch with curiosity as he looks up at Fox, his cheeks flushing pink again. *Interesting.*

Fox doesn't smile at him or say anything; he just turns and walks back to the kitchen, opening a drawer we use for junk. He pulls out a pen and paper I forgot were even in there, then comes back and puts them down in front of our guest.

"Give me her name, address, and phone number, and I'll do it."

The man quickly takes the offered pen and paper and writes it down. When he hands them back to Fox, I notice that my husband purposely brushes his fingers over the man's.

"T-thanks." He trips over the word, his voice an octave higher than it was before. I don't miss the way Fox's lip twitches from his reaction this time. I want to ask my husband what he's doing, but I think I know. However, I'm not sure why.

"And your name?" Fox asks.

"Nathan. Nathan Clark."

Fox turns his gaze to me. "Will you be okay while I go do this?"

I nod. Fox knows I can handle myself, but he's a protective guy. The man I now know as Nathan looks like he wouldn't hurt a fly even though he's packing muscles under that winter coat of his. Muscles I had no choice but to see when I was getting him warm again.

"I'll be right back." Fox shoots a menacing glare toward Nathan that tells him not to try anything, and I internally roll my eyes. He also kisses my forehead before walking toward the third bedroom, which we've made into an office.

When I hear the door click closed, my gaze falls back to Nathan, and I pull my cup of coffee toward me. It's time to get to know our guest.

CHAPTER SEVEN

Nathan

"So, Nathan, how are you feeling?"

"Who are you?" I ask, ignoring her polite question. My tone comes off rude, but I'm tired, my head still hurts, and I'm positive that the man who just walked out is either part of the Mafia or a drug dealer. He's scary as shit, and now he knows where my sister lives, a fact I realized after I gave all her information and my name freely. I'm going to blame the head injury.

The woman who I, just ten minutes ago, watched having her soul fucked out of her body takes a sip of her coffee then folds her hands in front of her. With the action, light reflects from something on her hand. When I look down, I see a large princess-cut diamond ring on her left finger and matching wedding band. For some unknown reason, my heart squeezes in my chest.

"My name is Morgan, and the grump who went to go radio the sheriff for you is my husband, Fox." I must not be good at hiding my reaction because she huffs a small laugh. "I know it's an odd name, but the more you get to know him, the more you'll understand why it suits him. It's also not a nickname."

I think of the man who just walked off. He's large, but there's something quiet and almost stealthy about him. Hearing his name reminds me of the fox carved into the fireplace mantel and the oddly beautiful painting in the room where I woke up. Then I vaguely remember him calling her "little lamb" while he screwed her brains out. He also called her something else I do not care to repeat.

My heart beats loudly in my ears, and I wonder if maybe I should risk swimming in the snow outside to get help. I know that's stupid, which is why I'm sitting here right now. And apparently, Fox has a direct line to the sheriff. So even if these people are Mafia drug dealers or just sex-crazed weirdos, what am I supposed to do? I'm stuck here, and I don't have a phone or a way to leave.

After another beat of silence, Morgan clears her throat.

"I'm sorry for what you saw. I should've been there when you woke up to explain what happened. I didn't mean for you to see that."

I think of her smiling face, of the way she looked at me while— "I don't think that's true."

She blinks at me, and honestly, I'm surprised I said it, too. Maybe it was finally standing up to Kathy and quitting my job, or maybe it was what I'm assuming was a near-death experience in that snowbank, but she's lying. I think she left the door open so I would see that. The question is why? The only thing I could come up with is it's some kind of kink. I saw that contraption on their floor—having someone watch seems like the least of the kinky things this couple likes.

Morgan takes another sip of her coffee, and I decide to do the same. The hot bitter liquid feels good going down my raw throat, and I could use the caffeine boost to clear my head and wake me up a bit. I don't want to fall asleep without knowing more about where I am and how I got here. It's been over four hours since I fell in that snowbank, and I'm missing that whole chunk of time.

"Nathan, I really didn't mean for you to see—" she starts, but I interrupt her.

"How am I here?"

She leans back against the dark wooden chair, sighing at my subject change, probably, but I don't need to debate her truthfulness over the matter.

"Fox and I were…" She pauses as if trying to choose her

next words carefully, "…out looking for a Christmas tree. I happened to see the lights of your car and got curious. I'm glad I did, because had we not come along, I'm positive you wouldn't be talking to me right now."

"A Christmas tree?" I ask disbelievingly, ignoring that she confirmed I could've died because I did not want to think about that.

She gestures around the cabin. "As you can see, we're a little late decorating this year. We also enjoy the snow and thought it would be festive. But like I said, I'm glad."

"I think I remember you rescuing me."

She takes another sip of her coffee. "Yes, you called me Lindsey."

"That's my sister." I'm not sure why I told her that, but she smiles at the information.

"You were out of it and freezing to death. I'm not surprised you were hallucinating or thinking of your family in that moment."

I subconsciously bring my hand to the bandage on my head.

"You're lucky it's just a little gash," Morgan continues.

"There was a lot of blood."

"Head wounds tend to bleed a lot. I imagine part of you passing out was the shock."

"What if I have a concussion?"

"It's possible, but it's a good sign that you're walking around and talking. How are you feeling?"

I want to say, *Besides waking up in a strange place to find two strangers fucking and being stuck in said place with said strangers for the foreseeable future while my family spends Christmas without me, I'm feeling fucking fantastic.* Not.

"I feel like I got hit by a truck," I say instead.

"Your body has gone through a lot. Now that you're awake, I'll give you some painkillers, and you can get some rest. As you saw, we can't take you anywhere, but if you feel dizzy or nauseous or anything of that sort, let us know, and we'll radio the sheriff again to see if any emergency team could get out here."

I shake my head. I do feel sore, but I don't think that's necessary. Though at least then I'd be out of this situation...

No. I can't cause all that hoopla just to leave here. I'd be risking multiple people's lives because I'm uncomfortable. I can stay in their spare room until the snow clears and hope this situation doesn't get any weirder than it already is.

Morgan leans forward. "Nathan?"

I look into her hazel eyes. In the brighter light, I see flecks of gold and brown in them, almost creating the effect of a kaleidoscope—I've never seen anything like them.

"I know we got off to a strange start. But I promise you, you're safe here. My husband and I are well-known in this community. We own a business with employees, have friends, and we're prepared for storms. I know it's probably not ideal for you to spend your holiday trapped here with us, but we'll take care of you."

I tap my fingers against the side of the mug, her words soaking into my tired mind. "How did you know what to do when you found me?"

She licks her lips, a small sigh escaping her. I suspect she was hoping I would respond to her statement, but I still haven't decided what to think of her...*them*.

"We own the lumber company here in Starlight Haven, and we can get hurt on the job during harvesting and other projects. Our employees can get hurt, too, and they do. You're not the first person I've cared for who's had a minor head injury or stayed out in the cold for too long with improper gear. We get a lot of transients looking for work, people with no experience. Sometimes they learn the hard way that what we do is dangerous."

"I woke up naked."

That makes her laugh a little. "Yes. If there were another

way to warm you up without removing your clothes, we would've, but they were wet."

We. My skin turns hotter, and I'm reminded then that I'm still wearing this hot winter coat. I can feel sweat starting to accumulate on my back and chest.

"We were as respectful as we could be. But like I said, had we not found you when we did…let's just say, your body was very cold. We had to get you warm gradually, so we removed your wet clothes and then put you in the bed. We used warm compresses on your body, and you woke up a few times, but you were still out of it."

"I don't remember."

"Like I said, you were out of it. You were calling me angel, though."

I do blush now as hazy memories start to come back into my mind, ones of a blurry soft face and a husky voice telling me everything was going to be okay. Of fingers stroking my hair and whispers of comfort. Her touch felt…good. Then there was another touch, too. Stronger, rougher—

I clear my throat. "I remember a little of that, I think."

"That's good. More might come back to you. And the good news is I don't think you'll have any lasting damage. You can move all your fingers and toes, right?"

I automatically curl my toes and wiggle my fingers before peering at her. "I can."

She smiles gently. "Good. Like I said, I'm glad we found you in time."

Her words strike me in the chest hard. Despite how I woke up, I'm grateful they did find me. Had they not, I most likely would be dead—or close to it. I didn't want to die—I wasn't ready to die.

I push my mug away, my body heavy with sleep and now emotion. The adrenaline I felt from waking up, seeing them in their bedroom, and trying to leave paired with the worry I felt because my family doesn't know where I am—it's all leaving my body. A yawn overtakes me before I can stop it. Then another one.

"We can talk more in the morning." Morgan chuckles. "Or I guess, afternoon. I think we'll all be sleeping in."

I nod, unsure of what to do next. She stands from her place at the table and takes my nearly full mug. I hear her move around in the kitchen and the sound of the faucet turning on and back off before she returns with a glass of water and two pills. I stare up at her dumbly, and she holds up the bottle so I can see what she's giving me.

"Not the good stuff you'll get in the hospital, but it should do the trick." She places the bottle of acetaminophen on the table. "You can take that into your room, and if you wake up in four hours and need more, take another two."

Images of her nearly naked in a naughty nurse uniform pop into my mind, and I blink them back. What the hell? I'm going to blame my current situation and what I saw in their bedroom for that image, because it's not something that would normally spring to mind. Actually, it's an image I've never entertained before. I'm not into role-play or kink.

I toss the two pills into my mouth and drink them down before taking the pill bottle in my hand. When I stand, I'm face-to-face with one of my rescuers for the first time—at least while I'm lucid.

I'm a hair shorter than her, but not by much. That doesn't bother me—it's kind of thrilling to be almost evenly matched with her. And wow, her eyes are even more beautiful up close. The different colors are pretty against the dark eyeliner and mascara she still wears. I also like the small mole above her lip and the vine tattoo creeping up the right side of her neck. I lean forward, a desire to both get a better look at the detailed lines of it and be closer to her overtaking me.

The clearing of a throat has me stepping back like a child caught with their hand in a cookie jar. Fox is standing a couple of feet from the table clad in his navy Henley and briefs, arms crossed over his barreled chest. I rub the back of my neck and look away from his piercing gaze, worried about him walking in on me studying his wife like a manual.

"Did you get a hold of the sheriff?" Morgan asks, apparently unbothered by what her husband just walked in on.

Fox walks closer and tugs Morgan into his side. It's possessive and a little rough, but she falls into him easily and places her hand on his chest, looking up at him while she waits for his answer.

"He's going to get in touch with Nathan's sister and radio us back later today. Luckily, everything in town seems to be working okay, including the power grids. We're getting the worst of it here since we're at the highest point."

Morgan nods and meets my eyes as if she expects me to say something. I would've preferred to know that my family knew I was safe, but some of my anxiety eases that they'll find out soon. I still feel sick that Lindsey's probably beside herself… and my poor mom. Hopefully, she's sleeping through all of it and is none the wiser. Maybe Lindsey is, too.

"Thank you," I finally say. "I appreciate it."

She tips her chin, and then I force my gaze to meet Fox's. His face is relaxed now, but I see the way his veins protrude from his tattooed neck and how his shoulders are set back, still in protector mode. When our eyes connect, I don't doubt for a second that he's studying me, sizing me up.

My skin itches, and I think of that painting in the bedroom, the cunning fox hunting the unsuspecting lamb. I know he called Morgan by that pet name, but why do I feel like the lamb is now me?

I shift on my feet and step away from the table. I need to go to sleep before I start compounding conspiracy theories about this couple in my head. Morgan told me what they do, and I'm assuming the lumber company they own is Starlight Lumber & Logging, the one that holds the games in the summer my sister wants to attend. They also rescued me, and they're allowing me to stay in their home. Fox may be scary, but I can do my best to try to ignore him—ignore the both of them—while I wait out the storm.

Fox and Morgan follow me with their eyes as I give them a wide berth, stepping around the table and them, much like I did with Kathy earlier tonight. Once I reach the mouth of the hallway, I stop and turn.

"Thank you for rescuing me."

The two of them stare at me, Fox still holding Morgan to his side. She grins, a breathtaking smile that makes her look like the angel I thought her to be earlier. A dark angel with tattoos and colored hair, but an angel, nonetheless.

"No thanks needed," she answers.

I don't wait for Fox to respond before I retreat to my temporary home. Once I'm safe inside the bedroom, I put the pill bottle down on the bedside table and take off my winter coat. It isn't until I look to the bed that I notice someone has been in here—not only because there are fresh logs on the fire, but there are clothes laid out for me on the bed. A brown Henley, a pair of gray sweatpants, and even underwear.

I step toward the bed and finger the soft material of the shirt. Then I sit down on the mattress, the springs sinking gently beneath my weight.

There's only one person who could've done this: Fox.

CHAPTER EIGHT

Fox

"You need to rest," Morgan says from her place on our bed. She's freshly showered, and her hair lies wet around her face, the glow of the fire only adding warmth to her cheeks.

"I need to shovel that drift before we're completely trapped in." I pull on a pair of long underwear and then go to our closet to get the rest of the clothes I'll need. I'm used to the elements, and I thrive in the cold, but digging through snow requires I wear layers so I don't get frostbite. I prefer having all my digits intact, thanks.

"You should at least wait until the sun comes up. Sleep for a couple of hours."

I walk out of the closet as I'm pulling a sweater over my head. Morgan has the sheet pulled down, offering me her perfect tits for feasting. I lick my lips, and the desire to suck her pert nipples as if they'll provide me sustenance until she's begging for me to stop builds in my stomach.

"Fox." She pouts. "Get into bed."

I grunt. My wife can be persuasive, and if my need to protect her wasn't so strong, I would do what she's asking. But I can't shut off my brain, the brain that was trained for many years to be on guard, to be smart, to pick off threats. I don't even like the idea of leaving her with a man I don't know down the hallway. If I could, I'd lock him in his room.

He may not be built like me and may come off as skittish, but I recognize a likeness in him. Not only could I feel it when I carried his limp body back to our cabin, but I saw the way he responded to seeing me fuck my wife. I heard the need he has to get to his family, the anger and fear at not being able to leave. He may present outwardly like a sheep, but I see the wolf lurking under his skin—and I wonder if it would be ready to come out and play with a little coaxing.

"Lock the door after I leave," I say.

Morgan rolls her eyes. "Baby, he's harmless."

I want to take her over my knee for that eye roll, to strap her back to the stockade and watch her come on that fake cock while she chokes on mine until the sun has long been in the sky. And I would be doing that if I didn't have work to do. If I didn't have two people now depending on me for survival.

I get on the mattress, the bed dipping under my weight until my hand is wrapped around the column of her throat. The letters MINE are inked on my knuckles, made bolder and more pronounced against her ivory tattooed skin by the light of the roaring fire. I smile every time I see those tattoos wrapped like a necklace around her pretty throat. Not only because she *is* mine, but because those tattoos were inked on me by the little lamb currently in my grip.

"Lock the door, Morgan."

I'm not gripping her throat hard, so she grins at my order. I bite my tongue at her brattiness, but my wife would not be mine if she'd didn't test me. It's the switch in her—something I admire, but not when I'm trying to take her safety seriously. My grip tightens, and I take her lower lip between my teeth and bite down until she's gasping into my mouth.

"Lock the door." I pull back so I can see her now dilated eyes. I know her cunt is soaking for me after that, but I'm not going to give in to her.

I release her throat, and she sucks in a deep breath, though the corners of her lips are still upturned. "What do I get if I listen?"

I chuckle, the tone deep and dark. "You get to continue wearing clothes in front of our guest."

Morgan's eyes widen. "You're a bad boy."

I kiss her forehead before standing. "I never claimed to be good—nor am I."

She shakes her head because I know she disagrees with that statement, but I don't take the bait. We've had this debate many times, and I'm not going to argue with her right now because I know she's attempting to distract me from leaving.

"I'll be back as soon as I can, and I'll use my key to get in if you're still sleeping. Which I hope you are."

Her smile turns mischievous at that. Morgan and I have been together since we were teens, so she knows me inside out, and we've done a lot of things. Waking her up by coming inside her would be one of the tamest things we've shared, and I know it's something she likes.

I grab a sky-blue beanie off the dresser and put it over my head before I lean down to give her a final kiss. "Get some rest."

She salutes me, and my palm itches to spank her as I exit our bedroom. Once I'm out the door, I wait for thirty seconds knowing Morgan will debate if she should follow my instructions or not. It takes forty seconds, but eventually I hear the lock click, and a warm satisfaction fills my stomach. Such a good little lamb.

Sometimes.

CHAPTER NINE

Nathan

AN INCESSANT NOISE IS bouncing around in my skull.

Thwack! Thwack! Thwack!

I groan, rolling over and pulling a pillow over my head.

Thwack! Thwack! Thwack!

"What the hell is that?" I mumble into the pillow. It smells oddly of pine needles and musk, like one of those fancy Christmas-scented candles my sister likes. The scent reminds me I'm not in my bed, and I'm not at my sister's, either. If I were, my niece would have come into my room to wake me up, bugging me to make my famous crunchy French toast with crushed-up Cinnamon Toast Crunch cereal on the dipped bread—which, according to my sister, rots your teeth. But who cares? Life is meant to be enjoyed.

Thwack!

I throw the pillow off my head, rolling over so I'm staring up at the exposed-beam ceiling. Gray daylight is streaming through the picture window, and if I had my phone, I'd check what time it is. I'm going to guess it's afternoon by how rested I feel, a surprising fact considering I went to bed last night feeling like garbage.

I bring my hand to my forehead and press down. It's a tiny bit sore but not as much as I expected it to be.

Did I really pass out and almost freeze to death from that tiny gash? I need to work on my tolerance to pain and shock. I also don't get why my chains broke. They were the right kind. I made sure of it. I even had the guy at the shop install them.

The more I think about all of it, the madder I get.

Thwack!

There's a long pause, and I think the noise is done. Then another series of *thwacks* meets my ears, followed by what sounds like Jenga pieces falling down but much louder.

I sit up slowly, happy I'm not dizzy or nauseous, then get out of bed to go look outside and see what's woken me up. My bare feet hit the carpeted floor, and I take a moment to ground myself, curling my toes into the softness before I stand up. My body is a little sore, but the painkillers and rest did me a lot of good. And since I'm stuck here, all I'll be doing is resting. By the time I leave, I'll be as good as new.

Thwack!

My feet carry me toward the window. It's frosted from the cold, and snow sticks to the edges. I glance down and see the wind has slung the snow so it covers part of the lower window. There's got to be at least two feet of fluff plus the drifts, and when I look out into the distance, all I see is the effects of the storm: white ground, snow-covered trees, and gray skies.

Thwack!

I turn my head to the side, and what I see has me blinking. Then blinking again. Broad shoulders, strong arms, and long hair covered in snowflakes that continue to fall from the sky, though at a less ferocious speed than last night.

I blink once more as if I'm in a dream, but what I'm seeing is real. It's Morgan—and she's chopping wood.

I step closer to the glass, the cold outside seeping through—which means it's freezing out there. But Morgan doesn't look cold. She's only wearing a beanie, a knitted forest-green long-sleeved shirt, and some type of cargo pants held up by red suspenders.

She swings the axe, and it comes down hard on the giant log in front of her, one that has to be at least twelve inches in diameter. She swings again, hitting the exact spot she did before. The log splits, and then she starts again, splitting those pieces into smaller ones until she's satisfied with the size.

I stare, my mouth gaping, as she stands among the mountains of snow, round cheeks pink as she swings the axe again. Her form looks perfect, and I know by watching that she's been doing this for a long time because she makes it look easy—graceful, even. More wood falls to the ground, and I study her clothed body the same way I studied her naked one.

Morgan is strong, like a Greek goddess. She's the type of woman that makes men bow down, the kind that deserves to be treasured and revered. She's the kind of woman that people used to bring gifts to, would beg to kiss her feet. She's a woman to be worshipped and coveted.

Her body is soft and feminine yet strong and masculine, a perfect yin and yang. I understand more why Fox drew her into his side last night, the way he possessed her while he fucked her.

My blood heats, and my body grows hot. I managed to get a good night's sleep with no dreams of seeing them like that. I shouldn't be thinking of it now—or ever. If I want to get through my time with them, I have to not think of them naked. Not think of them fucking. Not think of the way Fox's large hand gripped her throat—

Knock! Knock!

I jump, my heart racing in my chest as I turn from the window where I can see Morgan still chopping wood, then back to the door. The fire that was roaring as I passed out has long since died out, and the room is warm from their heater but cold enough I start to shiver. It also makes me realize I need to put a shirt on. I grab the brown Henley that was left for me out of the small closet I'd hung it in last night, then pad to the door. I know who is going to be on the other side, and it's not Morgan.

I inhale a breath and try to remind myself that Fox is just a man. He's frightening, but after seeing Morgan outside and getting some sleep, I think she's telling the truth about who they are. Unless they're Mafia lumberjacks. Lumberpeople?

I open the door, and sharp blue eyes meet mine. There's no smile on his face, and his long hair is in a bun at the top of his head. It makes the sharp planes of his bearded jaw more pronounced and his high cheekbones more—I don't know what word I'm going for. But high. He's got on an ice-blue sweater that makes the color of his eyes almost look like the ocean on a stormy day where the waves are turbulent and mighty.

"It's late; you need to eat," his deep voice barks at me, and my back straightens on instinct, as if he's my master and I'm his dog, ready to follow his orders. I open my mouth to answer, but he's already eating up the ground down the hallway toward the kitchen. The desire to tell him to fuck off bubbles in my stomach, but then it growls so loudly, I think my insides might be eating themselves. What time is it? It can't be that late.

I consider going back to the window to see if Morgan is still outside, to try to get her attention and beg her through telepathy to come inside so I don't have to sit with her husband alone. I may not necessarily like Morgan—to be honest, I don't know enough about her to like her—but she feels like the safer of the two options. She's working, though, and I need to not be a pansy.

Guess I have no other option than to starve. I walk across the hallway to the bathroom I used last night before I went to sleep, my bladder full and the desire to brush my teeth strong. Especially before I face Fox in the kitchen…who apparently cooked for me?

I think I've entered some strange world up here. Lindsey is going to flip when I tell her I stayed with real lumberpeople, ones who own the very company that hosts the Lumberjack Games. The thought makes me smile, because I know my sister is going to want to ask Morgan if she knows any single burly men who love children.

After I relieve myself, I splash some cold water on my face and prod at my injured forehead. I didn't want to remove the bandage last night, but since it feels okay now, I decide to take a look at it. I gently remove the bandage to find barely any dried blood, once again making me feel silly for passing out last night.

Sure, it's a little sore, and I'm going to have a small bruise, but no one would ever guess it was from a car accident. With how healed it looks, I wonder if they put something on it while I was out. I suppose it really doesn't matter—I'm alive, and I'm going to be fine. I should just be grateful and not think about if they iced my head.

After I've thrown out the bandage in the small trash next to the toilet, I start looking for an extra toothbrush and toothpaste. The moment I open the largest drawer under the sink, I find a toothbrush that looks to be eco-friendly and toothpaste tablets as well as a fresh bandage and a washcloth.

I stare at the dark-stained wood door, wondering if Fox left this for me like he left me clothes. The idea is a funny one, considering he doesn't come across as a caring and thoughtful man. But just like I don't know Morgan, I don't know him, either. All I know is he scares me. Or at least that's the only way I know how to describe the flip in my stomach every time I've seen him or thought of him in the last…however many hours it's been.

My stomach growls again, and I take out the toothbrush and tablets. Once I've wet the brush, I scrub my teeth thoroughly, including my tongue, before running a hand through my hair. I look okay, a little worse for wear, but who am I trying to impress? I'm staying with a married couple, and I don't need to look acceptable for them. Plus, I'm wearing clothes that are slightly too big for me—which reminds me of my car. Fuck, I hope it's still drivable after this. I make a mental note to ask Fox about it and if he's spoken to the sheriff again.

Feeling a little more human, I inhale a breath and decide I can't delay being alone with Fox any longer. He's just a man— and I need to grow a fucking pair.

CHAPTER TEN

Fox

I SPREAD THE WARM icing over the fresh cinnamon rolls, my gaze focused on the way the sweet liquid melts into the cracks and crevices of the breakfast treat.

They're not homemade, but they're Morgan's favorite. And since she insisted she go chop wood since I'd been up all morning shoveling snow, I decided to make myself useful in the kitchen. When she comes in and sees me, I know she'll be pissed, but I'm too wired to sleep like she ordered me to. She also knows I don't take orders unless I'm in the mood, which is rare.

There's also still a man I don't know in our home, though until a few minutes ago, he's been dead to the world. I checked on him earlier to make sure he wasn't actually dead, and he wasn't—just passed out from what I suspect was exhaustion.

I finish icing the rolls, then put them in the middle of the kitchen table. I can hear our guest in the bathroom, the faucet turning on and off. After a bit, I think he's taking his sweet time on purpose because I make him nervous. If I could smell fear, I know it'd be rolling off him.

This is nothing new to me. I'm a six-foot-five man with a beard, long hair, and ink on almost every inch of my body, so I'm scary to most. If I cared, it would upset me, but I'm used to it.

I've always been large with a permanent scowl on my face. The aversion people have for me only grew the more ink I placed on my skin and the bigger I got—especially after my time in the US Special Forces.

Morgan thinks it gets to me like it did when we were teens, but I don't give a fuck. People are either comfortable around me, learn to be, or never are. It's not my problem.

The sound of an axe connecting with wood has my eyes lifting to look out the window above our kitchen sink. Sadly for me, my view isn't the greatest, but I see the swing of my wife's powerful arms as she expertly turns logs into firewood. It didn't have to be done now, but Morgan woke up needing to work off some steam, so she's been out there for the last hour chopping away. I would've preferred that she got her energy out by sitting on my cock, but I know she wants to be more respectful with Nathan here.

I have other ideas.

He's stuck here until the plows can clear the roads, and I'm not going to keep my hands off my wife in my home. I also know that even though he was shocked, he enjoyed what he saw. I felt him the moment he peered through the open door, watching us curiously. Had he really been offended and upset, he would've heard my wife's cries and stayed far away from the door. But he made the choice to walk down the hall, and he made the choice to stay and watch. The question is: If he had the opportunity again, would he still claim he wanted to leave? Or would he be curious?

I hear one of the floorboards creak and turn from watching Morgan to the man currently occupying my thoughts. He rubs the back of his neck awkwardly, the shirt and pants I left him covering the muscular body hidden underneath. I'm glad the clothes mostly fit and that our old tenant had left some behind, because my clothes would've drowned him.

"Good morning," he says, his warm voice uneasy.

I could say "good morning" back, but I reserve frilly words for Morgan alone. Instead, I tip my chin down in greeting. "Coffee?" I ask.

He drops his hand back down to his side, his eyes pausing on the cinnamon rolls before meeting mine. "Um, yeah. Thanks."

"Black?"

"Yes."

I move to the coffeepot. The dark liquid is freshly brewed, and I pour him a cup before I place it on the table in front of an empty chair. "Sit."

Nathan blinks at me, his lips tightening. For a second, I think he's going to say something, but then he follows the order. Satisfaction stirs in my gut that he listened because I like when people listen, but again, I go back to my earlier assessment of a wolf in sheep's clothing. He wanted to tell me something—probably bark at me for sounding rude—but he'd held himself back.

I pour myself my own cup of coffee and take a sip before the oven dings. After draining half of it, the hot liquid burning on its way down, I grab the potholders and pull out the tray of crisp, thick-cut bacon. Nathan's eyes are on me as they were earlier, and just like then, he doesn't think I notice. But there's a reason I'm a good hunter, why the name Fox suits me in more ways than one. I observe, I notice, I plan and outwit…among other things.

Keeping my face neutral, I place the hot pan of bacon on top of the oven and set the potholders down before I turn my gaze to Nathan. Our eyes meet, and he holds the connection. It's brief, but he does it. When he looks down at his mug, I notice the tips of his ears are pink, and I find myself standing straighter.

I knew he was attracted to Morgan, not that I can blame him. My wife attracts everyone; it's just who she is. Yet I couldn't be sure if Nathan was interested in me beyond curiosity or fear, maybe both. Having his eyes on me while I fucked my wife is one thing—it's natural for someone to be turned on by the sight of it—but that reaction just now?

I start to catalog the details of every moment he's been here. The time has been brief, but unlike me, Nathan wears his feelings and emotions on his sleeve. He also expresses them. He may not have outwardly taken a shining to me, and I do sense fear there, but maybe I've mistaken his fear for attraction? Or he could be fearful because he is attracted to me. I suppose we have time to figure it out since the storm wants to keep us here.

I turn back toward the bacon, taking a plate down from the cabinet and lining it with a paper towel before putting the strips on it. Once I've finished, I place the plate next to the cinnamon rolls and grab my coffee before sitting at the head of the table, placing myself at Nathan's left. He doesn't make a move for the food, so I gesture to it.

"Eat."

My new order has his eyes snapping up to mine again. His jaw ticks as he asks, "Do you only speak in short commands?"

My lip twitches. Hmm, the wolf wants to play? I can play.

While keeping my eyes locked on his, I snatch a few strips of bacon and place them on my plate. "I speak what I need to."

"Wow. That was a full sentence *and* not a command—I'm impressed."

My skin prickles, and the image of his impressive body strapped to Morgan's stockade, his muscular ass bright red from the force of my hand, pops in my mind. It's an amusing image, one I'm not mad at. I think our guest could use a lesson—or several.

I rip off a piece of the fatty, crisp bacon with my teeth, licking my lips of grease. Nathan hasn't removed his eyes from me, but they aren't focused on *me*, either; instead, they're focused on my mouth. On the way I chew, the way my throat flexes as I swallow. When I lean forward to take a cinnamon roll, the movement snaps him back to reality, and I catalog this reaction, too, leaning toward the idea that he is attracted to me.

Nathan clears his throat, embarrassed I caught him, then

brings the mug shaped like a pine tree to his lips. After he collects himself, he takes a piece of bacon, then another, followed by a cinnamon roll.

Before he takes a bite, he's talking again. "What time is it? I forgot to ask."

I point to the clock on the wall, and his eyes follow my direction. I can see he's annoyed I didn't just tell him, but it was a test. I gave him a silent order—one that he once again followed.

"It's almost two in the afternoon?" he asks, blinking.

I don't respond, just take a bite of the gooey roll.

"I was out for almost ten hours," he continues. "Are the roads clear?"

His tone is hopeful, enough that I feel a little bad for him. I'd feel worse for him if he hadn't put the wrong chains on his tires—I saw what caused his accident before we came back to the cabin.

On top of that, he shouldn't have been driving in a storm like this in the first place.

"No." I take another large bite of the roll, only leaving a small bite remaining.

"I saw Morgan outside."

That explains why he was flushed when he answered the bedroom door earlier. I guess my beautiful wife and her axe skills woke him up—in more ways than one.

"I spent all morning clearing a pathway," I say. "The storm has slowed, but we're expected to get more snow tonight. The roads are closed, and the plows won't be around until the storm is completely over."

He blinks at me as if he's shocked I offered that many words and so much information. Then he leans back in his chair. "Did the sheriff get a hold of my sister?"

I chew and swallow the last bite of the sweet cinnamon bread. "Yes. They've also made the city aware of your car on the side of the road."

He exhales, his shoulders loosening. "Did he say anything else?"

"About what?"

Nathan's boyish features turn exasperated. "About my sister?"

"Why would they?"

The husky sound of Morgan's laughter makes both of us perk up. I'd faintly heard her open and close the door of our mudroom, so I knew she was coming, but I sit a little straighter nonetheless. Her winter-chilled hands land on my shoulders as she stands behind me, and I relish her touch. She squeezes me gently while I take another bite of bacon.

"You'll have to excuse my husband, Nathan. He's not one for fluff."

"I noticed."

Morgan chuckles at his response and squeezes my shoulders tighter. I think partially because she knows his comment irked me but also because he was brave enough to say it. Not many people can be snarky around me, and he's done it twice now.

As I continue to eat, Morgan does what I can't, reassuring Nathan that everything is going to be fine. While she does, I think of when we rescued him, the way he reached for Morgan and how he settled at her voice. How he sank into me as I carried him back as if his body knew to trust the people who were bringing him to safety.

I also can't shake the feeling in my gut I had when I first saw him, one I thought maybe I'd made up at the time. But it still sits heavy inside me, only growing the more I interact with him, the more I catch him looking at me. It was one of the reasons that compelled me to leave the door open beyond my own curiosity…

With a final squeeze to my shoulders, Morgan sits to the left of me, her eyes finding Nathan's across the table as she takes a cinnamon roll for herself. I observe the moment, absorbing every detail. The gentle smile on my partner's lips, the rosy pink of her cheeks from the biting cold outside and her exertion, and the ease to Nathan's shoulders despite him outwardly trying to prove his unease and anger with his words and glares.

It hits me then, like a spark catching dry tinder: Could he be the partner we've been wanting?

Morgan turns to me at the exact instant I think it, and she smiles. It's a smile of softness, of sweetness, of reverence—it's *my* smile, the one reserved only for me. When our eyes connect, I see the moment she knows what I'm thinking because her body tenses. She looks back at Nathan, who's cutting into his cinnamon roll as if he's at a five-star restaurant, then to me. Her eyebrow lifts, and I nod.

Morgan bites her lip and shifts in her chair, hesitance only I could recognize passing across her features. I know it stems from what happened with our last partner, Gabriel, but I also know that the idea of Nathan interests her.

I've established that she likes him, and he likes her. Then there's his interest in me, whether he's recognized it or not. But I think once I've convinced my wife that I'm right about him, we just need to see if our wolf wants to shed his sheep's clothing.

Though his clothes will do... to start.

Chapter Eleven

Nathan

I SWALLOW A BIT of bacon, the rich meat exploding on my taste buds. Fox may look like he'd never be caught in the kitchen, but this is the best-cooked bacon I've ever had. Not that I'd tell him that, and I won't be telling him the cinnamon roll is good, either. I think they're just the premade kind, but they're still fucking delicious. And the food and coffee is just what I needed to feel even more like myself, especially after sleeping for so long.

"Tell us about yourself, Nathan."

My eyes lift to Morgan's. There's an easy smile on her face as she takes another cinnamon roll from the pan.

I wipe my hands and mouth with a napkin after I finish my food, leaning back in the chair. Fox's eyes are on me again. I don't have to look to know, because I swear my body can sense he's observing me, as if I'm prey. It's unnerving, but I'm oddly starting to get used to it. Maybe even kind of like it.

"There's nothing much to tell," I say honestly. I could go into the details about my life, but it's not exactly exciting. They seem to lead way more exciting lives than I do. I mean, how many real-life lumberjacks—jills—does a person meet?

"I'm sure there's plenty," she volleys back. "Like how you ended up in a snowbank near our property line."

I stare down at my empty plate, feeling hot. I shouldn't be embarrassed, but I am, especially after seeing how small the cut was on my head. I think I passed out more from the shock of it all.

"He had the wrong chains on his tires."

My head snaps to Fox. "I didn't."

"You did."

I clench my jaw. "Are you an authority on tire chains?"

"I live and work in the mountains."

His answer is simple and straightforward, like all his verbalizations have been so far. Like a mountain troll of sorts, though not ugly, not at all…

I stop that thought in its tracks and scowl. "The man at the shop said—"

"Your chains were not meant for your car. You should sue the guy who put them on."

My hands, now on my thighs, dig into my skin. "You're sure?"

Fox nods, running his inked fingers over his neatly trimmed beard. In the light of day, I can see the letters MINE clearly tattooed on his index, middle, ring, and pinkie finger. Flashes of that hand wrapped around Morgan's throat, those letters clearer in my mind's eye now, send the blood from my brain downward.

I take a sip of my coffee to try to stop myself from imagining more but nearly choke on it when Fox raises a dark blond eyebrow at me. As if he knows what I just pictured.

I cough, setting the mug down as I try to regain my bearings.

"Nathan, are you okay?" Morgan asks.

"Fine." I cough several more times. "Wrong pipe."

Morgan gets up and grabs a glass of water, handing it to me from across the table before sitting back down again. I accept it gratefully, downing half the glass before placing it on the table. I keep my eyes off Fox as I thank Morgan.

"It's not your fault about the chains, Nathan. It could've happened to anyone," she says. "I've had things like that happen to me before."

I don't have to look at Fox to know she's lying to try to make me feel better. I appreciate her efforts, but I don't want her sympathy. "What's done is done," I say, taking another sip of water.

"On the bright side, at least they broke near us."

Part of me wants to ask her why that's a bright side, but I know she's right. Without them, I would have most likely frozen to death unless another miracle had happened. My sister would be without a brother, my niece without an uncle, and my mom without a son. I'd have left this world with my last thoughts being that something was missing in my life...or maybe missing inside me.

"Fox passed out in the snow once."

Interest pulls my focus to a growling Fox. I know Morgan isn't lying this time because he wouldn't be reacting this way if it wasn't true.

"Morgan," his deep voice warns.

A mischievous glint appears in her eyes, and my interest piques further. "Oh, come on, baby. Lighten up. Let me make our guest feel better."

I should say it's fine, that I don't need her to help me feel better, but I want this man of few words to seem a little more average and fallible than he appears.

Fox isn't looking at me—his eyes are fierce and locked on Morgan. With another silent conversation between them, one that looks practiced from probably years of knowing each other, he dips his chin. The harshness of his features, however, clues me in that he's getting something he wants out of it.

Morgan's eyes turn back to mine. "When we first started our business, there was a learning curve. There were a lot of sleepless nights, long hours, and physical work. Fox got sick and didn't tell me he wasn't feeling well. One morning, I accidentally sliced the tip of my pinkie finger off, and he passed out, right there in the snow, when he saw all the blood."

"That's not how it happened," he protests.

Morgan huffs a laugh. "If you say so."

"I was delirious, and with the way you came screaming at me, I thought your hand was gone."

She gives him a "really" look, and the two have a stare down that looks like a battle of wills. The interaction is amusing, and I'll admit, it does make me feel better that I'm not alone in my panic-induced fainting.

"Anyway, maybe men just need to be less squeamish."

"I'm not squeamish," Fox argues.

"I know, baby. But you were that morning."

Fox grunts and gets up from the table to take his plate to the kitchen sink. I don't know if he's truly upset or just embarrassed, but I find joy in it regardless.

Morgan grins at me, and I can't help but grin back. Even if last night was weird, Morgan is really starting to grow on me.

"Have you always wanted to be a lumber…person?" I ask.

She laughs at my question. "We like to use the term *logger*. And no, though I've always been into environmental science, specifically forestry, which I have a degree in. I also got into axe throwing—among other things—for stress relief while Fox was in Afghanistan. Then, after he left the military, we moved to Starlight Haven for some peace and quiet. That led us to take over the lumber company, and here we are. That's the short version, at least."

My brain absorbs everything she's saying. Fox having been in Afghanistan makes sense for his personality, the way he seems to slyly watch and protect, his hard exterior. The way he barks orders. How he reacted to being called squeamish…it all makes sense. The logging still seems like a stretch, but that was more Morgan's dream, I'm guessing.

"You have an interesting life."

Fox returns to take Morgan's plate and then mine. He doesn't look at me when he does, still lost in his thoughts.

"I suppose. It's hard work, but we both enjoy it," Morgan says.

"I noticed." I sit up straighter when the words are out of my mouth, not having meant to say them out loud.

"You did?"

"At least for you," I say. "I woke up to you chopping wood. It was impressive."

She shrugs. "If you can't chop wood, you probably shouldn't do what we do. Or live in a cabin in the woods."

That makes me chuckle. "Fair. But it was still impressive. You're strong and precise."

Morgan's hazel pools shine at my praise. Once again, I get lost in the colors of them, and my heart speeds up so quickly, I wouldn't be able to stop it even if I tried. God, she really is stunning.

The clearing of a throat snaps me from the moment, and my eyes dart to Fox. Instead of finding a man who should be jealous at the way I'm staring at his wife, I swear I see his cheek twitch as if he wants to smile, but I can't tell for sure.

"It's snowing hard again," Fox says, sitting back down in his chair.

Both Morgan and I look out of the living room window. Fuck, he's right. Disappointment burrows in my chest, confirming once more that I'm probably going to miss Christmas with my family. The fresh white powder also makes me wonder what we're going to do all day. Play cards? Watch movies?

While the tension between the three of us has lessened, it's still there. For a moment, I had considered asking Morgan if she would teach me how to chop wood, but that's not happening with another wave of the storm moving in.

A heavy pause falls between the three of us before Morgan taps her nails on the table, drawing our attention to her. "I have an idea." She smiles at Fox then back at me, an excited gleam in her eye. "Let's go in the sauna."

Heat creeps up the back of my neck as the picture of Morgan—and Fox—naked under a towel flashes in my mind.

I'll also be naked under a towel with them, a married couple. Isn't that weird?

"It'll be good for you, Nathan. Help ease the sore muscles," she says.

Then it occurs to me. "Wait—you have a sauna?"

She nods. "In the garage. I got it for Fox and—I got it for Fox as a gift to get through the winters almost two years back now."

For a moment, I wonder who else she got it for, but then she stands, and I can't help but appraise her curvy body, my mind again picturing sitting next to her in the sauna.

"You're welcome to join," she adds. "If not, we have cards or books in the office if you're a reader. Sorry there's not more to do. The downsides of the generator and no internet."

I glance at Fox—I should've figured he wasn't going to say anything—then to Morgan. Fuck it. When in a cabin in the woods, right? Plus, this is a far cry from anything I would've agreed to in the past. Maybe I need to do something different for once. I *have* been saying something is missing…

"Okay."

Morgan's smile widens. Fox stands to join her, his eyes showing no emotion, so I'm left to wonder if he's happy about my choice or not.

"We'll meet you back out here in fifteen minutes," Morgan says. "I put fresh towels under the sink in the guest bathroom. You can use one of those."

"Thanks."

She nods. "See you in a bit."

The couple walks away from me to their bedroom, and I stay at the kitchen table for a moment. I blow out a long breath as I attempt to figure out if I've been taken over by body snatchers. That's the only way I would have agreed to this crazy idea. Right?

CHAPTER TWELVE

Morgan

"THE SAUNA?" FOX ASKS once our door is closed.

I start to remove my suspenders, but before I have the chance to push the second one off my shoulder, Fox bats my hand away so he can take over. I smirk as he drops the strap then moves his hands down to the button of my pants.

"Do you have a better idea?" I ask.

"Not really." Fox pulls my sweater and sports bra up and over my head in one swift tug, purposefully covering my eye roll.

When my boobs are exposed to the air, my nipples harden. Fox doesn't waste a moment, his lips closing around one and sucking deeply.

I bite down a cry and grab the sides of his head, nails digging into his hair. If we ever decide to have children, I think he'd be on my breasts more than the baby. The man is obsessed and always has been—especially since I got them pierced years ago.

He tugs on one of the barbells, and a surge of arousal pools between my legs. When he goes to suck on the other one, I grab him by the beard and tug. His eyes narrow at me, and I tut. "We don't have time for you to play. Nathan is waiting."

"Patience is a virtue."

I chuckle, pulling away from my crazy husband to head to the closet and pull out two oversized white towels, my pants and long underwear still on my lower half.

When I exit, Fox has taken off his sweats and shirt, his body naked and cock half-hard. My mouth goes dry at the sight of him, and I allow myself to watch him for a moment, cool daylight highlighting his strong body. He's…intoxicating. It doesn't matter that we practically grew up together or that we've been married since we were eighteen, Fox Malone will always do it for me. He's perfect for me in every way possible, even when he doesn't think so.

"Wrap this around your waist."

Fox chucks his dirty clothes into the hamper, then turns toward me. "Why?"

I cock my head to the side and shove the towel into his chest so he's forced to take it. "You know why. It's not just us now. We can't walk in there naked."

"He saw us naked last night."

I turn away from him, setting my towel on the bed so I can remove the rest of my clothes. "Yeah, and that turned out *so* well."

Fox sits on the bed, and before I can protest, he's pulling me into his lap. His strong thighs support my weight, tattooed arms securing me. Muscle memory has me wrapping my arms around his neck as my fingers play with the hair at the nape of it.

"He's interested."

Fox wears the same look in his eyes that I saw at the kitchen table, the one that nearly threw me for a loop. At first, I thought I imagined it, but I took note of the way he looked at Nathan, confirming his thought process and where things could potentially lead with him.

I blow out a breath. "Just because he watched us a bit last night and is getting more comfortable around us doesn't mean he's interested in being with both of us."

"Do you trust me?"

"I'm not even going to answer that." Fox knows I trust him implicitly. There's no one on this planet I could ever trust more. He's held my life in the palm of his hands since the moment we locked eyes at fourteen, the troubled boy who stole my heart and never gave it back. Not that I'd want him to.

"I'll let you take the lead on this, Morgan, but he's interested. I don't think he knows it yet—or if he does, he wants to deny it. The question is: Do *you* want to deny it?"

I try to pull away from Fox, but his arms lock me in. Then he grasps my chin between his thumb and forefinger, connecting our gazes and holding me captive with his intense blue eyes.

"You feel it; I know you do. I've watched the both of you, and there's something there. I know what we went through with Gabriel was difficult, but I thought you were open to trying again if the right person came along."

At the mention of our ex's name, my stomach tightens, and my fingers that were playing with Fox's hair grip the nape of his neck. It's been almost a year since Gabe decided being with us wasn't for him, and while I no longer have feelings for him, the memory of how it ended still stings. He left so abruptly, and since then, Fox knows I've questioned if bringing a third person in is still right for us. Though he also knows I could never fully exclude the option.

"You really think the man we rescued from the snowbank could be ours?"

Fox's face softens, a rare thing for him. "I don't know, but I think we should see where things go."

My mouth hangs slightly open. "Who are you, and what have you done with my grumpy husband?"

I expect him to harden his features and roll back his shoulders, but instead, he strokes my cheek and tucks a piece of hair behind my ear. "I want you to be happy, Morgan."

My heart stops beating, and my breath catches in my chest. "You don't think I'm happy?"

"I don't know. Are you?"

"Of course I'm happy. I love our life together—it's more than enough for me. *You're* enough for me."

He shakes his head. "I know that. That's not what I mean, and you know it."

"Having a third in our relationship isn't a requirement."

"I know that, too."

"Are you happy, baby?"

I know Fox's argument for this; I've heard it countless times before. He's always struggled to really understand and know what true happiness is. He grew up in the foster care system, lived in a home with less-than-caring adults who wanted a free government handout instead of children. Then he joined the army at eighteen and probably would've stayed had he not been medically discharged for a knee injury that still aches from time to time, though he's learned how to manage it and make the muscle stronger over the years.

Fox leans in, pressing his lips to mine. I open for him, and his tongue licks into my mouth so I can taste the sweetness of the cinnamon rolls he made for me. I press our naked torsos together, my fingers winding into his hair until I'm pulling it free from the bun he'd put it in. My nails drag over his scalp, and he groans into me, cock stiff against the plush skin of my backside.

Fox has always claimed he's not good with words, that he likes to show instead of tell. And while that may be true in some ways, in others, he's actually very good with words—he just needs to feel comfortable enough to express them. I know he can't use them right now, so I let him tell me he's happy through his mouth, through the way his cock throbs under me, how his hands grip my face and his tongue strokes deeper into my mouth with every movement of his jaw.

When he eventually pulls back after a seemingly endless amount of time, he rests his forehead against mine. "If I'm with you," he says in a steady cadence, "I'm happy."

I nod between his cupped hands on my cheeks. "I know." And I do know that. But Fox and I, we've always been different. It's become more clear to us the longer we're together—not only in the way we play sexually, but in the way we've chosen to live our lives.

Having a third in our partnership has always felt right. Over the years, it's looked different, and when Gabriel was with us, I thought that was it—we'd live out our lives as the quirky polyamorous loggers of Starlight Haven. But then Gabe up and left, and I couldn't even blame him for it.

Being in a relationship with one person is hard, and being in a relationship with two people is even harder. Moments of jealousy will always pop up, and everyone has to be willing to talk through it, to speak freely with their partners and be okay with the things they're feeling. It's also not easy to come into a relationship with Fox and me given our long shared history.

That's why I'm hesitant to even entertain the thought that Nathan could be interested, let alone be the one for us, even though I felt a pull toward his car. Even though I sensed something the moment I found him in that snowbank. Even though I feel magnetically drawn to him now, something I think I've only felt with the man whose lap I'm sitting on: the love of my life.

My thoughts strike me hard, as if a lightning bolt has hit me in the chest. I pull back from Fox so I can look into his eyes. I see a knowing in his soulful blue irises, as if he heard my thoughts telepathically. Without any more words, I understand why my husband is prodding us in Nathan's direction. He felt that pull, too.

"He's skittish," I say.

"We've played with enough newbies to go easy."

"*You*, go easy?"

He chuckles. "That's why you take the lead, little lamb."

I smirk. "Giving me the proverbial reins, baby?"

He nips at my lips. "More like a leash."

I chuckle, my thighs clenching at his promise. My man always has to be in control, even when he says he's not. It's very rare for him to be fully free, but I know, love, and accept that about him and always have. It's part of the reason we've always gravitated toward a third in our partnership, someone to balance us out, to give me an outlet when I need control. My husband is also insatiable.

"Let's just be careful. He seems like a sweet guy; I don't want to push any boundaries."

"That's why we set them up early." Fox brings a thumb down to stroke the underside of my breast. "He may come off soft, but he's not. Give him a chance to show himself to you."

"You've really thought about this."

"I'm going with my instincts," he says plainly. "I've also had a lot of time to think."

Concern furrows my brow. "You should've been sleeping instead of thinking."

He flicks my nipple, which I take as my cue to jump off his lap.

He smacks my ass as I turn away, and I shoot him a chiding look. "Let's go before Nathan changes his mind."

Fox half smiles slyly as he stands, wrapping the towel around his waist. "Lead the way, lamb."

Chapter Thirteen

Nathan

Why did I agree to this again? is my first thought as I walk out of the bathroom, a towel wrapped snugly around my narrow waist. My second thought is: *Do they have tequila?* Because I could use a drink, maybe ten. This was a dumb idea. I should go find a book to read—

"You have a tattoo."

I jump, my eyes darting to the end of the hallway, where Morgan has emerged. I try to ignore that she's wrapped in a towel, her plump body hugged by the fluffy white material and the looming body of her husband behind her.

I look down at my biceps, where a black-and-gray wave encircles the muscle. They would've seen it already since they stripped me while I was unconscious to save my life, but I appreciate she's acting as if she hasn't. I'd rather start from scratch and pretend they didn't see me fully naked already.

"Just the one," I say.

She steps up so we're standing face-to-face, a smile on her lips. "Fox and I have a fascination with body art, if you can't tell."

My focus is drawn to an unsmiling Fox, the overhead light of the hallway illuminating his blond hair and broad tattooed features. It's hard to miss all his ink from the neck down. While sitting in the kitchen, I couldn't help but wonder if the detailed geometric shapes wrapping around his throat hurt like hell when he got them.

"I like it. Did you design it?" Morgan asks.

I pull my attention back to her and shake my head. "My dad did."

Her eyes light up. "It's amazing. The detail is incredible—it's so realistic."

"Thank you" is all I say. I don't want to talk about my dad. If I get into it, I'll have to bring up his passing, and I'd rather not go there, especially when I'm in a cabin almost naked with two people who are still strangers.

As if she read my mind, Morgan points down the hallway. "Walk down, then turn left. The door to the left of the fireplace will take you to the mudroom, then walk through the garage. It's going to be cold in there, but I got the sauna going earlier, so it should be nice and hot for us."

Her words spark my curiosity, and now I'm wondering if she was planning to invite me in here all along or if this is something they normally do on a Saturday afternoon and I'm just invading their plans. I try not to think about it as I follow her direction, taking in their home a bit more as I walk with unhurried steps.

I obviously haven't seen the outside, but from what I've seen of the interior, it's a decently sized log-cabin-style house. It's nice and appears to be on the newer side, which might explain their lack of decor. Or maybe they're just people who don't have time to decorate or don't care to. I think it would be good, however, if they at least had some Christmas decorations. If I'm stuck here for who knows how long, it would be nice to get in the holiday spirit a bit.

Once I've made my way into the mudroom, I notice the clothing I was in when they found me is hanging next to a washer and dryer.

"I didn't know if they were dryer safe," Morgan comments. I turn my head over my shoulder as I put my hand on the doorknob to the garage.

"Oh," I say, an odd feeling setting in my stomach upon

hearing that she cared enough not to shrink my clothes. "They can be put in the dryer."

She smiles, and I turn my head back to push open the door.

"Watch your step," Fox barks.

His voice pokes at my back and makes me stand straighter. And while the order was clipped, I decide I need to try to be nicer and warmer to the people who found me, people who obviously care about my well-being. I speak a quiet thanks for his warning as I step down into the garage. It's freezing like Morgan said it would be, but the space is large and a lot nicer than most garages I've seen.

Gym equipment sits in one corner with a black truck to its side. Next to the gym equipment is a wooden box I'm assuming is the sauna. It's funny—it never occurred to me that a regular person would have one in their home like this. I've only ever thought of them to be something found in a gym or a spa...or a wealthy person's home.

My feet freeze against the floor of the garage, and I pick up my pace, not caring if the two people who feel comfortable in the cold think it's funny. I'm not used to winter weather like this, and after last night, they know that. So why hide my thin skin?

Thankfully, they don't say anything as I walk briskly to the sauna, opening the door to the wooden box.

The hot cedar-scented air bathes my chilled skin, and I exhale a relieved breath. Morgan steps in behind me, and only when I feel the heat of her body and look at the size of the sauna do I realize how close the quarters are going to be. I mean, I kind a figured, but I guess I didn't really picture *how* close.

"Sit wherever you want," Morgan chimes, her breath skittering across the back of my neck.

My body shivers, and I try to hide it, taking another step in. I head to the back corner, seating myself on the top far bench.

I pick it because it's the shorter side of the L-shaped seating and my hosts can sit on the top of the longer side as well as the bench below it.

Once I'm seated, I'm slightly relieved the space is roomier than I first thought and we won't have to huddle together awkwardly. When Morgan sits, she seats herself exactly where I hoped she would, on the top bench to my right. Once Fox is inside, I notice he's so tall his head nearly touches the ceiling.

He swiftly closes the door, his broad back facing me now. After the door is sealed, he doesn't immediately turn around, allowing me to see a large black-and-gray forest scene covering the span of his corded shoulders and strong back.

The art is interesting. It's mostly forests that look like the ones surrounding us, but then I see a river flowing through it, leading downward until the water disappears below the line of his white towel—his very low-slung white towel.

I lean forward in my seat, my eyes drawing back up the art so I can observe along the waterline. As I drag my gaze over the sure black lines, I'm met with a depiction of a large and almost muscular fox, though its fine detail manages to make it look light on its feet, a swift and cunning predator. I squint to study more of the details, but the light of the sauna is too dim.

A hissing noise followed by steam filling the air pulls me from my perusal, and if my skin wasn't already turning hot from the sauna, it would be now.

Fox places more water on the hot stones above the heater, and another plume of cloudy steam fills the wooden space. I'll admit, the foggy atmosphere only makes the man seem more like a god among mere mortals.

"It's a nice piece, isn't it?" Morgan asks.

Embarrassment licks at my neck from being caught staring, and I turn my gaze to her amused one. It's pointless to try to hide that I was looking, so I nod. "It's very detailed."

"It's my work, though Fox drew some of it."

Fox takes a seat on the lower bench so his head is near

Morgan's knee, and I can look at them easily. He spreads his legs wide as he sits, the towel expanding until one side of it drops between his thighs.

I snap my head up from his crotch and try to quell whatever is coming over me. I've never been interested in men—or at least, I don't think I have. I'm not sure what's happening to me now or why I'm so intrigued by him. Or Morgan, for that matter. Not only are they married to each other, but they're also just people with interesting jobs.

Or at least that's what I tell myself when I ask the next question. "You're tattoo artists? I thought you were loggers."

"We're many things," Morgan says. "But when Fox was deployed, I had to do something to fill my time besides school. I've always loved art, and I fell in love with tattoos when I was fifteen. I forged my mom's signature to get this puppy."

She holds out her wrist for me to see. Two faded red hearts are overlapping each other, and in the middle are the letters F and M.

"Fox is my high school sweetheart," Morgan adds. "When my mom saw it, she grounded me for a month. Said I'd regret it when Fox left me." She looks down at Fox, and in an oddly tender move for a man who looks like him, he rests his head against her tattooed outer thigh.

"Guess you showed her."

Morgan smiles wistfully. "We did. We've been together for twenty-one years."

Fox squeezes her calf, and I have to admire them, because that's a long time.

"Anyway," she goes on, "I took drawing classes in high school and a few in college. Eventually, I ordered a tattoo machine online and started practicing on fruit and pig ears."

I screw up my nose, unable to miss the way the corner of Fox's mouth twitches at my reaction.

"After that, I did some apprentice work. Eventually, I worked at a shop while I was in school."

"Then you ended up a logger."

She chuckles. "I still tattoo Fox, myself, and people in town sometimes. But I enjoy the forestry work we do—it keeps us active." Morgan's eyes light up as if she's told an inside joke before she scratches her husband's scalp. The grunt of pleasure from his lips doesn't go unnoticed by my ears.

I shift on the bench, annoyed at the way the sound made my cock wake up and how the desire to have Morgan's nails running through my hair is now at the forefront of my mind. I shouldn't be having these thoughts about a married couple— a couple who's been together since they were fourteen. Seeing them being intimate doesn't give me the right to feel anything for them.

"Tell us what you do."

My muscles tense at Fox's low voice piercing through the air. I want to point out that again, he didn't ask a question. Well, he did in a way, but it was more of a demand. *Tell us what you do.*

"You don't have to," Morgan tacks on, shooting Fox an exasperated look.

I wipe at sweat that's accumulated above my lip and decide to answer. It's not like I have anything to lose. "I work— *worked*—in marketing."

Her eyebrow lifts. "'Worked'?"

"I quit a few hours before you found me."

"Oh shit."

Her response makes me laugh. "It was time. My manager was awful."

"I'm sorry to hear that."

I shrug. "It is what it is."

"What will you do now," Fox says, again a statement, not a question.

"Fox," Morgan chides.

"It's fine," I assure her. I turn my attention to Fox. His features are neutral, and with Morgan no longer touching him, his focus is completely on me. I find I'm getting used to his penetrating gaze. "I don't know. Get another job, hopefully."

"In marketing?" Morgan asks.

"It's what I'm good at."

"Do you enjoy it?" she follows up.

My mouth opens to answer yes, but then I stop. Do I enjoy it? I guess I never really stopped to ask myself that. I'm good at it, yes. But do I like it? Silence fills the sauna, and now all I can hear is the sound of breathing and my heart pounding in my ears.

"I—" I pause again. "I don't know. I've never really thought about it."

Morgan wipes a bit of sweat from her forehead. "Is there something you enjoy doing?" I hear an excited lilt in her tone as she asks.

"Surfing," I say without having to think about it.

She points to the wave cuff on my left biceps. "Explains the tattoo."

I nod. "There's not a career for me in that. I'm not good enough to do it professionally; nor would it make sense for me to start at twenty-eight."

"You could teach lessons?"

I shrug, moving my gaze to the hot rocks in the corner. Teaching surf lessons sounds fun for a weekend gig, but it wouldn't be enough to pay my bills.

More silence fills the space, and then I find myself speaking. "I'll figure it out. All I know is that I want to do something more than I was doing, because what I have been doing...it wasn't working for me."

"It sounds like you're talking about more than just your job."

I track my gaze to the couple staring at me. Morgan's eyes are soft and understanding, while Fox...he looks interested. Which surprises me, since he's not given me much more than a scowl or a blank stare.

"When I was in the snow last night…when I was—"

"—slowly freezing to death," Fox finishes for me.

Morgan directs a glare at him, but I nod, appreciating his bluntness in the moment. It makes me remember the gravity of the situation I was in.

"I kept thinking that something was missing from my life, but I don't know what. I have…*had* a good job. Easy life. I have friends, family. Just something is—" I trail off, wiping more sweat from my forehead. I wonder for a moment if the sauna is detoxing me in more ways than one. Normally, I wouldn't be so forthcoming.

I shift from side to side and consider getting up. Morgan can see it because her hand shoots out, her fingers gripping my forearm.

For a moment, there's tense silence. Besides my brush of fingers with Fox earlier this morning, I haven't been touched by my saviors, at least while lucid. Morgan's touch is hot, her hand slick from the heated air. My eyes flash to hers, and I feel as if she's trying to say something to me. My skin grows hotter, though this time, it's not from the sauna.

"Something's missing?" Her voice fills the space, finishing my thought for me.

"Yes."

Morgan's grip on my arm softens, but she doesn't remove it. Instead, she moves closer to me on the bench but doesn't let the rest of her body touch mine. With the heat of her next to me, I find myself wishing she would press her plush thigh into my own.

"We understand what you mean."

My brow furrows in confusion. "You seem to be doing just fine."

That makes her smile. "You never know what's going on beneath the surface of someone's life."

I exhale a short breath. "I suppose that's true."

Morgan's hand begins to trail up my forearm, the suggestiveness of it causing my heart to thump faster. I shift my eyes to Fox in near panic. His wife is touching me—she's close enough that if she wanted, she could lean in and kiss me.

What's more, we're all naked under these towels, and Morgan's is starting to slip down enough that it wouldn't take much for her breasts to fall free.

But just like when my eyes met Fox's in the kitchen earlier after the moment I had with Morgan, I don't find a jealous or angry man. I find an observing one, one who almost looks curious. Which both confuses and arouses me. Because he shouldn't look like that. And Morgan shouldn't be this close to me, touching me.

Yet I'm not stopping her.

"Is this okay?" she asks, her husky voice quiet.

"I—" Is it? My gaze bounces between the two of them, and fluttering builds low in my belly. Morgan's nail traces a vein in my forearm, and I shudder.

"Fox and I understand you more than you think, Nathan."

My name on her lips sends a jolt of desire through my body, and my eyes lock with hers. Her hazel ones are dark, and her breathing has picked up, causing her towel to creep lower now, her ample cleavage on display for me. I can also see the tattooed vines from her neck trail down between her breasts, red roses budding among the leaves and thorns. The overhead light makes the sweat on her body appear as fresh dewdrops that glitter, and I have the overwhelming desire to lean down and find out what the liquid tastes like against her silken skin.

I lick my lips, the salt of my own sweat bursting on my tongue. I shift, my cock half-hard beneath my towel. I want to be angry that I'm turned on, so I clench my fists almost in confusion, not knowing what to do or what to think.

Morgan must feel the muscles in my forearm tighten because she begins to pull back, lifting her hand from my arm.

The moment her touch leaves me, the flutter in my stomach disappears, and the warm room seems to grow cold. My arm reaches out of its own accord, snatching her hand. Fox doesn't react to the movement—he only continues to watch while Morgan's eyes widen in surprise.

"What is it you both want from me?" My bold question once again shocks my system. The Nathan of yesterday would not have asked it. He would've left the sauna feeling ashamed of being turned on. He would've retreated to his room to wait out the storm and then eventually gone home and tried to forget the whole thing. But I'm not the Nathan of yesterday—and something tells me I never will be again.

"If you haven't noticed, my husband and I are a bit different."

I huff a laugh. "You don't say."

Morgan smirks as she uses the hand she's holding as leverage to get closer to me. The air thickens, and I feel unbearably hot now that she's so close, close enough that I can see the fascinating colors in her kaleidoscope eyes.

"Can I kiss you, Nathan?"

My gaze moves to her puffy lips, and blood thrums in my ears. "I don't understand."

Morgan's palm glides up my skin, and my hand drops to my thigh, allowing her to trace the veins in my arm until she reaches my tattoo. She gives the etched lines of each wave a swipe, and I'm no longer half-hard. I'm tenting my towel like a hormone-crazed teenager. I'd hide it if I thought they hadn't already seen it—it's hard to miss in such a small space.

"Do you need to understand?" she asks.

I blink at her words, and her tracing stills. "You're married." My words come out quiet, as if Fox won't be able to hear them.

"We want you."

We.

My eyes catch the gaze of the man I haven't quite been able to figure out. He's leaning against the back of the top bench, his legs still spread wide and looking like the tattooed Norse god he must have been in another life. His gaze is intense, again like a hunter watching his prey.

He wants me?

Goose bumps appear on my flesh despite the heat, and I bring my eyes back to Morgan's. "I don't—I'm not—" But the words I'm trying to say stick to the roof of my mouth. I want to say I'm not bi, I'm not polyamorous, but the words won't come out. Because to be honest, I don't know what or who I am anymore.

"Fox won't touch you unless you ask him to."

My breaths come heavier now, and Morgan's easy smile and gentle touch on my arm relax me slightly. "I—" My eyes bounce between the couple. "This is new to me. I've never..." Had a threesome? Been trapped in a cabin with loggers who apparently are swingers or something? Maybe I did hit my head harder than I thought.

Her hand moves down to grip mine. "Let us take the lead, Nathan. Maybe you'll find what's been missing."

Morgan's declaration sucks me out of my spiral. Her gentle gaze and soft touch remind me that I'm alive and here right now in this moment. This may be an interesting situation I've found myself in, but I'm here now. This is real, and I'm being propositioned by a married couple I saw having very intense and dirty sex last night. Sex that made me feel things I haven't felt in... well, ever.

"You really want this?" I ask.

"Only if you do," she says with conviction. "We realize this isn't something a lot of people do. And if you want us to walk out of this sauna and never speak of it again, we will. You're in charge here, Nathan. I promise you that."

If I had alcohol in my system, I think I'd understand my response more. But I'm sober, I'm thinking clearly, and my body wants this. Maybe something like this *is* what I've been looking for. Because as I sit here now, with yesterday's thoughts swirling in my head, I realize I spend so much time making my family proud, trying to be the good boy I was raised to be, that I never allow myself to just be. Experience.

I always do things with a purpose—and that ends now. "Kiss me, Morgan."

Chapter Fourteen

Fox

MORGAN DOESN'T GIVE NATHAN time to rethink his decision. My wife leans forward and captures Nathan's lips in hers as if she's done it a million times before. My shoulders relax, and my legs fall open wider as I watch.

In the years that Morgan and I have played with others, our interactions and the way we approach them has varied. Our last partner was the one to approach us; he was already familiar with our kind of lifestyle. Nathan is a unique situation, and he's skittish. Which I can understand—or at least I'm trying to.

It's been a long time since I've had to let Morgan lead and allow things to happen. I also know what Nathan was going to say—he's not into men. But his hesitancy in saying it and all the times he's looked at me with more than just curiosity in his eyes says otherwise.

I'm not going to force anything on him or make assumptions, though. I would've never wanted that placed on me when I was figuring out who and what I liked. I'm just going to do my best to see where the night leads—and there's plenty I can do to my wife that doesn't involve touching Nathan.

"Fuck," he groans.

My gaze focuses solely on him.

Nathan's head drops back, and his eyes are now closed. Morgan's fingers are in his tousled brown locks, tugging at the root as her lips explore the light shadow of stubble on his neck. When she sucks his pulse point, I notice the way his dick bobs under his towel. My own cock stirs, and I deny the touch my body wants.

Nathan needs to feel safe and comfortable, and while I'm good with jerking off to the show that's about to be put on for me, I don't know if Nathan is. If this goes further, we'll all have to discuss boundaries. The last thing we need is for him to panic again and try to run out into the snow.

"How does this feel?" Morgan asks before sucking his neck harder, to the point I'm sure she's going to leave a nice strawberry on his skin.

His earthy brown eyes open, remaining hooded as his chest heaves with short breaths. "Good," he says, his usual baritone voice deeper.

"Do you have limits on where I can touch and what I can do?" she asks between sucks, her fingers tugging on his hair just a little harder.

Nathan's fists are clenched at his sides, and then he stretches them open, his fingers clearly itching to touch Morgan. I open my mouth to command him to do it, to put those long digits of his to good use, but I bite my tongue. I tell myself I'll get to play later, that I'll get to test how far this man is willing to go for me and my wife. How far he's willing to go for himself.

He opens his downturned lips. But before he answers, his head turns to me, and our eyes lock like they have several times since he arrived here and opened them after coming back to the world. This time, they look different—while still unsure, they're determined. Braver. But there's also a question in them: He's asking permission.

It's sweet he thinks I'd be letting him do this if he didn't have permission. The thought makes me want to laugh. But his action gives me a layer of respect for him that I didn't have before. I soften my hard gaze and nod.

Nathan swallows, the knot in his throat bobbing, before his blown-out pupils turn to Morgan's. "No limits."

This time, I do have to bite my inner cheek to keep my

laughter away—because this man has limits. He just doesn't know what they are or how to speak them yet. But by the end of our time snowed in together, he will.

My beautiful lamb scoots closer to him and nips at his diamond-shaped jaw, which is covered in stubble from not having shaved today.

"That's a dangerous thing to say to me." She says it so quietly I almost don't hear it, and my lip twitches until I'm almost smirking.

"How so?"

Morgan removes her hands from his hair, and I hear him grunt softly at the loss. She leans back, and before he can ask her what she's doing, she undoes the already falling knot of her towel, and the white fabric pools around her ample waist.

Nathan's breath catches in his chest, and his focus drops to her heavy breasts and tight pierced nipples. He licks his lips, his eyes almost closed as he takes in her breathtaking form. I know what's going through his mind—because the same thoughts go through my mind every time I see my wife, no matter how many years we're together. She's stunning, round and soft in all the places I like. Her skin is dimpled and marked in ink, telling the story of her life and everything that matters to her.

"Well, Nathan. I like a lot of things—things I don't think you're ready for." She reaches for one of his hands, and he willingly gives it to her. Then she places it over one of her tits and squeezes it so they're playing with her soft flesh together.

Nathan's eyes study the picture they make, his pale skin covered by her hand with only five small tattoos inking it. I see the moment he reads the letters Y O U R S on the knuckles of my wife's left hand, the letters matching the exact style of the one that spells *mine* on my right. He eyes me briefly before shying away, his gaze moving back to Morgan's.

"Tell me what you're thinking," he bravely asks.

She hums, making him squeeze her breast harder. "You really want to know?"

He nods on an exhale. "I do."

Morgan leans forward and pulls his earlobe between her teeth, biting down until he gasps. "I want to ride that pretty face of yours so it's hard for you to breathe—make it messy with my cum."

Nathan's cheeks stain pink from her declaration, and I take the moment of his distraction to gently crack open the sauna door, letting cool air creep into the cedar box. If Nathan agrees to what my wife wants, we're going to be in here for a while, and I don't need our guest on death's door again—even if I'm sure he'd happily go there while drowning in my wife's cunt. I know because I would feel the same.

"I'll do it." The words spill from his mouth like warm syrup.

Morgan doesn't react to his eagerness like I expected—no surprise or shock is in her eyes. Instead, she takes his hand from her breast, then kisses his palm tenderly.

"I'm glad to hear it, Nathan," she says, her eyes gleaming with satisfaction as they meet his. "But first, I want what's hiding under that towel in my mouth." With that, she pulls said towel open and drops down onto the bench below.

CHAPTER FIFTEEN

Nathan

MORGAN'S COY EYES STARE up at me from the bench below—hazel, nearly black—as a tiny bead of sweat drips down from her temple.

"If you want me to stop, tell me," she says.

Stop? While this may be the wildest thing I've done, I'm not going to stop it, especially not now. Not with one of the most beautiful women I've ever seen on her knees in front of me, her perfect pink lips parted and ready for my cock.

"I will," I say, my voice no longer sounding like my own. "But I won't."

My words hang in the heat of the sauna, and I'm still hyper-aware that Fox—her husband—is watching. There's no way not to feel that intense gaze on us, and I wonder if this is just a kink of his, watching another man with his wife. But again, I can't find it in myself to care. It's been a while since I've had a woman like this—since I've wanted a woman like this—and I'm not going to let this pass me by. If I feel bad about it later, I can always blame my head injury. Or at least that's what I'm going to tell myself.

Morgan shifts so her towel is under her knees before placing her hands on my ankles. She grips them tightly before swiftly spreading my legs wide, the force sudden and hard enough my steel erection bobs, and I feel more exposed than I ever have in my life. The slight humiliation only sends more blood rushing to my already hard cock, precum leaking from the tip.

"This okay?" she asks, her tits heaving. Tits that are pierced by little silver barbells, ones I didn't notice in my shock last night.

I dip my chin sharply, wishing she wouldn't check in on me. I'm fine, and for the first time in my life, I want to grab the back of a woman's head and shut her up by filling her mouth with my dick. I blink and push that down, not wanting to entertain my unhinged thoughts any more than I want to ana-lyze this new side of me. There will be time for that later.

Morgan's hands begin to travel up my calves. She mas-sages the sore muscles, her hands slipping over my damp skin. Every time she kneads a knot, she bobs closer to the tip of my engorged head, teasing me, taunting me, and I know she's doing it on purpose. But I don't say anything, letting her take the lead—she is about to suck my cock, after all.

Though I'm still thinking about her offer to ride my face.

"*Fuuuck!*" The word slips from my mouth as her tongue darts out to lap at the salty liquid gathered at my slit.

She answers with a naughty smile before she pulls back again, her hands working up my legs until they're on my knees. With more leverage, she shifts so she's poised over my crotch, her long hair tickling my pelvis as she drags her sharp nails up my inner thighs. My cock literally pulses, and I have to strain my lower ab muscles so I don't come early on her face and embarrass myself in front of her—in front of him.

Morgan's dark eyelashes flutter at me. "How do you like it?"

I swallow. "What?"

She gently blows air over the ruddy crown of my cock, and my stomach clenches. "Hard"—Her hand appears and grips my shaft, the squeeze strong and almost brutal. My lips part, and I groan, then she lets up and strokes me from root to tip with delicate precision. "—Or soft?"

My chin drops to my chest, and I exhale a shaky breath. "Both."

"Hmm. A man after my own heart."

Her fist goes tight around my length, and I'm gasping again. Her mouth parts, and instead of placing her lips on me like

I so desperately crave, she spits on my cock. The warm saliva travels down the thick vein running along the underside of my shaft before pooling around her thumb and forefinger where they're circling the base.

"Holy shit." My head drops back against the sauna wall, my neck straining as I inhale a breath to hold myself together. Has a woman ever spit on my dick before? No. Fuck no. I would've remembered it.

"Do that again, lamb. He liked it."

My eyes shoot open, and I'm reminded that Fox is here, watching. And now he's given her, his lamb, instructions.

"Sorry." Morgan chuckles, drawing my attention down to her. "He can't help himself."

Fox doesn't respond. Instead, he continues to observe, his body still, almost like a marble statue. Even so, I can see his own erection bulging beneath his parted towel. I'm curious why he's not touching himself.

Morgan turns her fist, allowing some of her spit to slip down onto my tight sac. "Did you like that, Nate?"

Nate. At the sound of my shortened name on her lips, I clench my fists at my sides and become more turned on—if that's even possible. "Yes," I whisper.

Morgan spits on my cock again, but this time, she uses it as lubricant to jack me. She pumps, alternating between hard and soft. Women I've slept with in the past, their hands were dainty, delicate. Morgan's are strong, calloused—worker's hands. Yet there's a softness to her movements that's feminine and completely hers alone. It's...*fucking incredible.*

She pumps me a few more times and inhales a slow breath. "You can touch me if you want, *Nate,*" she singsongs. Morgan wraps her lips around my leaking head, sucking the tip until her round cheeks hollow. I curse, my head falling back again as she takes more of me in her mouth, her nails digging into my thigh muscle as the hand near the base of my shaft moves down to cup my balls.

She squeezes, the pressure heavy and just right. All the actions together cause my spine to tingle, and one of my hands flies up to grip the back of her skull. My touch is meant to stop her movement, which it does.

Morgan looks up at me, eyes shining and puffy lips stretched around my cock. I've never really taken the time to admire the beauty of a woman at my mercy, but *goddamn* is it a thing of beauty. I have no doubt that this is a moment I'll remember forever.

Morgan's eyebrow quirks—a silent question asking what I plan to do. My hand moves through her silken hair, damp from the sauna, and I palm the back of her head.

"Use her."

My movement stops at Fox's order, and Morgan takes my distraction and starts to suck again, her hand rolling my balls. I mutter a string of gibberish, and my fingers pulse against the back of her head, but I manage to bring my attention to the man who can't seem to keep his mouth closed.

"Pardon?"

Fox rubs his thumb and forefinger over his beard, and it's then I see he's propped the door open a sliver so we don't die of heatstroke. *Smart.*

"You heard me." His grumbling words are challenging, as if he wants me to bark something back.

Morgan manages to take more of me in her mouth, and my head nearly slams back against the wooden panels. I dig my blunt nails into her scalp as a warning of sorts, but I don't push her down further or pull her off.

Fox is almost smirking, causing annoyance to crawl up my neck, yet my fingers twitch as if they want to follow his instruction. As if they have a mind of their own.

"I'm not sure what you want," I grit out, my words directed at him.

"It's not what *I* want," he says plainly. "It's what you want."

Morgan slides up my cock, her lips moving so high I think

she's going to completely slide off. But just as she reaches the tip, I apply pressure to her skull, stopping her. The action surprises us both.

"That's it," Fox says. "Use my wife's smart mouth, Nathan. It's yours."

Morgan flattens her tongue along the underside of my shaft, lips still sealed around the head like she could drink from me and die happy. The idea should be too dirty, too crass, but my balls tighten almost painfully, and I hold back a shudder. I can't believe this is real—but it is.

Morgan hums, and the thrumming vibrations seal her fate. My hands become possessed, and I cage her head with my palms. Our eyes connect for a moment, and I see her submission lying within. My resolve snaps, and my hips piston up as my hands push her down on my cock. She gags but makes no move to try to pull off me; instead, I swear she takes more of me down.

"Fuck, Morgan," I grunt.

A hiss sounds, then steam from the rocks fills the room. The white fog rises around us, and I become lost in a haze of heat and sensation. There's more steam, and Morgan moans around my dick. I clench my ass and lift off the bench, my hands forcing her down until I feel her nose brush against my pubic bone.

Morgan's palms are now planted on my thighs, and she digs them in. I take the cue and loosen my grip so she can slide up my cock, her dark gaze penetrating me through the steam as she takes a breath in through her nose. I pull to let her up, but she braces against me, her eyes shining with tears, spit leaking from the corner of her mouth. I want to ask if she's okay, if she needs a break, but the smile in her eyes sends me a clear message: *More.*

Another hiss, more steam, and my lack of ability to see clearly lends itself to a newfound feeling of freedom. My hips come up again, and I unleash myself.

"Suck, Morgan." She does as I command, her cheeks caving and tongue flattening. God, she's amazing at this. "Yes, just like that."

I dig my nails into the sides of her head, working her down my length again, then back up. I repeat the motion, each push and pull of my hands getting quicker with each pass. "Oh, fuck."

Morgan hums, and I thrust up, the crown of my cock hitting the back of her throat. I hold her there, relishing the way her muscles constrict around me. Her nails press into my thighs, and the sting sends me to another plane altogether. The only thing that would make this better is if we were on a bed and I could hang her head off the edge, see my cock moving in her throat as I played with the little bars in her nipples.

My eyes close as I imagine it, and then, as if he can't help but insert himself even in my dirty daydreams, Fox's head appears between Morgan's legs in my mental image, his blue eyes on mine as he licks her wet pussy dry.

"*Fuuuck*, I'm going to come." I open my eyes to my current reality and drop them to watch Morgan. Sweat and tears roll down her pink cheeks, and her lips are red and swollen from being abused by my dick. Warmth coils in my low belly, and my balls draw tight as my eyes drop to where I can see her breasts jiggling from her ministrations. If I wasn't so close, I'd ask her to touch herself and come with me so we could both fall over the edge together.

Every muscle in my body tightens, and I tug her hair in warning, trying to pull her off my cock before I come down her throat. "Morgan, I'm—"

"Make her swallow it," Fox barks. "Make her drink down every last drop."

"Jesus," I mutter. Morgan sucks around the crown of my pulsing head, and then I'm pushing her down so there's no question that she has to swallow it. My hips jerk, and I feel her throat muscles clench around me as I orgasm, white sparks flashing behind my eyelids.

"Morgan, fuck," I chant as I press my head back against the wall, the heat of the space almost too much as my desperate hips continue to seek the warmth of her wet mouth. For a time, the world around me fades, and all I know is the feeling of her slick heat around me and the ecstasy of coming, and coming, and coming.

It's the best orgasm of my life, and I don't want it to end. I don't want this moment to end. But when it finally does, I drop my hips back down to the bench, taking a shaky breath as my muscles begin to relax and my grip loosens on Morgan's head. She pops off my cock, my still-hard length sliding from her mouth along with a little bit of spit and my cum.

The high from my orgasm drops, and my chest tightens as I take in her abused appearance. She smiles in assurance, but I can't quite process it. A war with myself starts as I try to grapple with what I just allowed myself to do to her—of what I pictured in my mind right before I came.

"Nathan," she says quietly, but I hold up my hand to stop her.

"I should—" I say, but the rest of the words die on my tongue. Because I'm not sure what I was going to say. *Thank you? I'm sorry? What the hell did we just do?*

"Nate," she tries again, but I'm already grabbing my towel and moving as quickly as I can on my shaky post-orgasm legs.

"I'm sorry" is what I choose to finally say. Then I slip out the door without making eye contact with either of them, semi-glad that neither of them try to stop me.

CHAPTER SIXTEEN

Morgan

I SNATCH MY TOWEL off the bench and wipe down my face and mouth before turning to glare at my idiot husband.

"I told you to let me lead."

"You did."

I take a few steps to where he's sitting. The desire to grab the cock I know is hard under his towel and give it a swift tug and twist is very strong right now. "I was, until you inserted yourself."

"He needed the push; he was too afraid to let himself go."

"He would've—"

"You know better than me that's not true, Morgan. I could see it in his body language—he was afraid to let himself do what he wanted. He needed the instruction to get him there, and it did. Now he needs a minute to work it out in his head, that's all."

Fox stares at me, a stare that scares most grown men, but it doesn't scare me. It never has and never will. I wipe some sweat dripping from my forehead off, then step between his legs and cross my arms over my chest.

"I'm worried we went too far too quickly," I admit.

Fox remains still as I take in glimpses of bare skin—the skin showing between the intricate tattoos covering his body—that is flushed red from the heat and the effort of holding himself back. He's an interesting mirror to Nathan. I exhale a small sigh, then bend so I can take Fox's damp cheeks in my hands.

"Why do you want this so badly, baby?"

His gaze intensifies, and his brow furrows. "I thought you wanted to see where things went."

"I do." I stroke his cheek with my thumb. "But you're trying to force it."

"I'd argue that I'm not—I'm going at the pace he needs."

"Sometimes you have to let people set their own pace."

His jaw clenches beneath my touch. I know he's thinking about Gabe and everything that happened with him, and for a second, I feel bad that I said it. But sometimes my husband needs a reminder that not everyone likes to be pushed.

Fox swallows, then brings his hands up so they're placed over mine. "Are you trying to tell me something, Morgan?"

I pull my hands from under his and stand up straight. I love my husband, and we have a great relationship, but we're just like any other couple. We argue and have disagreements, and when a couple has been together for as long as we have, it's easy to push their partner's buttons because they often know them better than they know themselves.

"I'm just trying to understand why you felt you had to push him and why you feel so strongly about him. It's clear Nathan has never done anything like this before. How do you know he could be the right one for us, that he's not another Gabe? Is it just based on the pull we both feel toward him, or...?"

In a swift movement, Fox tugs me by the waist and plants me on his lap. My towel falls as he crushes his lips to mine, my mouth opening to his naturally as he licks inside. His tongue strokes and massages mine, searching, tasting, teasing. It takes me a second to understand what he's doing. Not only is he using his body to convey once again how much he loves and needs me, but he's tasting Nathan on my tongue.

Logically, it shouldn't prove anything. In the end, it doesn't really. But the flavor of another man on my lips while Fox adds his own makes me feel like I understand his desire to see where things go even more now.

My low belly warms like it did when Nathan and I met, and

my body thrums with a newfound energy. I wrap my arms around Fox's slick neck and hungrily return his kiss, meeting him stroke for stroke but allowing him to consume me. When he pulls back a short minute later, his breath is choppy, and he's rock hard beneath me.

"Trust me, Morgan." His letter-inked hands rest over my heart. *Mine.* "Trust your gut."

I swallow the emotions constricting my throat. "You know that's hard for me after everything."

Fox delicately kisses the corner of my mouth. "I know, but given what you just experienced with him, you can't tell me that I'm wrong. That display only proved what I've been thinking…what *my* gut has been feeling."

I huff out a long breath, knowing that he's right. "I just don't want to get hurt again."

My husband squeezes me to him. "I'll always do my best to protect you, Morgan. Especially your heart."

I play with a strand of his damp hair. "I know, baby."

Fox's pointer finger tilts my chin up so he can look me in the eye. "Trust me," he reiterates. "Let me do for him what you did for me."

My eyes widen, and my body stills as I'm thrown back to a time when we were so much younger than we are now. We were just kids trying to figure out life and young love, especially how to exist in a world that told us we were different and weird at every turn. Back then, I helped Fox pull back his layers, figure out how to channel his anger and feelings into hobbies and a lifestyle that suited him—suited *us*—and how to accept himself. Just as he did for me.

I press my forehead to his and inhale a deep breath, the scent of sweat, sex, and cedar heavy in the air. Since we found Nathan, I've been trying to figure out what drew me to him… why there was something so familiar about him. Now I truly understand. He's so much more like us than I originally thought.

"Okay." I exhale, laying a kiss on his lips. "Just let me lead this time. Let me talk to him."

Fox nods. "Okay."

"Okay," I repeat. "I love you."

Fox's body melts, and he presses his cheek into mine, soaking me in like he so often does, as if he needs me to keep him grounded, just like I need him. "I love you, too, little lamb."

CHAPTER SEVENTEEN

Nathan

COLD WATER RAINS DOWN from the shower, chilling my overheated skin. I've already washed off the last twenty-four hours, but no soap in the world can erase the feeling of Morgan's lips wrapped around my cock and Fox's intense gaze on my body.

I drop my head back and release a groan as my erection makes itself known. I thought I'd spent everything I had down Morgan's throat, but regardless of whether my eyes are open or closed, I can't stop my brain from remembering what just happened, how it felt to be so out of control yet controlled at the same time. How it felt to do something so wild that even my fantasies could never have dreamed it up.

Fuck.

I completely panicked afterward, which is another reason I'm still in this shower. I'm embarrassed, and I don't know if I can look Morgan in the eye. But the way she looked afterward… I've never done that to a woman, never used one like a toy and lost myself to the feeling of pleasure alone.

What's worse is that I liked it. I liked it a lot. More than I feel I should. And while I keep trying to tell myself it was all consensual—that compared to what I saw them doing in their bedroom, this was tame—I can't help but feel like I did something wrong. Like I should find a church and go repent.

I rub water out of my eyes, and my fingers prune against my now icy skin. With a bit of resistance and a still-hard cock, I shut the water off and grab the fresh towel I'd placed on the hook before I got in. I dry off my body, hissing when the terry cloth rubs over the sensitive head of my length.

"Get it together, Nathan," I grit out. "You can be an adult about this." *Or can you?* a nagging voice in the back of my mind chimes. I bite the inside of my cheek and push the thought away before hanging the towel back up.

Once I'm dressed in the gray sweatpants and brown Henley from earlier, I stare at myself in the mirror. The same brown eyes that've stared back at me for the last twenty-seven years are there, but this time...

They're different.

They're still the warm earthy brown they've always been—of course that didn't change—but now? Now there's something more to them. They seem to shine in the light of the mirror, and my pupils are larger and darker. I try to remember if I've ever seen them look like this, like there's something more to them than what someone can see on the surface.

That's crazy, though, right? Because a blowjob doesn't change a person that much. Even as I contemplate it, I think that while it might be crazy, it also might be true. I feel as if what happened in that sauna altered my brain chemistry, or maybe the last day has. Not only did I quit my job, but I almost died, was saved by two hot kinky loggers in the woods, then had the best blowjob of my life. So yeah, maybe my brain is altered—or maybe *I'm* the one who's changed.

I pause. Two hot kinky loggers. Not one, *two*.

My eyes stay locked on my own gaze in the mirror, and I wonder if it's my soul staring back at me. A creepy thought, maybe—I don't fucking know anymore. I've never considered myself to be gay or bi, but I've never thought about it. But now that my brain has been opened to it, the idea of Fox, the idea of Fox and Morgan, I'm starting to think the reason I never questioned my sexuality is because I've never given myself the chance to.

From the moment I was born, my parents, and then eventually my sister, have been planning my marriage. I was to marry a nice girl, have a nice wedding, buy a house, get a dog, and have a couple of kids. The expectation has only gotten greater since my dad's death and Lindsey's divorce.

Is it something *I* want, though? Has it ever been?

I think of my relationship with Sasha, how before the car accident, I was contemplating our time together. I would have married her if something hadn't been missing.

But what was that missing piece?

It had nothing to do with her and everything to do with me. I know that because every girlfriend or sexual partner I've ever had has always felt the same. The sex was okay, the orgasms were okay, the time we spent together was okay, but it was never great. It was never like it was in the sauna with Morgan—with Fox. Which is even more confusing, because it's *two* people, not one. I'm not sure how to deal with that, either. It's not like I could bring them both home for Christmas dinner and not expect my family to freak out.

Also, why am I thinking of bringing them home to meet my family? Not only are they married—*married*—but I walked out on them after what just happened as well. Plus, we don't know each other.

This is all happening way too fast, and I'm beginning to wonder if we all just have a case of cabin fever, even if I know that's not true. Because Morgan was clear they've done something like this before, and now I'm questioning if the clothes I have on are from a past lover instead of someone platonic. Because these aren't Morgan's clothes, and they're too small to be Fox's.

I bring my hands up to the cool stone sink, my knuckles turning white from how hard I'm gripping it. Fox's icy-blue gaze flashes behind my eyelids, and his barking orders still rattle in my mind. *Use my wife's smart mouth, Nathan. It's yours.*

My cock aches, and I groan. I can't leave this bathroom with a fucking hard-on—I just can't.

Knock! Knock! Knock!

My back stiffens, and I squeeze my eyes shut. Really? One of them had to knock now?

"Nathan?" Morgan's voice calls from behind the door. "Are you okay?"

I exhale and rub my hands over my face, feeling the stubble from my growing beard. If I don't ask for a razor soon, I'll leave this place looking like a mountain man.

"I'm fine," I manage to get out, though my voice is raspy and lacks confidence. Which I'm sure Morgan heard.

"I'm having a glass of mulled wine by the fire if you'd like to join."

I inhale another breath, glad she didn't ask me how I was again. My attention drops to my crotch, and I beg it to deflate. It would be nice if I at least had a pair of pants that didn't show the outline of my dick. I'm not as gifted as I believe Fox to be, but I'm not small, either. Especially when I'm this hard.

"Nate?"

I lick my lips. Again, the shortened name sounds so good coming from her mouth. "Yeah," I answer. "I'll be out in a minute."

"Great!" she chimes, and even through the door, I can hear her genuine excitement and relief.

I eye myself again in the mirror, counting to ten and thinking of anything else but sex and what happened in the sauna. Instead, I think of Kathy at work with her blue forehead vein pulsing and that horrible red lipstick.

My face screws up—yeah, that did it.

CHAPTER EIGHTEEN

Morgan

I'M PLACING TWO CLEAR glass mugs of mulled red wine on the coffee table in front of the couch as Nathan walks out of the bathroom. He's freshly showered and wearing the clothes Fox set out for him last night.

"Hey," he says as he approaches.

He rubs the stubble that's grown in on his jaw as blood rushes to his cheeks. It's cute—Nathan is cute. With his short floppy brown hair, brown eyes, boyish features, and cut muscles, he's enough to make anyone's mouth water. I suppose he may like the word "handsome" better, but there's a sweetness to him I'm not used to.

The men I'm around, Fox included, are rough around the edges. We get a lot of unsavory people looking for work up here, and many are untrustworthy. Which is why Fox was so on me about locking the door last night. He's right to be wary of strangers, even though he very obviously has a good feeling about Nathan now.

"Hey," I say back, gesturing to the space on the couch next to me. "Please, sit."

Nathan glances around the room, and I feel my heart rate pick up because I know he's looking for Fox.

"Fox had some work he needed to take care of, and I wanted to chat with you." He looks sheepish that I've pointed out the obvious, but I don't give him the chance to dwell. "I hope you like mulled wine."

Nathan clears his throat as he sits. "I've never had it."

My eyebrows shoot up. "Really?"

He takes the mug off the table and holds it in his palms. "If I drink, it's usually a beer with my friends while we watch a game."

The image of Nathan drinking a beer with his friends in a sports bar makes me smile for some reason. It's so normal. I can't remember the last time I was in a bar drinking a beer. Fox and I are homebodies, especially since we built this cabin. If we do go out, it's to get breakfast at the diner in downtown Starlight Haven.

"I think there's some beer in the garage if you'd prefer," I say as he sniffs the mug.

"It's fine. I'm sure this is great." He sniffs again, and a bit of laughter sneaks past my lips. Nathan stops sniffing and cracks a bashful smile. "Sorry, it smells like Christmas."

"Hmm." I pick up my own mug and smell. "It does, doesn't it?"

The shy look disappears, and in its place is a true smile. It's stunning and sweet, a smile that makes my toes curl in the slipper socks I put on.

He sips it carefully, and at first I think he doesn't like it because his nose bunches up. But then he relaxes and takes another sip, then another.

"Verdict?"

He leans back into the soft red couch, still holding the mug in his hands. "It's good. I thought it would taste like trees, but it's spicy and sweet—and a little earthy."

I chuckle. "It's the cloves and cinnamon. Normally, I'd put a stick of cinnamon and a dried orange slice on top, but I ran out."

He nods before taking another sip and then staring into the crackling fire I lit. For a few minutes, we don't speak—we simply drink our wine and watch the flames, enjoying each other's company. Eventually, Nathan breaks the silence.

"Do you not like Christmas?" he asks, placing his mug on the coffee table before settling back again.

His question surprises me, as that's not what I thought would be the first conversation topic to leave his mouth considering how he left the sauna. "I love Christmas."

He cocks his head, confusion on his face. "You only have two stockings hung."

I point to two brown boxes in the corner of the room. "All my decorations are in there."

"Do you often keep your decorations in their storage boxes?"

I snort from his snark. "No, but like I mentioned, we were out getting our tree when we found you. We were going to come back and decorate."

The skin around Nathan's eyes tightens. "Do you like searching for Christmas trees in blizzards?"

I press my lips together to hide my smile. "The snow makes it more fun."

He screws up his face. "I'm not sure how cutting down a Christmas tree in a whiteout is fun."

I place my mug on the table, thinking of how much fun Fox and I would've had in the snow had I not found Nathan. But then he wouldn't be sitting here right now.

I gently clear my throat. "We love the snow. In recent years with the droughts, we haven't gotten much of it, so we were excited to play in it."

That confuses Nathan again. I'm sure he's imagining us building a snowman or something of that nature, and the image of Fox putting a scarf around a snowball puts a smile on my face.

If Nathan hadn't run out of the sauna, I'd be more inclined to divulge what kind of "play" my husband and I like to indulge in during our yearly Christmas tradition, but hopefully, I can tell him later. Maybe he can even participate, if he's open.

A thrill tingles in the back of my throat as I imagine Nathan chasing me, his feet crunching in the snow echoing in my mind. But then the vision twists—Fox has Nathan pinned against a tree, his teeth tracing the rhythm of Nathan's racing pulse.

I shift on the couch, glad Nathan has yet to figure out my tells. If Fox were in the room, he'd know exactly what I just thought—he'd probably have thought the same thing. However, I'm sure I'd be pinned down or tied up next to Nathan in his imagination.

My skin tightens, and my breasts grow heavy underneath the cream sweater I threw on. I bite the inside of my cheek, silently cursing how aroused I am. My little fantasy, plus the fact that I didn't get relief in the sauna, has me feeling as if I'm walking on a tightrope. If Nathan were to touch me right now, I'd come without much effort.

Nathan's face morphs from curiosity to concern. "Are you okay?"

I guess he is more observant than I gave him credit for. "Yes, I'm fine." But my tone says I'm not fine.

"You sure? Your cheeks are flushed."

I touch the back of my hand to my cheek and feel the warmth there. I debate lying to him by making something up about the fire and the wine causing my cheeks to heat, but I don't want to lie. We should be adults and talk about what happened. It's important to be honest with Nathan about our intentions, even if we've been clear about our attraction—or at least my attraction to him.

"I want to talk about what happened in the sauna."

Nathan blinks, probably surprised that I just came out with it. To his credit, he recovers quickly. With a gentle exhale, he lifts his mug from the coffee table and takes several large gulps, nearly finishing it. My stomach coils with nerves. That's not exactly the reaction I was hoping for, but I understand it.

"If you don't want to, we don't have to. But despite how your time here started out, I do want you to be comfortable with us, Nathan."

He squirms in his seat, and for a split second, I think he's going to get up and walk off again. But instead, he settles back into the couch. When he turns his warm gaze back on me, I'm happy to see he doesn't look upset, just nervous.

"I'm—" He rubs his jaw. "I don't know what to say."

I uncross my legs and shift so I'm a bit closer to him. When he doesn't move away, my body relaxes a bit. "Can I say something then?" He swallows, his chin dipping in permission. "I understand what we did in the sauna was—"

"—different," he finishes.

I cock my head to the side, a half smile tugging at the corner of my lip.

"Yes. And I wasn't upset by what happened, Nathan. I enjoyed it—I would've stopped it if I hadn't."

Nathan takes time to observe me, his gaze trailing over my face as if he's trying to spot a lie or any damage he may have caused. It makes my heart squeeze and my breath feel sticky in my chest.

"I've never done something like that," he mutters.

I nod in understanding. I knew that to be the case, but I'm glad he's speaking the words out loud. "I know it can be scary, especially after the endorphins have left your body. The first time I dominated a partner, I went through a lot of emotions."

Nathan's eyes bore into mine, and I can tell I've made him curious.

I continue. "I'm what people in my lifestyle would call a switch. I have both dominant and submissive tendencies. With Fox, I allow him to take charge, but sometimes, when I'm in the mood, I like to have complete control. It was a part of myself that couldn't flourish until I allowed it to. And the first time I did, it took a bit of time to process it and own it."

"Lifestyle?" Nathan asks, clearly confused.

I consider for a moment how to tackle this. "Yes," I say, deciding not to complicate it. "Fox and I are not only poly-amorous, but we actively participate in a dominant and submissive lifestyle. Usually only in the bedroom, but sometimes we like to play outside of it."

Nathan's brow furrows. "I have no idea what that means."

"It's okay—a lot of people don't. Or when they think of BDSM, they think of what they see in movies or in porn. It's much more layered and nuanced than that, in my opinion. But essentially, in the bedroom, Fox dominates me. Then, if we choose to, our scene continues outside the bedroom. It doesn't always involve sex or sexual acts— it's the little things. Sometimes it's as simple as serving him his coffee the way he likes or kneeling at his feet."

Nathan leans back on the couch. "And you dominate Fox as well?"

I shake my head. "Not in the bedroom; that's not something he likes." Fox has switched before, and on the very rare occasion, he'll do it for me when he feels I need it and we don't have another partner to fulfill that need, but I can count on one hand how many times he has since we started living this way.

Nathan nods. "And out of the bedroom?"

My grin grows wider. "He'd say no, but like I said, we don't live the lifestyle twenty-four seven. It doesn't suit either of us. I know it sounds a bit odd, but we're just like any other couple. We love each other, care for each other, and annoy each other. We just choose to express ourselves and our love differently than society expects."

Nathan scratches his jaw. "Is that why you live in the woods?"

A guttural laugh bursts from my lips at his unexpected tease. "No, but it helps." Nathan's eyes shine with a smile as he moves on the couch so our knees are nearly touching.

After a moment, he murmurs, "I like your laugh."

"I like you." My abrupt declaration hangs in the air, but I'm not embarrassed by it. It's the truth. I may not know Nathan that well, but in the short time since we met, it's clear he cares. Not only about my well-being, but also the way he responded to his family needing to know where he was shows me the kind of person he is. And like Fox, my gut is telling me something about him, too. Even if it's a bit scary to acknowledge.

"I really didn't hurt you?" His question is so quiet, I almost don't hear it.

I place my hand over his. He doesn't flinch or pull away, so I wrap his hand in mine, giving it a squeeze.

"A little." He cringes like I knew he would, but I squeeze his hand harder until he looks me in the eye. "But I liked it, Nathan. And I wanted it." I pause so I know he'll really hear me. "And I wanted more of it."

His eyes widen. "More?"

"I know you may have tried to forget what you saw happening between Fox and me in our bedroom, but did that look gentle?"

His cheeks tinge pink, and he shakes his head. "The opposite."

"And that was tame."

Our eyes remain locked for a time, and then he nods.

I exhale to relax as I rack my brain for how to approach this. If I lay everything out for Nathan all at once, it could be too much. But if I'm not completely honest, I risk him being upset later, which I don't want, either.

"Nathan—"

"Morgan—"

We speak at the same time, causing us both to laugh.

"You first," he says.

I press my lips together before letting out a calm breath. "If I were to say that Fox and I are interested in playing with you more while you're here, would that be an option?"

The muscles of Nathan's arms bunch, and his jaw goes taut. I study his features, and what I find there makes my stomach sink. He's going to say no, and I'm going to have to accept it—no matter how much I like him or want to take things further with him.

Nathan sucks in a breath, and time seems to slow as I wait for his answer. Eventually, his eyes tick back to mine, and they've softened a bit, giving me a little hope. "Before I answer, I have a couple of questions."

"Anything."

He exhales. "Why me? Is it just because I'm here and available?"

I fiddle with the wedding ring on my finger as Nathan watches the movement. "No, of course not. We don't go around just asking people to have sex with us."

Nathan's eyebrow rises, and I can't help but laugh.

"I swear we don't."

"Then why me?"

"Like I said, I like you. And while Fox is terrible at using his words sometimes, he likes you, too. He wouldn't have let us play together in the sauna if he didn't."

Disbelief crosses Nathan's features. "But we don't even know each other."

"Fox and I—" I take a breath, trying to choose my words carefully. "We've been together for a long time. We know what we like, and we get feelings about people. Fox's gut instincts are incredible. Maybe he was born with them, or maybe he honed them in the military; I don't know. But he thought you'd be open to what we're offering, that you're compatible with us. And I have to agree with him, especially after what happened between us in the sauna. I'll admit, I've felt drawn to you, Nathan."

Nathan blinks at me like I'm speaking gibberish, and I think I've gone too far. Fox and I may believe in fate and gut feelings, but Nathan may not. It all sounds so silly when I say it out loud, and I'm starting to think this was all a mistake. This isn't normally how we seek out or find a partner. I'm playing in a whole new ball game here.

"I'm sorry," I say honestly. "That was a lot. I can be a lot sometimes. Do you want anything to eat?" I ask, starting to stand up.

"Morgan," Nathan says, snatching my wrist.

I sit back down. "It's okay, Nate. Really." I feel insecurities bubble up and once again curse Gabe's abrupt departure for putting them there.

"Morgan," Nathan repeats. His voice is calm, and I realize I'm panicking a bit. I blow out a breath, and my eyes dart to his fingers still holding my wrist. He strokes the skin over my pulse gently, and I shiver. "You're not a lot—you're just the right amount."

My panic eases as his sweet words settle into me. "I'm not weirding you out?"

A boyish grin appears on his lips, and I mirror it, feeling shy for the first time in, well, a long time.

"I mean, I'm a little weirded out, but not by you," he says.

"By what, then?"

"Like I said, I've never done this before. It's everything you're saying. Everything I'm feeling right now. It's all new, sudden. My brain doesn't know what to think."

"Could be your accident," I chirp, attempting to lighten the mood.

He chuckles. "I *was* questioning if this was real or if I'm dead."

"I can guarantee you're one hundred percent alive, Nathan. Because if you aren't, then I'm dead, too. And I don't remember freezing in a snowbank."

His shoulders shake with quiet laughter, and I join in. After a moment, he pulls my hand up to his lips, and my eyes follow his movement as he exposes my palm and kisses it. The action stuns me but also makes my heart speed up.

"I like you, too, Morgan."

My cheeks flush, and I dip my chin. "I'm glad to hear that."

Nathan kisses my palm again, then places my hand in his

lap, trailing over the lifelines before moving up to trace the heart tattoo I showed him earlier.

"What happens next?" he asks, our eyes meeting.

"What do you want to happen next?"

Nathan's fingers still, and he swallows. "If I were to say I'd be willing to see what happens while I'm here, what is the expectation? Is this a Christmas fling? Am I a fun game for you both?"

I shake my head. "There are no expectations, and we're both happy to see where things go if you are." I swallow. "And, Nathan, you're not a game. I promise you that." I flip my hand so I'm now holding his. "I understand we got off on a strange foot. I'm sorry if you felt that way or if we made you feel uncomfortable. But I'd like to start with a clean slate. Is that all right with you?"

"And Fox?"

"Yes."

Nathan and I jump slightly at the sound of my husband's gruff answer, and we both turn to find him walking in from the hallway entrance.

Nathan registers that I'm still holding his hand, and he tries to pull away, but I don't let him. I want him to understand that Fox is okay with us being close, with touching. My husband isn't a jealous man—not because he can't be, but because he doesn't have to be.

Nathan looks at our joined hands, then back to Fox, who's now standing near the couch. "Can I sit?" he asks Nathan.

Their gazes lock as Fox waits for his decision. While this may not seem like much, I know this is the determining factor. If Fox and I read things wrong and Nathan actually isn't okay with Fox or feels uncomfortable with him at least being in the room while we play, we'll enter a no-fly zone. I can't be with someone who isn't accepting of the man who quite literally has been my everything since we were teens. It would just never work, even if it was only for an evening.

I gently grip Nathan's hand, and his shoulders slowly ease. "Yes," he says with a steady, even tone. "Please sit."

Chapter Nineteen

Fox

I TRY TO KEEP my face clear of emotion as I sit down on the chair next to the couch so I'm closer to Nathan than my wife. I only heard the tail end of their conversation, not wanting to spy on them. But I understood Morgan's desire to ask Nathan to start again with a clean slate.

While I stand by what I told her in the sauna, that I didn't go too far with Nathan by giving him instruction, I know we broke a lot of the rules we normally have in place when we bring a third person in. Nathan is, for lack of a better word, vanilla. Even though he has shown his desire to be otherwise, Morgan and I know what it's like to question those desires, to be unsure of what you like and feeling as if it's not okay to like it.

Morgan and I have had many years to explore our boundaries and figure out likes and dislikes. Nathan is much like a freshman in college when it comes to this, and he's also in a situation with strangers, so his emotions are heightened. I'll admit, I've probably made this harder than it had to be, and if Nathan wants to talk to me about it, I'll use my words and do just that.

"So," Nathan says shyly after a few beats of silence.

My cheek twitches at his awkwardness. I know I make him uneasy, and while it tickles my sadistic side, I want him to feel comfortable with me, a realization I had while I cooled off in the office.

It's easy for me to see things others don't and to use that

information to my advantage. But as Morgan's been helping me see, I can't always use that information to get what I want, which is what I was doing with Nathan. Again, I stand by what I did because I did it. But I'm going to try to be less of a dick from now on.

Key word: try.

"I'd like to start over," I say.

My eyes leave Nathan's for a moment to catch Morgan's. She's smiling warmly at me, and my frozen heart thaws.

"And if I don't want to start over?" Nathan asks.

Morgan and I both turn to him. I can see the shock on her face out of the corner of my eye, but I'm not surprised by his statement. Like I said, I see things other people don't.

"What is it you want, Nathan?" I ask, enjoying the way his name feels on my tongue. The tongue that still has a lingering taste of him I gleaned from my wife's mouth.

"I…" He looks down at his hand, the one that's joined with Morgan's. His still-damp hair from his shower flops over onto his forehead, and I stop myself from reaching out to tuck it away.

I may be a big man who demands what he wants and doesn't take shit, but that doesn't mean I can't be soft, that I don't enjoy the small things or taking care of people. I *live* to take care of people—and not just my wife but our employees and our land. And I always take care of our partners, even if it sometimes doesn't feel that way to them.

"Nathan." My tone is laced with an edge of dominance. When he looks back up at me, I soften my eyes to reassure him, as if I'm reaching out my hand. "Say what you want."

"There's no judgment," Morgan adds.

Nathan inhales. "I want to explore more, but I don't know what that looks like. I don't understand how this all works. I don't know what to say or do. It feels overwhelming."

Morgan uses her hand in his to scoot closer to him, giving him the comfort he needs. I feel my hand itch to do the same, to reach out and touch him. But while I'm confident that Nathan is attracted to me, he made it clear he's not ready for me to do anything, so I'm keeping my hands to myself. Even if, deep down, it feels like a rejection—an emotion I haven't had to feel since I was much younger and naive about love and feelings.

"We'll set clear boundaries so you feel good about everything. We should've done it before, but we jumped into things too quickly," Morgan says.

She's right. Not being responsible right off the bat is so unlike us. It's also why we're having this conversation right now and I'm not balls deep in my wife while she sucks Nathan off or some variation of that image. And it's my fault, because I came to realize that there's a reason I've been acting like this, and it has nothing to do with Gabe or my past and everything to do with the man we saved.

The man now sitting across from me with color in his cheeks and determination in his eyes. Even if I didn't admit it right away, I knew the moment I laid eyes on him that he was different. I let my gut feeling and that sappy kismet moment cloud my ability to keep order. And now I have to be responsible and set things right so we don't lose Nathan before we even have him.

"Boundaries?" he asks.

"We go over what you're okay with exploring and your limits—and it doesn't have to be complicated," Morgan says. "Then, once that's settled, we let things happen naturally. We're stuck here for a while; we don't need to rush things. You can set the pace, Nathan."

I glance at Morgan, the words she echoed earlier cycling in my brain. The cheeky grin on her lips tells me everything I needed to know. She's baiting me, but she's right. I've let her take the lead to keep Nathan from spiraling, and now we need to let him set the pace.

"And if I like the pace you set?" Nathan asks, his voice tentative.

Now it's my turn to gloat. The very immature response would be to yell "I told you so!" at my wife and stick out my tongue, but I won't do that. Also, I'm positive she knows I'm thinking it because her jaw is hardened, and I'm betting she's biting her tongue.

I clear my throat and steady my features. "Then we can lead. But we need boundaries."

Nathan rubs the stubble on his jaw, looking timid. "I don't know where to start. I'm...well, I'm—"

"You're a missionary man?"

"Fox!" Morgan scolds.

I hold up my hands. "Nothing wrong with that."

My gaze turns to Nathan's, and instead of finding him embarrassed, I see that he's trying not to smile. "He's not wrong."

Two points for "I told you so."

I lean back in my chair, satisfied with his answer, and cross my arms over my chest. Nathan watches the movement, eyes tracking the muscles and veins bulging in my arms beneath my sleeves of black and gray ink. The attention only makes me preen, and I create more tension in my muscles so that he knows I've got his number.

When his eyes meet mine again, I smirk at him, almost in challenge. One that begs him to deny he wasn't paying attention and liking what he saw but not enough to put him on the spot. Thankfully, he still doesn't turn away or become embarrassed like he did earlier. It makes me think the sauna helped erase a little bit of his hesitation.

Morgan sighs, the kind of sigh she uses when she's around men being idiots. My head turns to her, and while she's exasperated, she's also smiling. My chest tightens when I see it. It's been a hard year for her—for us—and I'm happy to see her smile. Not that she doesn't smile with me, but this one is softer. It's a smile I missed, one that says she's at ease and hopeful about where this may lead.

"First, I think it's important we let you know that Fox and I have been tested recently."

Nathan blinks. "I didn't even think of that."

"Good thing you have us, then," Morgan assures him.

Nathan's body softens, and he smiles at her. "I, um, I had a physical and got tested last month. Nothing to report."

An emotion I can only describe as giddy kicks up in my stomach. I was fully prepared to use condoms, but my ideas about what we can expose Nathan to have shifted if he's open to it. I know Morgan's thinking it, too, because I see her wiggle on the couch. The image of Nathan's cum leaking from her tight asshole while mine pushes free from her cunt is a pretty one that I plan to make come true for her—for us.

"Do you have any hard limits?" I ask next.

Nathan eyes me. "Meaning?"

"Things you don't like."

He shrugs. "I honestly don't know."

"What porn do you watch?"

Nathan flushes, but he wants us to set the pace. And with him, I think it's better to get to the point instead of beating around the bush.

"I, um…"

"No judgment," Morgan coos.

Nathan settles back on the couch before his gaze finally returns to mine. "I don't watch porn that often, but when I do, it's either amateur videos or a bit like what we did in the sauna." He adds the last part quickly, like he's embarrassed to admit he's been curious about domination.

I nod. "Do you like pain?"

"Meaning?" he responds, a lilt of curiosity in his tone.

I lean forward in my seat. "Meaning, if Morgan or I put you over our knees, would you like a good spanking, or would that be too much?"

The air sucks out of the room, and the popping of a log in the fireplace makes Nathan flinch. Morgan is watching him closely, and I know she thinks I've asked too much. But I saw the way he responded to the idea of her riding his face, suffocating him with her pussy, and now I see the way he's responding to my question.

Nathan's chest is rising and falling rapidly, and his skin has more color. I also don't miss the outline of his impressive cock in his gray sweatpants. If I were nicer, I'd take that as my answer. But I want to hear him say it. It's important that he learns to use his words before we truly begin playing.

"I think I would be interested, but I'm not sure."

Satisfaction wells inside me. He didn't balk at that or the fact I included myself in that scenario. It's not something I'd do yet, or ever. But it's good information to have.

"Nathan." Morgan draws his attention to her. "Remember what I told you about me being a switch?" He nods. "I got a taste of your dominant side, but given what Fox just asked you, would you be interested in the reverse, then?"

His skin turns redder. "I think so. I mean, I think that's how I've tended to be with my partners in the past."

"You experimented as a submissive?" I ask.

He shakes his head. "No, not that, just—I like to take direction. I like to make my partners feel good."

I absorb the information that's not new to me but good confirmation, nonetheless. Nathan followed my direction in the sauna perfectly, and despite his reaction to using Morgan in a way he wasn't used to, he was checking in with her, making sure she was okay. Had he not left, I'm positive he would've insisted on reciprocating, letting her use his face for her pleasure.

"I'm going to give you a couple of options, Nathan."

His and Morgan's eyes both snap to mine. My tone is stronger now, commanding. I'm done with talking, and I have enough information and experience as a Dom to know how to make this comfortable for everyone. Morgan does, too.

Nathan's gaze flicks to Morgan's, then back to mine. Morgan

doesn't know what I have planned or what I'm going to say. But I think she gets why I'm moving this along.

"What if I don't like the options?" he asks, a snarky tone coloring his question.

Morgan smirks, and I cock my head at his smart mouth. Once again, he's showing me what I already know—he's very much like my wife. He doesn't know how to own the dominant side of him, but he also hasn't really explored his submissive side. He just existed in this space between, floundering and looking for a lifeline—or two.

"I think you'll like them if you can keep your mouth from opening again so I can speak."

I don't know if he means to, but Nathan's body responds to me, his lips pressing shut like a good boy. Fuck if that doesn't make me hard. I refrain from saying the praise out loud and sit straighter in my chair. "Your first option is we keep talking. We can do that all night if you want—"

"And the second?" he asks, interrupting me with his impatience. I guess his ability to stop himself from speaking only lasts so long.

I smirk sadistically, keeping score of how many punishments I want to give him for his insolence. "The second is you get on your knees and lick my greedy little lamb's cunt clean."

Chapter Twenty

Nathan

Fox's blue eyes dominate me from across the room, setting my already-heated skin ablaze. A part of me wants to ask if he's serious, but after the conversation we just had, I know he's not bluffing.

I also know my answer already. I've been thinking about putting my face between Morgan's thighs since she mentioned riding it in the sauna, and now that I get the opportunity to taste her, I'm not going to waste it. I still have so many questions I want to ask them, and I'm still unsure of what—if anything—I want to happen between Fox and myself, but I don't want to talk anymore. I'm not sure if Fox knew that, but I'm glad he cut our talk short.

I do like plans and knowing what I'm in for, but I don't want to think about this too much, or I'll probably question my sanity. There was a reason I let myself go in the sauna, and what Morgan said earlier got me thinking about the idea of fate.

I was raised going to church, and even though I don't consider myself an overly religious man, I do believe in a higher power, so fate isn't exactly a far-fetched idea for me. And while it seems insane that my fate would be to crash into a snowbank three days before Christmas and be rescued by polyamorous loggers, here I am.

As the minutes I'm here turn into hours, I find the idea of letting myself go with them to be freeing. And now that I've spoken to Morgan, now that I know she's okay, that I understand where this could be heading and what I'll be exploring, it's easier for me to give myself permission.

"I'm waiting," Fox says.

I run my tongue along the back of my teeth as Fox's head tilts to the side, a twinkle of mischief sparkling in his eyes. He knows what my answer will be, yet he's going to make me say it. Too bad two can play this game.

I know this man likes to be dominant, and despite my desire to also explore the other side of the coin, he knows I like it, too. Or I should say it's what I think I've secretly craved—or didn't know I was craving—until I let myself have it in the sauna.

So instead of answering, I stand from my spot on the couch.

Fox's intense focus tracks my movement with interest. He's leaning back against the chair now, his legs spread wide like they had been in the sauna. His eyebrow is still up in challenge, daring me to try something. As if he *wants* me to try something.

A picture of me on my knees, Fox's hand in my hair, my fingers digging into the tattooed muscles of his thighs as my head bobs on his cock flashes so quickly in my mind that I almost drop to my knees. I swallow the knot in my throat, my dick so painfully hard that my eyes start to water.

The Nathan of twenty minutes ago might have run out of the room at that image, but I don't want to now. I'll have time to think about what that image means for me later. Right now, I want to feast on Morgan.

I pull away from Fox's stare and find her soft hazel gaze watching me carefully. Her breathing is choppy, and the apples of her cheeks are flushed. I wonder if her nipples are hard underneath her sweater, if her pussy is weeping for me like my cock is weeping for her.

Morgan's mouth parts, and her pink tongue darts out to lick her sultry lips. The action does me in, and as if some magical force pushes me down, I get to my knees in front of her. We stare at each other like we did in the sauna, but this time, our positions are reversed. I'm the one at her feet now. And fuck if I understand it completely, but I want her to use me like I used her.

"Morgan." Fox's assertive voice cuts through the air.

Her eyes shift to his, and one of their silent conversations passes between them. When Morgan looks back at me, her gaze has transformed. There's still a sweetness to her, the one I've come to realize is part of her natural demeanor, but now the same mischief I saw in Fox's eyes are in hers.

Blood pounds in my ears as Morgan's hand comes up from her lap. My eyes track the action, but my body remains still as she runs a thumb over my stubble.

"You're going to give my inner thighs beard burn." She hums.

"Do you want me to shave?" I ask without thinking.

She smiles, her thumb still brushing over the coarse hair. "Good answer."

My lips tip up to mirror her smile, and a warmth fills my stomach. I start to open my mouth, but she silences me with a finger over my lips.

"I don't want you to shave, but I like that you were willing to for me." My smile grows beneath her finger, and when she removes it, I have the urge to snatch it back and suck it into my mouth, tease it like I'm going to tease her clit. But Morgan distracts me by placing her hands at the base of her sweater.

In a swift movement, she pulls it over her head and drops it to the ground. I expect there to be a bra underneath, but instead, her full tits are on display, just like they were in the sauna. This time, though, the barbells I saw are now small silver rings that make me want to lean forward and tug on them with my teeth. I can also see the vine and rose tattoo better in this light, making me want to trace every line and curve of it with my tongue.

Morgan lifts my chin up. "I'm in charge, all right?" I nod my acceptance. "But if you need to stop, just say stop, and I will."

"Okay," I say clearly, though I know there's no way in hell that word will be leaving my lips. At least not in this scenario.

"Are you okay if Fox gives you instructions as well?" I think back to the sauna, and my cock throbs, my length heavy and leaking precum against the soft fabric of my sweats.

"Yes." My agreement comes out breathy. "I'm okay with that."

She smiles. "Good. Now take off your shirt for me. I want to see that gorgeous body of yours while you make me come."

CHAPTER TWENTY-ONE

Morgan

NATHAN REMOVES HIS SHIRT and places it on the floor by my sweater. The smooth expanse of his chest is easy on the eyes, and if I didn't already have an objective, I'd be running my hands over his muscles and tracing the deep V of his hips. The clear skin also has me contemplating all the art that would look amazing on him. So much space to work with—unlike my husband's body, which I've helped decorate over the years.

I lift my eyes to Fox, who's perusing Nathan's back. If I didn't know him as well as I do, I'd think he was uninterested and just observing casually. But he's always been like this, training his expressions so that no one knows what he's thinking or feeling. The only thing that gives him away is the bulge of his cock beneath the pair of jeans he's thrown on. When he senses me watching, he lifts his gaze to mine while Nathan waits patiently on his knees for my instruction.

Fox's icy-blue irises warm like they do only for me, and then he purses his lips in an air kiss. The action has me grinning, because had Nathan been looking, Fox wouldn't have been caught dead doing it.

"Are you waiting for the snow to stop, Morgan?" Fox teases.

"Impatient, baby?"

He eyes me up and down to show his casual dominance, a look that always makes my knees weak and my pussy wet. "Show Nathan your pretty cunt, lamb, before I come over there and spread you for him."

His threat tingles throughout my body, and I'm half tempted

to stall so he does. But I asked to take the lead, so I'm going to do it. I've given Fox permission to instruct when needed, but this is my show, and I intend to take advantage of it.

I shift on the couch and look down at Nathan. "Remove my leggings."

Nathan's nostrils flare, and he licks his lips, almost like he can taste me already. But before his hands get to my waistband, he stops, his eyes catching mine. "If I do anything you don't like, will you tell me?"

My stomach flip-flops at his care. "Yes. I'm in charge, remember?" I wink at him, because while I am going to be in control for this, Nathan's got all the power.

A little of his brown hair falls on his forehead, and I reach out to twirl my finger around one of the strands. "Now remove my leggings, Nathan."

Nathan smirks and gives a mock salute. "Yes, ma'am."

Fox chuckles at his sass, and while it's cute, the urge to edge the shit out of him for being sassy wells inside me. I know Fox is already conjuring up ideas and uses for his smart mouth, but I know he has ideas for mine, too. My man is full of ideas— some frightening yet wonderful all the same.

Nathan's fingers hook into my pants, his brown eyes glinting in a way I haven't seen before. They're pretty, like warm pools of hot chocolate or fresh soil. When he starts to pull down, I place my hands on his broad shoulders so I can lift my hips. Not once does he remove eye contact with me, which makes the action erotic—made even more so with my husband watching.

Nathan tugs on my pants and shuffles on his knees. I take the cue, letting go of his shoulders so he can remove the rest of my leggings, leaving me completely in the nude. I was hoping we'd end up in a position like this, so what was the point of underwear?

I think Nathan stops breathing when he notices, and I know he's itching to touch me because I see his hands flexing at his sides. I move backward on the couch so I'm propped up against the pillows. Nathan continues to watch as I spread my legs open, one knee resting against the back of the couch and the other dropped open on the cushion.

"Tell me, Nathan," I say, dragging my pointer finger down my sternum. He watches the digit with rapt attention as I trail it over my breasts, toying with the piercing on my right nipple, tugging just enough that I release a small gasp. "If I let you touch me right now, where would you touch first?"

"Your clit."

"Hmm, greedy boy." I look to Fox, a question in my gaze.

"Yes, lamb?"

"Get the lube and the waterproof towel."

Fox rumbles a sound akin to a growl.

"Get the lube and the towel, *please*," I ask again with a soft smile.

He expels a satisfied grumble and gets up from his chair before leaving the room. I turn my attention back to a now confused Nathan and reach my hand down to trace my thumb over the apple of his cheek.

"I'm going to ask you to trust me."

"Okay." He inhales. "But may I ask what the lube is for?" His gaze flashes to my pussy, and I can guess what he's thinking. I'm wet, very wet.

I release a breathy chuckle. "It's for something later. But I promise that when the time comes, I'll make sure you want to do it. Like I said, if you want to stop, we'll stop."

He nods, and I brush my finger over the skin of his lower lip.

"Now, lick me up before I ruin my couch."

Nathan blinks as my words register, and then a wicked grin plays at his lips. "As you wish."

My chest tightens with a thrill, and I hardly have time to fully lie back before Nathan joins me on the couch, placing his head between my legs.

Chapter Twenty-Two

Nathan

Liquid heat coats my tongue, and I groan, my cock throbbing in my pants as if I'm about to come from just tasting Morgan's pussy. Her flavor is tangy, spicy, and a little sweet. It's better than the mulled wine, and I want to drink her up or drown in her, something I never thought I'd say.

Without a doubt, I've enjoyed going down on my partners and giving pleasure, but I've never wanted to eat someone alive like this, consume them as if they're my last meal. The idea of her riding my face, soaking me like I know she wanted to do in the sauna, seems like a fucking great idea right now. But I'm following her orders, so I remain in my position and suck her swollen clit between my lips.

"Yes, Nathan," she moans. "God, that feels good."

Her confirmation that she likes what I'm doing only makes me more ravenous. I press against her inner thighs, pushing her open for me. I'm not sure if I'm supposed to be touching her, but she doesn't stop me. I continue licking up her arousal as I alternate between using my tongue and my lips to please her.

One of her hands spears through my dark tresses, and then she's shoving my face into her pussy until my senses are consumed with nothing but her.

"Use your fingers," she commands, her hips bucking up from the couch to seek even more contact.

I take my hand from her inner thigh and seek out her wet opening. I dip one finger inside, my lips sucking on her clit as I do. The action makes her inner walls clench, and I add another finger. God, she's tight—and wet. So fucking wet.

I pull away just slightly, and Morgan lets me, so I inhale a breath and watch some of her arousal leak out around my fingers. I lean down to lap it up, flattening my tongue to catch every drop of her so none of it falls to her couch.

Morgan squirms as my tongue licks the sensitive skin between her tight rosebud and her cunt. When I press my tongue to her back entrance, she squirms, giving me ideas of other things I'd like to do to her. I've never taken a woman in the ass before, but maybe I can with Morgan.

I grind my dick on the couch, just imagining what it would feel like to have her tight ass milking my length while her husband fucked this dripping pussy. I wonder if I could feel him moving inside her, fucking her hard like I saw him do last night.

A small groan leaves my lips, and I turn it into a hum as I seal my mouth around Morgan's clit again and curl two fingers inside her. Her hand on my hair pulls the strands tight enough that my scalp stings, but I like it.

I plunge my fingers deeper until I hit her G-spot. The action makes her shove my face harder into her cunt so I can't move this time, her hips undulating as if she's trying to ride me.

"Harder, Nathan."

My lips suction, and then I release her hard bud, scraping my teeth lightly over the swollen skin as I thrust my fingers in and out of her.

Morgan cries, the sound a cinematic score as her legs begin to shake and her nails dig into my skull.

"Add a third finger."

I almost jump at the sudden stark command, but I can't turn to look at Fox because Morgan is still holding my face against her sex, using me like I used her in the sauna.

My cock aches at the memory, and now I understand why she liked it, why she wanted me to use her like a toy. Not only is it incredibly intimate, but the trust such an act requires is a turn-on in itself. It makes me feel useful, wanted, and powerful, knowing that she loves what I'm doing so much she's lost to the sensation of it—lost to me.

My tongue rolls over Morgan's clit as I add a third finger, my long digits stretching her. God, she's still so tight. I can feel how close she is to coming, though, and I want—no, *need*—to feel her orgasm. I need her to come around my fingers and on my tongue. I need to taste her release and have her tell me how much I satisfied her.

"Harder," Morgan demands at the same time I feel a presence to my left. I know it's Fox, and for a moment, I wonder why he's there. I can't look at him, but a second later, Morgan's pelvis lifts, and a towel is placed under her hips. The action forces my nose against her slippery pussy, and for a couple of seconds, I think I actually may drown.

I naturally pull back, but her hand on my head holds me there. I take the hint and suck my lips around her clit as I curl my fingers deeper inside her.

"Add another finger, Nathan." Fox's bark is so commanding and my senses are so overtaken that I obey him readily, adding a fourth finger.

Good god. If I wanted to, I could probably fit my whole hand inside her pussy. My hips rock at the image of it, how dirty it is, and I thrust my fingers up and curl them toward me again and again.

Morgan's orgasm hits her hard then, and she cries out my name. Her inner walls spasm around me, and her cum floods down my hand until it drips onto the towel below as she continues to use me for her pleasure.

"Oh my god," she moans. "Such a good boy."

My heart stops in my chest, and my hips move against the couch in a rougher pattern. I've never been called a good boy before, at least not as an adult nor in a sexual situation. Had my cock been in her pussy, I would've come hard. I'm honestly surprised I didn't come in my sweats because I liked it. I liked it a lot.

Morgan bucks again, and as I'm about to force myself away to breathe, her hips drop down, and I suck in a breath, the heady scent of her sex coating my face and permeating the air.

I look up from between her legs with hooded eyes, my four fingers still inside her as she quakes with the aftershocks of her orgasm. Morgan's head is back against the pillows, one of her arms thrown over her eyes while her chest heaves, her breasts rising and falling as she catches her breath.

"You okay, lamb?" Fox's low voice teases.

I rest my cheek on Morgan's shaking inner thigh, her hand relaxing against my scalp so I can turn my head toward him.

Fox is sitting on the coffee table, still fully clothed. He's got his hand resting on her inner knee, his thumb stroking the pale skin there. When I look closer, the skin is tinged pink as if he'd been holding her open for me while I feasted.

"He's good, baby." Morgan chuckles breathlessly. "Amazing."

If my skin wasn't already flushed from getting her off, it would be now. The praise mixed with a tiny bit of humiliation has my skin prickling. My dick strains, and I think my sweats are soaked from the leaking head. I don't know why, but the way they're speaking about me as if I'm not here is turning me on.

Fox turns his gaze to me, his hand still on Morgan's knee. Between the sauna and now this, I'm not sure how to act around him. This is his wife—shouldn't he be participating beyond barking orders and holding her open for me to feast on?

I've thought more than once about how it would be to touch him, to have him touching me. The more I explore with Morgan, and considering how I feel right now, I'm starting to think I'd be okay with it. But I don't know how I'll feel when it's happening.

Fox shifts on the table so he can begin to trail his hand

down Morgan's thigh. She makes a small noise of pleasure, and I watch as his tattooed fingers creep closer to my hand, the one that's still inside her. I should take it out, but I want to see what he's planning.

My stomach coils with anticipation, and Morgan's fingers in my hair only add to the multitude of sensations in my body. Just as he's about to reach my wrist, he stops.

I move my gaze to his so our eyes lock, and I see the silent question within his blue depths without him having to speak it. *Can I touch you?*

I don't blink, don't move—I just look into his eyes. I don't know what I'm looking for, but I keep looking. Then finally, I nod.

If I had blinked, I would've missed the corner of Fox's lips twitch. But he quickly erases it, his eyes remaining on me as he shifts. When his fingers graze the skin of my wrist, I don't flinch or try to pull away. I just let my body light up as if it's been set ablaze from within by his touch.

When I don't shy away, his touch grows bolder, his fingers encircling my wrist. My curiosity grows, but I don't have to wonder what he plans to do for long, because he tugs my hand free from Morgan's pussy.

She adjusts under me, a low moan escaping her throat that makes me once again aware that my cock is begging to be touched. I go to turn my head to her, but Fox's other hand grabs my jaw.

"Eyes here," he barks.

The forcefulness of his tone makes every muscle in my body clench, but he doesn't give me time to relish his grip because he drops his hand and pulls my wrist to guide my wet fingers to his mouth. I watch in stunned silence as he parts his lips, and my pointer finger disappears between them.

A different kind of wet heat envelops the gleaming digit, and he doesn't hesitate to suck it clean. A sound I've never heard before bubbles from my throat, and he sucks harder, his rough tongue seeking all of Morgan's heady arousal. He does the same thing with every one of my fingers, only letting my hand go after he's licked up every drop.

The room is quiet except for our breathing as my brain races with what to do next while my eyes stare at my glistening hand.

Morgan's fingers gently tug on my hair, and I snap out of my trance. "Nathan," she croons, "do you want to continue?"

I don't hesitate to answer, my hooded gaze bouncing between the woman still splayed out for me and the domineering man who just sucked on my fingers. "Yes, please."

Morgan scratches my scalp like I'm her pet and smiles at me with a lazy warmth that heats my soul. "Then let's take care of my husband."

CHAPTER TWENTY-THREE

Nathan

FOX STANDS AND LEAVES my side as Morgan starts to sit up, but I halt her by placing a hand on her stomach. The tentative look on her face tells me she thinks I'm going to say I changed my mind about going further, but that's not what I want to do.

I turn my attention to the space between her legs and take the corner of the towel Fox placed under her to gently clean up some of her arousal. If they took care to put a towel down, I imagine she wouldn't want to drip on her floors, either.

When I turn my attention back to her, Morgan's gaze is soft, and a small smile plays at her lips. "Thank you," she says in a hushed tone.

I lean down and place a kiss on the soft mound between her legs. "My pleasure." Then I release her and sit up, unfolding my body from the position I was in and stretching out my legs.

When I lift my head, Fox has retreated to the recliner. His jeans remain, but his shirt is gone. The fire still crackles, though it's subdued now, and the room is darkening with the fading winter light. A dimmed overhead light casts a soft glow, making Fox appear like a king on his throne—not a king of riches or men but something entirely his own. He looks almost ethereal, like a fallen Lucifer, with his ink-covered body and hair cascading around his shoulders.

I stand on shaky legs and help Morgan up. Then we walk the few steps to him side by side. A small voice in the back of my mind still wants to say I'm pulled to him by some magical force, but it's all me. I want to be near him. I want to take care of him. Even if it doesn't make any sense. Even if I'm not sure what this means about me or my sexuality—or if it has to mean anything at all.

Fox flexes his chest muscles, and my eyes track down his barreled body, over his corded inked forearms to his strong hands. One of said hands is gripping the bottle of lube Morgan had him get.

"Nathan."

My name on his lips makes my body tremble. My throat bobs with a swallow before I suck in a breath. "Fox."

His cheek twitches with what I assume would've been a smile if he'd let it form. "I'm going to give you options again."

Our eyes remain connected, and his one brow lifts, challenging me to be smart with him like I was earlier. If I didn't know any better, I'd think he's hoping that I will, but this time I give in, wanting to keep him on his toes.

"All right," I say.

He licks his lips, trying to cover his surprise at my acquiescence.

"Go back to the couch, sit there like a good boy, and I'll show you how to properly face fuck my wife…"

Heat licks at the back of my neck, not only from his words but the challenge in his tone. This dominant man is trying to get a rise out of me by commenting on my earlier performance in the sauna.

I decide not to take the bait and suck in a breath through my nose. The cunning Fox wants to play, and I'll admit, if I wasn't so curious about his second option, I would've said something back to challenge him—which is another thing I normally wouldn't think of doing.

"Or?" I ask as his words still hang in the air.

"Join my wife on your knees like a good whore, and do as you're told." Fox claps his hands, and Morgan drops to her knees next to me at the nonverbal command.

A rumbling noise of satisfaction leaves his chest, and my eyes travel to the top of Morgan's head. Her chin is tipped down toward the ground, and her palms are facing upward on her bent knees, which are spread open. Before I can study the tattoos inked down her spine, Fox clears his throat.

I bring my gaze back to his waiting one, my stomach clenching as the warm air crackles with a taste of the unknown. Faint thoughts in the back of my mind question me, but they are not the questions I would've expected to have at this moment. Instead, my softening cock turns hard as I think of all the things I could ask Morgan to do while she's in this position. Of all the things Fox could ask us both to do if I join her on my knees.

I breathe in another slow breath as Fox silently waits for my answer. With a tip of my chin, I relay my choice and give in to the itch in my kneecaps, joining Morgan.

CHAPTER TWENTY-FOUR

Fox

NATHAN KNEELS NEXT TO my wife, and it's a beautiful sight. He flounders, trying to decide what to do once he's there, his eyes bouncing to the ground where Morgan kneels, then back up to me before repeating the process.

Morgan has been my submissive since our young selves even understood what it was. She knows what I like, my cues, what to do and what not to do—not that she always follows the rules I've set in place when we're playing. But she wouldn't be my brat of a wife if she didn't disobey and do it often.

"Nathan." My tone is strong yet lighter than my normal default.

His brown eyes look darker in the fading light, yet the flicker of the fire catches their depths. I take a moment to absorb him, to read the words inside his mind playing like a movie across his face. He's nervous, and I can't blame him.

Even though I knew I was attracted to both men and women by the time I was a teenager, my first experience was one I shamed myself over for a long time. Then Morgan came along and helped me realize there was nothing wrong with the way I was, and everything changed for me. I was finally able to learn and accept every aspect of who I am without judgment.

Since then, during every new intimate experience I have, she's been with me or I with her. Not only have we found it's best for our relationship to share those times with each other, but Morgan's presence is grounding and comforting, unlike mine. I often say that she could tame a feral animal if given the opportunity.

Her response is always *Why would I need to do that, when I've already trained my feral Fox?*

"Yes?" Nathan's honeyed tone breaks me from my trip down memory lane. If Morgan's head wasn't down, she'd be questioning me with her eyes, asking why I spaced out.

I consider my next move for a moment. It's been a long time since I've felt tentative in my actions, and my only explanation for it now is that I see a part of myself in Nathan. I want this experience to be good for him. Regardless of whether he walks out of this cabin when the snow clears or if this turns into something more, I don't want to hurt him. At least not in a way he doesn't ask for.

My hand flexes on the arm of the recliner, and I surrender to my instincts. I lean forward slightly, aware of Nathan's gaze as I reach out to trace my finger down his jaw before cupping his cheek. The roughness of his stubble feels unfamiliar against my work-worn fingers, sending a shiver through me. Nathan reacts the same way, but he doesn't hide it—his body vibrates, eyes locked with mine. Yet, despite the trembling, he doesn't pull away. Instead, he surprises me, leaning his face into my touch, so obviously craving more.

I allow him to do it, waiting for him to exhale and for his shoulders to relax. As if he knows that's what I'm looking for, his hot breath blows across the skin of my wrist where I have a heart tattoo identical to Morgan's on my skin.

His eyes start to flutter closed. Though it's sweet, I don't want him to look away. I tap his cheek lightly, just enough to startle him. "Eyes open."

His pupils go wide, and he adjusts on his knees. He doesn't say anything, which is fine for now, though I would've preferred to have heard a "Yes, Sir" from his sweet mouth—which I hope will come in time.

Nathan licks his lips, and I watch his pink tongue dart in and out before I trail a finger over the wet skin. They're soft like Morgan's, though not as plump. If this wasn't our first time, I'd have them wrapped around my dick already, but I'm trying to be patient because it's what Nathan needs. Even if it's not my strong suit.

"Kiss Morgan."

Nathan blinks, and his body freezes. I almost smirk because he gave me the reaction I was hoping for. I'm sure he was expecting me to ask him to kiss me or take my cock out, but that'll come.

"Morgan, eyes up," I command.

Her gaze locks with mine, and my dick hardens from her quick acquiescence. Fuck, I love her like this. It never gets old. Her hazel irises are tender and gleam with anticipation, and I see a surrender in them that is all mine.

"Kiss her, Nathan. Make my wife taste herself on your tongue."

I snap my fingers, and that does the trick. Like a puppy with clicker training, he jumps into action, repositioning his body so he can pull her into him.

Nathan drives his tongue into Morgan's waiting mouth, his hands spearing through her already tangled hair as if he's a man on death row and she's his last taste of life.

Morgan moans from the sensations and presses her breasts against the muscles of his chest, rubbing her hard nipples over him so he kisses her deeper.

When Nathan grinds his cock into her round belly, I grip the back of his neck, pulling him off her. I force his attention to me, expecting to see shock on his face or maybe even a little fear. Instead, a grin—a wolfish grin—is on his lips.

Great. Two brats on my hands.

I squeeze his nape, my blunt nails digging into the skin in warning. "Naughty boy."

Nathan's mouth parts, but he's smart and doesn't say anything. I tilt my head at him in challenge, but he must get the message that if he speaks, there will be consequences.

I glance between the two of them, seeing my wife trying not to smile from their insolence. "Do I have to tie you both up and use your mouths how I want instead?"

Nathan's eyes darken at the threat, and there's no way I could miss how his cock bobs in his sweats.

"If that's what you want, Sir," Morgan says, her tone sweet and saccharine.

I release my grip on Nathan's neck, then sit back in the recliner. Both my playthings are breathing harder now, their naked chests rising and falling.

"No," I say nonchalantly, unbuttoning the top button of my jeans. Nathan's hungry gaze watches, his swollen lips parted. "Do you want to do it for me?" I ask.

His eyes snap to mine, and his cheeks tinge pink, but then he nods.

Morgan's breath stops, and I'd be lying if I said mine didn't as well. Nathan tentatively brings his hands to the zipper of my jeans, and my lower stomach tenses as the pressure from his fingers grips the metal tab. When he slowly starts to slide it down, the metallic sound of the teeth opening seems to echo throughout the living room. I understand this is a huge moment for Nathan, and I don't take it lightly.

My attention remains on him, and I study every aspect of his posture and facial expressions to ensure he's not forcing himself to do something he's not ready for, but I see no sign of that. Yes, he's nervous, but he's eager. Willing.

Once the zipper is down, his fingers flex as if he's not sure what to do next.

"Do you want to continue?" I ask.

"Yes."

His tone is even. Self-assured. Which is what I was hoping for. "Yes, what?"

He blinks, his brain putting the pieces together before he says, "Yes, *Sir*."

I hum in satisfaction, and I don't miss the way Nathan's lips tip up at the corners as if he's proud of himself. "Then don't make me wait, Nathan. Take my cock out."

"Yes, Sir."

CHAPTER TWENTY-FIVE

Nathan

THE WORDS LEAVE MY lips without hesitation before I pull at the band of his jeans, my fingers curling around the rough fabric and the elastic of the navy briefs hiding a prominent bulge underneath.

A quiet part of my brain says this is crazy, that I can't believe I'm doing this. I'm on my knees for a man, calling him Sir. I'm about to do something I've never done before with people I hardly know. But then, a bigger part of me wants this. Wants him. Wants Morgan. Wants to experience this with them.

Whatever "this" is.

Fox lifts his hips without me asking him to, and anticipation swells in my gut. While I've seen him fuck Morgan, I couldn't exactly see his entire cock. But from what I *did* see and from what I can guess from the outline of it, I know it's going to be massive—much like the rest of him.

While I've never had an issue with my dick size or really cared about it for that matter, my stomach is in knots wanting to know what *his* looks like. And from this vantage point, I'll be able to see every vein and curve of it.

With one final tug, his length bobs free, and all the moisture in my mouth dissipates as it taps against the plush skin of the bold dragon tattoo inked on his stomach. The noise of the skin-to-skin contact does nothing to help the throbbing between my legs—my own cock has become heavier at the sight of his.

Then I see it. *Jesus. Fucking. Christ.*

Is that a dick piercing?

Fox expels a gruff chuckle that confirms what I'm seeing is real. But I don't look up at the sound, unable to take my eyes off this man's glorious cock—a true God-given gift.

The head of it is dark pink and swollen, precum leaking from the slit. He's long and thick, and the veins are so prominent I could see them from across the room. I'd wondered if maybe his shaft would be tattooed as well, but no. In place of ink, though, there is, in fact, a piercing just under the head on the frenum. A small silver bar goes under the skin and is held in place by two small silver balls on each end.

The sound of a cap opening is the only thing that draws my attention away from it.

"Morgan," Fox says as he dribbles some of the lube over the head of his dick, the viscous liquid pooling in his slit alongside his precum before making its way down the tight engorged skin. "Be a good little lamb, and do a little show-and-tell. Nathan needs to know how I like to be touched."

Morgan shifts beside me, her warm body brushing against my arm as she wraps her hand around his cock and begins to pump roughly, working the lubricant over him.

Fox growls low in his throat, and the picture they make together is downright sinful—exactly how they looked when I came upon them last night. But this time, I'm front and center, a part of the show.

The realization throws me back into my body, and I remember my forearms are on his thighs and my hands are still gripping the fabric of his bunched clothes. Given how Morgan's positioned herself, the cool metal of her nipple ring brushes against my right arm, and I debate what I should do. Does he want me to touch him? Touch Morgan?

"Use your words, Wife."

Her head turns to me, and she grins. "Don't be gentle." She twists her hand as she says it, then brings her other one to the base of his tight sac, gripping and squeezing until Fox's head falls back against the recliner. He curses under his breath. Pre-cum spurts from the tip, and for a split second, I wonder what it tastes like.

"Firm strokes. He also loves it when you do this." Her fingers gently tug on the piercing, and Fox's hips buck, his cock thrusting upward.

"Careful," he warns. "I didn't tell you to make me come."

Morgan's smile is devilish now, which says she did that on purpose, and more excitement builds within me. She has so much power here on her knees. Fox may be in charge, but he's at her mercy.

Now I want him to be at mine.

"May I try?" The words are out of my mouth before I can truly process them, but there's no awkward pause or question to ask me if I'm sure.

Morgan defaults to Fox for direction, and my gaze follows hers. His head is leaning back against the recliner, his hooded eyes dark with need.

"Ask nicely," he demands.

My balls tighten, and my spine tingles, the already sauna-like heat in my body skyrocketing at his command. "May I please try?"

"Try what?" he volleys.

Frustration ticks in my chest, but I understand why he's pushing me to say what I want. If I can't speak my desires out loud, I shouldn't be doing this. But I want to. I really fucking want to.

"May I please touch your cock?" Fox lifts an eyebrow like he did before. "Sir," I add quickly, the title easier to say this time even if it feels strange to do it.

He doesn't speak his permission. Instead, he tips his bearded chin.

Morgan moves her hands for me, and Fox's intense stare never leaves me as I slide my hands to his erection, the feeling of his jeans and skin starchy on my palms.

I've never touched anyone's dick besides my own. If I'm being honest with myself, though, I think there were times that I imagined it, especially when I was younger. But I brushed it off because that "wasn't me."

The tips of my fingers brush over his coarse, trimmed blond curls on his pubic area, and Fox's lower belly contracts. Knowing he's anticipating my touch, wants my touch, makes my lip twitch.

At the first contact of my fingers on his balls, I suck in a quiet breath. The tight heat of his skin only makes me want this more. On instinct, I gather some of the lube and draw it up the base of his shaft, the skin so hot it almost burns me.

When I finally clamp my hand around his cock, my fingers barely touching around its girth, I squeeze him the way Morgan showed me. His cock pulses beneath my grip, leaking more precum from the pressure.

Fox releases a low sound of pleasure that goes straight to my own cock, so I do it again, moving my hand up and down, coating my palm in the lube and his own arousal.

"That's it," Morgan praises. "Change the pressure as you go."

I nod and lick my lips, my other hand digging into Fox's thigh for balance as I jack him in varying kinds of strokes. Stronger and then lighter, gripping and then firm, but never too light. I become almost lost in the motion of it, watching the skin move up and down, his dick twitching under me as the massive man beneath me gets more and more worked up.

"Play with his piercing," Morgan says softly, "but don't pull too hard."

I bite the inside of my cheek and nod again, taking the foreign object in my fingers and tugging on it lightly. Fox lets out a throaty moan, and once again, I'm struck by how powerful this feels. My body naturally leans closer, and I can feel Morgan's hot breath on my cheek.

"You can tell him how much you like it," she says against my ear, "how pretty his cock is."

I swallow, unsure if I can speak that out loud. I've never talked that much during sex, and this... this is completely new.

Morgan sees my hesitancy and places her hand over mine so we're both gripping Fox together. Her fist clenches around me, increasing the pressure on his cock. Then she leans forward and spits on the crown, just as she did in the sauna with me.

Her saliva slides between our fingers, and she does it again before looking up at a very pleased Fox.

"Your cock is beautiful, Sir," she purrs. "It's so big. So fucking perfect. I love the way Nathan's hand looks on you, tucked underneath mine. You're so fucking massive, he almost can't close his hand around it."

"Fuck," Fox groans, his hips once again thrusting up, seeking more from us.

I squeeze harder without Morgan's help, and then I cup his balls. The sac tightens beneath my grip as I roll them how I like it. I don't know if it's universal for all men, but Fox grunts in pleasure.

"He likes that, Nathan. Keep doing it."

I continue the motion, observing Fox as the skin beneath his beard flushes and a bead of sweat drops down from his forehead. His eyes connect with mine, and the icy blue has turned into that stormy color. He's close. Very close.

Fuck. I'm going to make a man come with my hand.

My hips move forward of their own accord, and I grind my erection against Fox's leg. My brow furrows from the sensation, and I press my lips together to keep myself from unloading in my sweats.

"Do you want to come, Nathan?" Fox's strained voice slices through the heated air.

I press my lips together harder at being caught. Of course he felt that. How could he not? I was just rubbing my dick into him like a teenage boy dry humping his girlfriend in his parents' basement.

"I—" My words fall flat on my tongue. I could say no, but

that's clearly a lie. I'm leaning into this, right? I'm already lean-ing into this. I have been.

"Yes," I say on an exhale. But Fox doesn't address me; instead, he turns his attention to Morgan.

"Touch yourself, lamb. Put that free hand of yours to good use."

I track the movement of Morgan's other hand, the one that's not under mine, and see her fingers skating down her body and disappearing between her legs. She releases a soft cry as she touches herself, her hand squeezing me on impulse.

Fox clears his throat, bringing my gaze to his. He looks more domineering than I've ever seen him yet vulnerable somehow. "Use my leg to get yourself off, but do not come until I do," he barks at me. "Same goes for you, Wife."

"Yes, Sir." Morgan sighs, her hand still working her clit while the other helps me jack him off.

I want to ask what happens if I come before he does, but if Morgan is listening, I decide I don't want to find out. I look down at my crotch and see a wet stain on the front from my precum. My entire body heats when I think about the mess I'm going to make.

There's a shift, and then Fox's finger is lifting my gaze to his. "Make a fucking mess, Nathan. That's what a washer is for."

His filthy words send a lightning bolt to the base of my spine. As if my hips have a mind of their own, I grind against him and release a groan, my hands around his balls and cock gripping him so tightly I feel his body shudder.

"That's it," he praises, settling back in his chair. "Such good little whores for me."

My head drops back, and my brain tells me I shouldn't like that, but fuck. I thrust my hips against his leg, seeking more pressure. When the bone of his shin rubs against my sensitive crown, I almost fall face forward into his lap but somehow manage to keep myself upright.

"Good boy, Nathan," he grunts. "Work my fat cock harder."

"Oh god," I mutter, my eyes closing as I get lost in everything I'm feeling. My dick against Fox's leg, Morgan's heated body beside me making mewling noises as she chases her own release, and my hand around Fox's thick and heavy erection.

"Sir." Morgan exhales, her husky voice strained. "I can't wait too much longer."

"Do not come, or I won't let Nathan's dick anywhere near those pretty holes of yours."

"*Please*, Sir," she pleads desperately, the sound only making me grip Fox tighter.

He grunts. "Suck me, lamb. And don't waste a fucking drop of my cum."

Morgan releases her grip around my hand. She maneuvers herself so she's still rubbing her clit but is able to lean forward until her mouth is closing around the head of Fox's cock. Her thick hair curtains her face as she begins to bob, the soft strands brushing against my arm and Fox's groin.

"Suck harder," Fox demands.

The noisy sound of her sucking and licking only adds to my arousal. My hand manages to find a rhythm with Morgan's bobbing head, her tongue and lips touching my fingers as I pump Fox.

"Tell me, Nathan. Do you like what you see?"

I press my hips harder into his leg. "Yes," I say in a needy voice that doesn't sound anything like mine. "I like seeing her lips around your big cock."

Fox vibrates in agreement, and my cheeks heat at the words I said, but then I'm distracted by his fingers tucking the hair away from Morgan's face to give us both a better view of her sucking.

"My wife is such a beautiful whore. A whore who's thirsty for her husband's cum."

She moans, and without warning, Fox shoves her head down when my hand slides near the base of his shaft. She gags violently, but he doesn't let up, holding her down until her cheeks become red. The sight should appall me, but the muscles in my low abs clench, and I punch my hips forward against Fox's leg.

"Oh, shit. I'm—" I cry. "I'm going—"

Fox chuckles, his palm still holding Morgan on his cock, her nose flaring wide so she can breathe. "Better be quick and make me come, then."

Morgan must do something with her throat because Fox hisses and grunts. I use the moment of his ecstasy to my advantage and squeeze the base of him, rolling his balls before gripping them tight.

"Come," he growls, his command echoing in my ears.

Morgan makes a keening noise around Fox's cock as her body shudders from her orgasm, and I feel Fox's dick throb as his balls unload his release down his wife's throat. The pulsing heat of it and the noise of Fox's loud grunt triggers me, too, and I fall over the edge with them.

My hips jerk against his leg, and I can't stop my head from falling near his pelvis, his musky scent filling my nose as I come violent and fast. My fingers squeeze around him as I ride out the complete and utter nirvana racking my body.

I don't know if it's seconds or minutes later, but I only manage to turn my head when I feel warm, wet fluid dripping over my fist that's still gripping the base of Fox's cock. My eyes track from my hand to Morgan's lips, which are still sucking his length, and I watch his spend leak from her swollen mouth and drip down onto my skin.

I've never seen anything like it, not even in the porn I've watched. My dick jumps again as if an invisible hand is milking it, and I exhale a shaky breath. After a few more moments, Fox gently guides Morgan from his cock.

I automatically loosen my grip around him as I lift my head.

"Every last drop," he tells her, the words an order.

Morgan doesn't balk as her mouth returns to where my hand still is. She laps up Fox's release, cleaning both his still-hard length and then my hand, humming and moaning while Fox tucks her hair behind her ear lovingly.

When Morgan's head turns to meet my eyes, she's smiling despite her abused lips and red cheeks. I half smile at her, not quite believing what we just did.

After she gets in another few licks and lays a short kiss on my hand, Fox turns her chin to him. "Good girl," he praises, cupping her cheeks.

With their focus now zeroed in on each other, they go still. He doesn't blink until she nods at him, a silent and tender check-in to make sure she's okay. My stomach twists, and a longing fills me as I continue to come down from my high. It's a longing that, for the first time ever, makes me wish I had something like that, someone who loves and cares for me as much as they clearly do for each other.

I begin to pull away, but before I can go too far, Fox's hand grips my wrist. When I meet his eyes, I expect to find them icy or see that godforsaken neutral expression of his on his face, but I don't.

His stare is searching, soft. A similar tenderness to what he just gave Morgan is now being given to me. "You good?" he asks.

My heart stops beating in my chest at his question. It's a real, genuine question, not a command or a gruff-sounding bark. Instead, it's kind and almost unsure, like he's afraid I'll say I'm not and that we took things too far.

But we didn't, because I'm fine. Better than fine. I feel… great. Or better yet, I feel lighter than I've felt in a long time, as if this was something I needed to do, something I needed to experience.

"I'm good." I exhale, knowing I could say more but that I don't need to.

Fox holds my wrist for another beat before he releases it. "Good, because we're just getting started."

My nostrils flare, and my cock stirs against the mess I made in my sweats. "More?"

Fox chuckles, a dark sound that has the hairs standing up on my arms. But I can't deny I'm curious about what that "more" will be. "Yes. But first, we should clean up and eat."

Morgan, whose head has been resting on Fox's thigh, reaches over to squeeze my hand. "Do you like steak?"

My lips press into a line, and I try to hold myself together, but I burst out laughing. The question is so ridiculous, especially with her nude form at Fox's feet and my hand still resting near his half-hard cock.

Morgan eyes me before joining in, her husky laugh warming something deep inside me, filling the empty space that was there just hours ago. I even feel Fox's body vibrate with amusement, though no laughter leaves his lips.

"I do like steak," I say, once I manage a breath.

Morgan grins. "Perfect. If you didn't, we'd have to throw you out in the snowbank."

I huff another laugh and squeeze her hand back, the promise of a nice dinner and more debauchery hanging easily around us.

Chapter Twenty-Six

Fox

I POUR WATER FROM the kettle over a bag of chamomile tea. Morgan and Nathan are asleep, having gone to bed shortly after dinner. I had planned to see where else we could take Nathan tonight, but the exhaustion coming from both of them was palpable. I was exhausted, too, but I woke up shortly after midnight, the house too quiet from the snow that continued to fall outside.

I tried to go back to sleep, but my mind began to race. And while I love cuddling with my wife or using her body to my liking while she rests, the last time I cleared the snow was this morning. So I'd gotten up and dressed quietly before heading to the mudroom to put on my winter gear and a headlamp.

Thankfully, the snow had reduced to a light flurry, and I was able to clear a lot of it from the front door and walkway. By the time I was done, my body was tired, but my mind was still wired, which brought me to the kitchen after I'd changed into a pair of flannel pants and a long-sleeved cotton shirt.

I sit down at the kitchen table, dipping the tea bag in and out of the green mug, watching the water turn a yellowish color. Thoughts of what happened in the living room with Nathan are at the forefront of my mind. He'd done more than I expected him to, even going so far as to get himself off on my leg. Not only did that prove to me yet again that I was right about him, but he also impressed me. I liked that he was willing to push himself outside his comfort zone so quickly and enjoy himself.

I thought that maybe after the hormones cooled off, he'd regret what happened. But after we'd cleaned up and had dinner, he was in a good mood. We got to know him better over dinner, learning more of his past and why he quit his job. Eventually, he even started joking with Morgan—his belly laughs alongside my wife's were still humming in my ears.

Nathan even attempted to ask me questions, though most of them were related to the storm. He wanted to know what the sheriff had said earlier and if there was any news on the weather. There wasn't. We were still stuck here, and I could feel his disappointment when I reiterated he would probably miss Christmas with his family.

A thought strikes me, one I hadn't fully considered before: Nathan would be spending this holiday with us, a day that seems to mean a great deal to him. Sure, Morgan and I like Christmas, but aside from the tradition he disrupted, a good meal, and a lot of sex, it is just another day for us. For Nathan, it appears to be different. I wonder about his family's traditions, whether they exchange gifts and if he takes pleasure in giving them.

"Um, hey."

My heart jumps in my chest as I lift my gaze to Nathan's. He's staring down at me with bleary eyes, his face apologetic.

I inhale and attempt to regain my bearings without him noticing I was off to begin with. I don't like that I didn't hear him approach. It's rare that I'm not paying attention to my surroundings, and I'm annoyed that I was distracted by thoughts of the very person now in front of me getting and giving Christmas presents.

When I don't say anything, he takes a tentative step forward. He's shirtless, and the sweats he was in earlier are in the wash, so he's got on a pair of mine. They're several sizes too big, so he has them rolled down around his trim waist so they don't fall.

"Sorry if I startled you; I couldn't sleep."

"You didn't," I lie.

He stares at me for a moment in the dim light. Not wanting to wake anyone, I only turned on the light over the kitchen sink, so it leaves Nathan mostly in darkness, lighting him only from the front.

"Are you okay?" he asks.

I don't remove my eyes from his, dropping the tea bag in my mug before standing. "Fine."

Nathan doesn't move, but I can feel him watching my back. When I get to the cupboard, I turn my head toward him. "Do you like tea?"

He blinks at me, his eyes clearer now as he becomes more coherent. "Can't say I drink too much of it. But it sounds good."

I pull down a red mug for him and then a bag of chamomile. The water is still hot in the kettle, so I pour it over the bag before I approach the kitchen table again. To my surprise, Nathan is seated. But that's not what gets me—it's the fact that he's chosen the seat at the head of the table so he's sitting close to me instead of across from me.

I school my features to show no reaction and put the mug in front of him before taking my place again. For a few minutes, Nathan and I sip our tea in silence. The sound of his breathing and the creak of the wood from him shifting in his chair only adds to me being on edge. It's not Nathan's fault, either. I think my mind is trying to catch up with everything that's happened today and the unexpected feelings being with him has brought up—all of which led to me being distracted.

Nathan's voice cuts through my thoughts. "Thank you for the tea."

I lift my eyes from my mug and nod in response.

The corner of his lip twitches. "You *really* don't like to talk much, do you?"

"Like I said before, I speak when I need to."

Hurt flashes across Nathan's face at the implication of my

words, and I clench my jaw. I don't like that I hurt him, but I struggle to know what to say to make it better. This is just how I am.

After another awkward moment, Nathan moves to stand. On impulse, my hand darts out and wraps around his wrist, my fingers pressing gently into his thrumming pulse point.

"Stay."

Nathan's unsure eyes meet mine, and I hold the contact, passing a silent apology through them. I watch as he thinks through his options, vulnerability pooling in the earth tones of his irises before he finally sits back down.

If I allowed it, I would've exhaled a breath of relief, but I swallow it down. I gently release his wrist, trailing my fingers over the top of his hand. I don't miss how he shivers from the gentle caress or how he clears his throat as if that'll hide his reaction.

"I was in the military." The confession spills from me as I sit back in my chair. It's the only thing I could think to say. It's also an offering of sorts, to help him understand me a bit more. Yet a part of me wonders why I felt compelled to do it.

Nathan stills as he absorbs my words. Then a little bit of the tension in his shoulders dissipates as he eases back into his own chair. "I remember Morgan saying that. Afghanistan?"

Right. I forgot she'd mentioned it to him earlier. "Yes. I was in the infantry at eighteen. Then I went into Special Forces."

"I'll admit, I don't know much about the military. But that sounds impressive."

I finger the string of my tea bag but don't break eye contact with him. It is considered impressive, but to me, it's just part of my past. "It's a job," I state.

A gentle smile plays on his lips. "Silent *and* humble." I glare at him, and he chuckles. "So did you retire, then?"

My knee twinges at the question. "Injured on a mission."

Nathan's brow pinches in concern. "Badly?"

"Shrapnel to the knee."

He nods, tapping the side of his mug. I can tell he wants to ask more but is afraid to, so I throw him a bone.

"In the end, I was lucky," I supply, but that is all I give him. What's done is done, and speaking about it again and again won't change what happened. I'm also starting to edge into territory I don't like to cross with people other than Morgan. I didn't even share a lot of my past with Gabriel—it's one of the reasons he left.

"How long ago was that?"

"Ten years."

Nathan cocks his head to the side. "How old were you?"

"Twenty-five."

Nathan pauses again, thinking over his words carefully before his lips part. "But you're okay now?" His question is soft, a deeper question behind it. One that tells me he's not only asking about my knee.

"Most days." The honesty of my answer brings a flash of sympathy to his face, reminding me why I tend to keep things to myself.

Likely sensing the change in my energy, Nathan lights up his expression with a gentle smile. "I'm curious, though. How does a man who was once in Special Forces decide to be a lumberjack?"

"Logger," I correct, grateful for the segue.

"Right. Logger."

"Morgan's doing. Like she mentioned, she has a degree in forestry, and it's one of her passions."

"You don't like it?"

I think of the life I live with my wife, the only woman I've ever loved and have since the moment she kneed a douchey kid in the balls for calling me a freak with no parents. The memory still makes my heart expand to this day. "I like it. It's a job."

"That wasn't convincing."

"She deserves to do something she loves after putting up with me and the military for seven years."

Nathan taps the side of his mug again. "So you do this work for her?"

"Yes. But also for me." And that's the truth. "I like the woods. I like physical labor and the work we do for the planet. Her passion has become my passion."

Nathan nods, though he doesn't seem convinced. Not that he has to be, and I understand why since I didn't exactly sell my love for what we do. But I do enjoy it, and not just the physical work of logging—it also requires a lot of mental work on the back end since we own the business.

I run numbers, do paperwork, work on government contracts, and manage employees alongside my wife. I also love that we do it together. It makes me happy to see how proud Morgan is of what we've built over the years, and she gets to use her degree. As far as I'm concerned, we'll do this work until the day we decide to retire—or until Morgan wants to quit, which I don't ever see happening.

"Maybe if the snow lets up, you and Morgan could teach me."

My eyebrows lift in question, wondering what he'd want to learn given his love for surfing and the beach.

"Teach you what?" I ask.

"How to chop wood."

My eyebrows stay up as I study Nathan. If I ignore that I know he loves the beach, the visual of him swinging an axe is a nice one. He's an attractive man, a strong one, and with the stubble growing on his jaw, he'd fit right in among me and the other scruffy men who work with us in no time.

"It's okay if you don't want to," Nathan says.

I shake my head, feeling bad that he took my silence as a no. "If you want, we can show you."

His small grin returns. "That would be nice."

The kitchen goes quiet again, and I push my near-empty mug away, feeling more awake than I did before. In the silence, I debate what to say next or if I should say anything at all. But once again, Nathan fills the dead air, as if the lack of talking makes him anxious.

"Can I ask you something?" His question is unsure, and by the way he rubs his jaw shyly, I think he wants to take the question back. But I nod my permission and gesture with my hand for him to continue before he can.

His fingers flex around his mug. "I guess it's not really a question, but this afternoon was…" His gaze drops down to his hands as he pauses. "The first time I've…well, the first time I've touched another man like that."

I wait for his eyes to meet mine. I knew that already, but some of the edge I've been feeling settles inside at his willingness to talk about it.

"How do you feel now that you have?" I ask.

Nathan sits up straighter in his chair as if he didn't expect me to respond the way I had. "Good, I think. Fine. But I'm confused."

I tip my chin in understanding. "It's okay to feel that way."

Nathan pushes his own mug away. "Can you tell me how it felt for you?"

"The first time I was with a man?"

He nods.

"Freeing."

Nathan stares at me, his gaze intense as if he's trying to read every thought and feeling in my head. "Did you always know?"

"That I like men and women?"

Nathan nods again.

"Since I was a teen, though Morgan helped me realize it was okay that I did."

A warm grin caresses his lips, as if he's thinking about his time with Morgan today. It hits me in the gut more than I thought it would, and I'm glad that he already feels safe with her, that she clearly has the same effect on him that she has on me. That she has on many people. It's what makes Morgan *Morgan*.

"You know what's strange? I never thought about it until—" He runs his fingertips over the grain of the table before meeting my eyes. "Until I saw you."

My heart thuds in my chest, and I think my breathing stops for a moment.

He exhales roughly and shakes his head at himself. "Sorry, that was weird. I should say, I guess, I never let myself think about it. Or at least, not that I can remember."

I swallow hard, the muscles in my throat tense. "Sometimes we ignore what's right in front of us or what we already know because it's easier than seeing the truth."

Nathan stares at me like I have three heads.

"What?" I question.

He lets out a tense chuckle. "I guess I just never thought I'd hear you say something like that."

"Just because I don't talk a lot doesn't mean I can't be insightful."

He holds up his hands. "I didn't mean it in a bad way; I liked it." After a beat of silence, he speaks again. "I've been racking my brain, wondering how I could've ignored something like that about myself. Was I that repressed in my life?"

"I don't think I can answer that for you, Nathan."

He scratches his chin nervously. "Yeah, I know. Sorry—it's why I couldn't sleep. I kept thinking that maybe something's wrong with me, you know?"

I nod, because I *do* know. I spent many years believing that, and only by stopping was I free from the dark ideas and thoughts that plagued me. Ideas and thoughts I only had because of hateful and naive people.

I scoot my chair forward, then lean in so I'm closer to Nathan. He watches me with interest, but he doesn't tense or move away.

"Close your eyes," I say.

He blinks, the knot in his throat bobbing. I know he's nervous at my closeness, but there's nothing in his body language that tells me he wants me to move away. His eyes even track to my mouth, his tongue darting out to wet his lips as if he's anticipating a kiss.

When his eyes move back to meet mine, he finally nods and closes them.

"Take a breath, Nathan."

He immediately inhales, and I smile gently at his submission.

"Now exhale it out."

He does that, too.

"Now again."

I have him complete the cycle a few more times until his shoulders fall and his jaw relaxes enough that his mouth parts slightly.

"Now open your eyes for me."

His eyes flutter open. They're softer now, his trepidation replaced with curiosity, the same curiosity I saw when he watched me and Morgan together and again when he was at my feet. I place my hand on his and gently squeeze it, making sure his eyes are focused on me before I speak in a commanding tone.

"Nothing is wrong with you, Nathan." I squeeze his hand harder. "Nothing."

He sucks in another breath, and for a moment, I'm afraid I went too far. Yes, we've been intimate, but not in this way. This is something bigger, deeper. It's a moment he'll carry with him for the rest of his life, regardless of whether this thing between the three of us continues.

I go to pull my hand away, but he grabs it, stopping its movement.

Nathan's eyes are open and clear when I study them now, an emotion I can't place shining in their depths. "Fox." He pauses, running his thumb over the heart tattoo on my wrist. I don't know if he knows he's doing it, but the action is tender and sweet. "Will you kiss me?"

Blood thrums in my veins, and my body feels as if it's become a live wire. For a split second, I almost grant his request, the desire to taste him almost winning out. But it's not in my nature to fold that easily.

"No, Nathan." His face falls, and he leans back like I thought he might, but now I'm the one stopping him. "But you can kiss me."

His eyes saucer, but the reaction is fleeting. Before I can quite register his action, Nathan's lips are on mine, and his fresh scent is surrounding me.

I let it happen, knowing that he needs this. Needs to take the lead right now and feel me open to him. His tongue pushes at the seam of my lips, begging for entry, so I let him in. His lips are dominating, hard, and his taste is minty, which tells me he brushed his teeth before coming out here, a sign that maybe he was hoping this would happen.

The knowledge of this flips a switch inside me. All my prior thoughts exit my mind, and it instead fills with the reasons I felt he could be a good partner for us in the first place. I don't need to think about anything else right now except him and that feeling in my gut.

My hand clamps onto the back of his neck, and Nathan groans as my fingers dig into the muscle there. I tighten my grip, taking full control of the kiss. Instinctively, he understands, surrendering the lead. His mouth opens, and I draw his tongue into mine as he leans in closer.

Acting on impulse, I pull him toward me until he's practically in my lap. He doesn't hesitate—instead, his hand cups my cheek, fingers threading through my beard as he pulls us even closer until our bodies fit together like perfect puzzle pieces.

My chest smarts, and I push it away, kissing him harder, taking him in and burning this moment into my memory before I finally force myself to pull away. I want this to go further, but I also need it to stop. Not because I want it to or because I don't think Nathan wants it to, but because Morgan needs to be here with us. She'll already be sad she missed our first kiss, and I never play without my wife. It's just how we work together.

We take a moment to catch our breath, Nathan's hand still gripping the hair of my beard and my fingers still holding on to the back of his neck. Our eyes meet, both of our mouths swollen and our chests still heaving.

Nathan's mouth opens to say something, but I silence him with a short kiss. "Did that feel wrong to you?"

Nathan shakes his head. "No." He drops his hand to my shoulder, and a smile tugs at his lips. "It felt right."

With his answer filling my chest, I pull back and stand. He's confused for a moment, but then I gesture for him to follow me.

"Where are we going?"

"To bed." Nathan's face morphs to that of hurt and confusion, and I grab his jaw before his thoughts run wild. "My wife is probably cold without us, don't you think?"

His sadness transforms to mischief like a budding leaf in spring.

"Yes, you're probably right."

My eyes crinkle at the corners, and I tap his cheek. "I'm always right, Nathan."

CHAPTER TWENTY-SEVEN

Nathan

FUCK, I FEEL GREAT. Not just because I had one of the best kisses of my life, one that's still tingling on my lips and lingering on my tongue, but because I'm finally just allowing myself to be... me.

I want to laugh, cry, or maybe both. Because I thought I knew myself. I thought I understood who I was and was okay with it. Until now.

Now... now I feel entirely different and yet the same. I'm Nathan two-point-oh, and it's all because of Fox and Morgan.

"Nathan," Fox says quietly as we reach the closed bedroom door.

The way he says my name has goose bumps fanning out over my arms as I stop behind him. There's no light on in the hallway, so I can't see him well—mostly the outline of his tall form. But the dominating nature of him makes me shiver, and the phantom touch from his fingers on my neck itch as if the skin is begging for him to touch me like that again.

"Yes?" I ask.

Fox takes a small step forward so his lips brush the shell of my ear. My breath catches in my throat at his nearness, and arousal heats my body. He runs his nose over my sensitive skin, his beard tickling me as he does. "How far do you want to take this?"

My hands flex at my sides, wanting to reach out and touch him, to feel more of his skin beneath mine. To trace his tattoos and learn the strong yet soft lines of him.

I swallow. "How far do *you* want to take this?"

A low and quiet chuckle brushes against my ear, and my cock twitches from the devilish sound, one that promises so many dirty things. "I'll take it further than you think is possible, Nathan." He nips at my ear, and my body quakes.

I think of the contraption I saw yesterday and wonder if he'd strap me to that. Being tied up like that would be another first for me, and the anticipation of what I'd allow myself to do, where I'd be willing to go for him, for Morgan—it's a beautiful yet frightening thought. But I can't find it within myself to think any of it is wrong, not anymore.

Fox nips my ear playfully, but this time, his bite is harder. I gasp and automatically thrust my hips forward, my groin connecting with his. He's hard, very hard, and now all I can imagine is sinking to my knees right here in this hallway, his tattooed hand gripping my hair and making me take him until I physically can't anymore.

"Do you want that, Nathan?"

Blood pounds in my ears, and I nod at the same time I speak. "I do."

A low grumble erupts from his chest, an answering purr of satisfaction. "We're going to make my wife feel good together. Do you understand?"

My thoughts shift from me on my knees to Morgan on all fours, her plump ass in the air with my cock sliding in and out of that beautiful pussy. My dick turns to steel, and I lick my lips. "I understand."

He pulls back, his fingers holding my chin as I'm discovering he likes to do. My eyes have adjusted to the dark enough that I can see his lips as he speaks. "I want to see your wolf come out, Nathan. Make my wife beg for you."

I lift my chin up in his grasp and put my shoulders back. "My wolf?" I ask curiously.

His head tilts forward, and he places a soft kiss on my lips. My body wants to melt into his, to taste him again like I did in the kitchen, but he pulls back before I can.

Fox chuckles at my eagerness but doesn't remove his fingers from my chin. "Let your dominant instincts guide you. Trust me, my lamb can take it."

He pulls back and pushes the door open so the light from the fire inside makes him glow. The tiny sly smirk on his lips is now visible as his eyes silently ask me the final question: *Do you want this?*

I answer by pushing the door completely open, my gaze finding Morgan's sleeping and completely nude form on the bed.

Hell yes, I want this.

Chapter Twenty-Eight

Morgan

There's something so nice about the beach. I haven't been in a long time, at least not to an ocean beach. The lake one in Starlight Haven is nice but too rocky for sunbathing unless we go to a private beach or use a chair.

But here, where Nathan has taken us, the sand is warm, and my body is, too. So warm.

"You smell like summer," Nathan's breathy voice says in my ear before his lips suck on the sensitive skin of my neck. His dark tresses tickle my nose, and I inhale his clean scent, hooking my leg over his hip so I can grind my pussy into his erection. He groans, and I do it again, feeling him grow against me.

Hmm, his cock is nice. Not as thick as my husband's, but it's long and slightly curved at the tip. It's perfect.

Nathan sucks on my neck, surely leaving a mark, and I buck into him, seeking more friction. A deep chuckle against my ear has me smiling.

"You're so needy, lamb."

Fox's warm body molds against me from behind, the sand moving beneath us as his thick erection pokes into my backside.

"Fox," I moan, my hips rocking forward against Nathan and then back against my husband. They're both so hot and so hard, like molten steel against my pliant and willing body.

I want both their cocks inside me. I want to feel how different they are and have them bring me to the point of no return together. I don't care that we're on the beach or that people might see us. I need them—and I need them now.

"Open your eyes, Morgan," Fox commands against my ear.

Are my eyes closed? I see the beach, the waves, the sand.

"Morgan," Fox says again, his hand slipping down the curve of my ass, my ass that has now become bare. I thought I was wearing a swimsuit.

Fox circles the ring of my back entrance with his finger, and I whimper. When the tip of his thumb slips in, I shoot my hips forward toward Nathan in surprise.

"Open your eyes, or you'll sleep through the show," Fox murmurs. "I'd rather you remember what we do to you."

Sleep? I'm dreaming?

Fox pulls his finger away, then smacks the round globe of my ass. I jump, my eyes flying open to meet the dim light of our bedroom.

"Welcome to the land of the living," Nathan says.

I blink several times, my brain waking up and my eyes adjusting to my surroundings. I may not be on a beach, but I'll argue being in my bedroom on a plush king-sized bed is better. No sand, no onlookers, and I'm sandwiched between two very aroused men giving me all their attention.

"Is this okay?" Nathan asks between licks and sucks on my throat, his path moving toward my naked breasts.

I moan through a yes as he reaches my nipple, pulling on the ring gently with his teeth. Fox's chest rumbles against my back, his hand still stroking my ass as I turn my head so his lips press to mine. The angle is a bit awkward, but I part for him, and his tongue lazily strokes mine until I'm fully awake and ready for whatever they have planned.

Fox strokes my cheek, and I open my eyes to meet his. There's something different in his gaze—it's softer, lighter than it's been for a long time. "Nathan and I have come to an agreement," he says.

"Oh?" I ask. "About what?"

Fox extricates himself from me, shifting his position on the bed so he can pull Nathan from my chest. The man groans with annoyance, but before he can protest further, Fox seals his lips over Nathan's. My heart pounds in my chest as I lie on my back, watching the two men kiss. Apparently, sleep caused me to miss more than just an agreement.

My stomach clenches, and arousal floods my pussy as Fox takes and dominates Nathan's mouth as if he already knows exactly how Nathan likes and needs to be kissed. I also can't help but think that Nathan isn't the man we found in a snow-bank. Because this man is confident and assured in his actions, letting Fox have control in the way he needs.

I wet my lips as I bring one of my hands to cup my breast, rolling my hard nipple between my fingers as my other travels between my legs.

If they let me, I could watch them kiss until the sun rose. They're beautiful together. Fox's long blond hair, his strong tattooed hand on the other man's cheek, bearded lips against Nathan's. And Nathan himself, he's in many ways Fox's oppo-site. But he's also powerful and masculine in his own right, though his sweetness comes through in his gentler move-ments and the way he gives in to Fox's unyielding strokes and touches.

My fingers rub the sensitive skin above my clit, but before I can touch the tight bundle of nerves, a hand wraps around my wrist, stopping me. Had my eyes been closed, I would have thought it was Fox, at least until I felt the softness of the hand.

My eyes meet Nathan's, his lips swollen and wet from Fox's brutal kiss. "Did we say you could touch yourself?" He tsks.

My eyebrows fly up, but Nathan doesn't waver, his brown eyes darker than before. "No, you didn't."

"Then why are you?"

Fox makes a sound of satisfaction at Nathan's question, and butterflies develop low in my stomach. "I'm sorry."

Nathan cocks his head to the side. "Are you?"

I consider my next move. I could say that I am, but Fox will see through it. Nathan might not, but my odds are better if I'm truthful. It's also more fun that way. "No." I smirk.

Fox chuckles, then puts his mouth near Nathan's ear. "I think our little whore deserves to be punished for that, don't you?"

More arousal leaks from my pussy as Fox's words heat my core and make me squirm. I cheer internally because I know what's coming next: They're both going to use me, the two of them, *together*. And now they're getting comfortable with each other, which means it's going to be much different from the sauna. So much different.

My nipples tighten painfully as my focus remains on Nathan. His lips turn up when he sees how aroused this situation has made me, and I nod at him, giving him the final permission I think he's seeking, letting him know I want this. Want him and Fox together this way.

He has no idea how much. Our time in the living room earlier, followed by our easy and light conversations at dinner, only confirmed that for me. I'd told Fox as much before I fell asleep in his arms, which is how I know he let Nathan touch me while I was still dreaming.

"Yes." Nathan's grin widens. "I think she does need to be punished."

Fox whispers something to Nathan, and when he pulls away, I don't miss the tiny dark smirk tugging the corners of his lips or the way he moves off the bed as if Nathan just gave him the best Christmas present of his life.

"Morgan, what's your safe word?" Nathan asks as he leans back on his knees, the muscles of his chest tight as he flexes.

My heart squeezes, and warmth blooms in my low belly. I wonder if Fox told him to ask me that. While I do have a safe word, Fox knows my limits, and I've never had to use it. Thankfully, I've never had to use it with any of our past partners, either. But I know this will make Nathan feel safer as he's exploring.

"Unicorn," I say.

Nathan chuckles. "I'll remember that."

My lips press together in a small smile, and then Nathan is crawling over me until his body is flush against mine. He leans in as if he's going to kiss me, but instead, he tucks a strand of hair behind my ear. "I've never done this before, Morgan. Please use the word if you need me to stop."

I nod in agreement, his care once again filling my chest and confirming everything that Fox thought he could be to us. It also sends the hesitation I was feeling before out the window. We hardly know Nathan, and yet I know in my heart that I'm already falling for him, faster than I've fallen for anyone outside of my husband. And watching Fox with him, how they kissed—I think he is, too.

"Give me your worst." I smile.

He licks his lips and closes his eyes. When he opens them again, I wonder if I'm going to regret saying that.

Chapter Twenty-Nine

Morgan

"Blindfold her," Fox says as he walks swiftly back to the bed. He's removed his shirt but kept his sweats on, and with the way the fire backlights him, the orange glow dancing along his tattooed skin and strong muscles, he looks exactly like his namesake.

He may be a large man, but his every movement appears easy. He's always had a lightness on his feet, even more so after his time in the Special Forces—and that makes him the great hunter that he is. My hunter. My cunning, kinky, caring, and beautiful hunter.

My body grows heavy with lust, and a moan sneaks past my lips as Nathan slides off my body. I feel the heat of his cock through his pants dragging over my sensitive skin until he pulls away, sitting on his haunches.

The two men ignore my noise, and Fox hands Nathan a black silk blindfold. I don't miss the way their fingers brush and their eyes meet, words passing between them again that the world can't hear. It's an image I'll keep playing behind my blindfold as they use me to their liking.

Nathan crawls over me again, and I lift my head up without him having to ask. He smiles, his eyes firm and colder now yet pleased at my minimal offering. He ties the blindfold around my eyes and then tests it to make sure I can't see. When he's done, he leaves my body, but I don't have time to complain. Two hands grab me by my ankles and pull me toward the edge of the bed.

I squeal at the sudden movement, and Nathan chuckles. "I like that sound," he says.

"You'll hear it plenty," Fox answers gruffly.

"Only if it's good." Both men go quiet at my retort, and I smile demurely.

The energy in the air gets thick, and I know I'm not going to get away with that comment. But that's the reason I did it. I could follow the rules and be a good little lamb for them, but while I do like that side of myself, I also like to be a brat. And Fox likes to be a brat tamer.

"Are you testing us, Morgan?" Fox snaps.

I feel a whoosh of air brush my chest, and a smack resounds through the room. I cry out from the sudden sting, my breast moving from the force of a calloused palm—Fox's palm. Before I can recover, he smacks my other breast right on my piercing. My nipple is so hard around it that my eyes water from the sensation, but I bite my tongue to keep from crying out. After another succession of swats, the onslaught stops, and my chest heaves as I catch my breath.

"I think Morgan needs a little reminder of what her mouth is good for," Fox says.

"What do you have in mind?" Nathan replies easily.

Fox doesn't verbally respond. Instead, I hear movement, and I think one of them walks over to the corner of our room, where we keep a cedar chest of toys. My brain starts firing off, attempting to guess what they're going to get, and several things come to mind.

When soft yet firm fingers push against my cheeks, forcing my mouth to part in an O, I eagerly open to find out what it is.

"Brats don't get our cocks," Fox says near my ear as Nathan starts to slide the silicone gag into my mouth. I know it's him because his movements are gentle and his hands are soft.

I whimper when I realize what gag it is. It's one we've only used a couple of times, one reserved for when I've been very naughty or when Fox wants to test my gag reflex.

Instead of a small ball or the O-ring gag my husband tends to favor, they've given me a "deep-throat gag." The small penis-shaped dildo with a ball on the opposite end will force me not only to suck on a cock that isn't real, but my lips will remain wide around the ball. It's uncomfortable and messy, but I can't deny it excites me. I like to be punished, and even more, I like to please Fox—and now Nathan.

Once it's secure, I feel Fox's strong fingers check it to make sure Nathan's fastened it correctly. My mouth begins to water from the intrusion and strange taste, my body temperature rising as I work to swallow around the silicone. A moment later, a small clicker is placed in my hand.

"If it's too much, you know what to do," Fox says.

I nod, unable to use my words. Fox goes on to tell Nathan why he's doing this. Since my eyes are covered and now my mouth is occupied, the clicker is here for me in case I need them to stop.

"Roll onto your belly," Fox says next. "Don't keep us waiting."

I do as he asks, careful not to hit my clicker. The new position has the spit that was accumulating around the fake cock seeping from my lips and down my chin. I swallow, the small cock annoying yet doing the work it's supposed to do: reminding me that if I was a good girl, my mouth would be free and my breath easier.

A hand runs down my head, again a softer and gentler touch so I know it's Nathan. "Good girl. You look so..." His words trail off, but then I hear him say quietly, "...sexy."

His praise hits me differently than my husband's. While Fox's is true and sure, the kind of praise that settles deep in my bones and grounds me, Nathan's is sweet and innocent, as if he's in awe of me. I like them both, and I like that Nathan isn't trying to run out of the room. It's not like the position I'm in is very tame. It may be for me and Fox, but not for him.

But he's staying.

Nathan's hand drags down my head to my back, his fingers trailing my spine till he reaches my ass. I wait impatiently to see what he's doing, my pussy screaming for him to dip his fingers inside, but he grips my ass cheeks and spreads them wide. A split second later, his saliva drips onto my tight ring of muscle. I moan around my gag, more of my own spit falling from my lips to the comforter.

There's a click and then a buzzing noise followed by cold lube being spread over my back entrance. My hands clench on the comforter, and I swallow around the phallic gag as Nathan holds my ass cheeks open and Fox's finger plays with my tight hole. He teases the muscle, dipping the lube inside, but the bastard doesn't give me more than the tip.

Nathan squeezes the globes of my ass harder while Fox continues to torture me, both of them playing me like a fiddle but never giving me more of what I want. After another minute of teasing, the vibrating tip of a butt plug is pressed into my back entrance.

More lube is applied, and then there's a fair amount of pressure as Fox inserts the silicone bulb past the flexing muscle until it's halfway in.

"Fuck!" I cry, but the sound that comes out of my mouth is nothing like the word. The men playing with me chuckle as the vibrating plug seats itself all the way to its hilt, and I squirm on the bed from the feeling.

"That's it, lamb," Fox praises as he puts pressure against the base of the plug. "Such a good whore for us, taking what you deserve."

My eyes water at the fullness I feel. I don't even have their cocks in me, but between the gag, the plug, and their hands on me, my body is in sensory overload. Especially with the blindfold.

"Nathan," Fox says, moving his fingers from the plug to my wet pussy. "Look at how she's dripping for us. For you." He spreads my outer labia with his thumbs to illustrate his point, exposing my inner walls to him.

"Goddamn, Morgan. I can see you clenching that tight pussy." Nathan groans. "You want our cocks, don't you?"

I nod, moaning around the gag. Nathan squeezes my ass, his fingers trailing down toward Fox's where they are still holding me open.

"Can I touch?" he asks, though I know the question isn't directed at me.

"She's our toy, Nathan. Play with her how you want."

God, my husband. He knows exactly what I like to hear. My clit throbs, and my hips move of their own accord against the bed. But before I can get any type of relief, a hand comes down on my ass in four quick swats, much like what Fox did to my breasts. "So fucking naughty."

My spine tingles, because the words and spanks didn't come from Fox this time—they came from Nathan. When he's done, I hardly have time to register movement before I'm being flipped onto my back. The plug is still vibrating, and the sudden change in position seats it further inside my ass. My head falls back against the bed, and I moan wildly around the gag, making a mess of myself as more spit seeps from my lips onto my face and neck.

"This is a spreader bar," Fox says to Nathan as he begins buckling padded cuffs around my wrists and ankles. "It will keep her from being able to get away."

More arousal floods my pussy at his devious tone and the promise of all the dirty things they can do to me while I'm confined by this device. I swallow around my gag as the two men work to maneuver my body so my legs are bent and spread open, feet in the air, and my hands are hooked near my ankles on the bar, leaving me in what is almost a lewd crunch.

"Beautiful," Nathan whispers.

The bed shifts near my head, and then breath is fanning across the side of my face. "Are you okay, lamb?" Fox asks.

I nod at him in response.

"Are you comfortable?"

I shake my head from side to side, and he ghosts a kiss on my cheek before taking my earlobe between his teeth and biting down.

"Good."

Chapter Thirty

Nathan

I FEEL AS IF my eyes were closed for the first twenty-eight years of my life and now they've been blown wide open. I keep thinking I should feel weird about what we're doing, or at least guilty that I'm liking this, but I don't. It's obvious Morgan likes this, that she wants it. And I want to give it to her.

Fox pulls away from Morgan and comes to stand next to me. For another moment, we admire her ample form. The way her thighs have begun to shake from how she's fastened to the spreader bar, how her pussy is dripping onto the bed just like the spit from her mouth. She's ours for the taking, the using, in every single way possible.

"You know," Fox says, "we could leave her like this, let her teeter on the edge of pleasure and pain for hours. We could drink mulled wine from her and eat off her back like our own personal table. She would do it, too, for us. Wouldn't you, Wife?"

Morgan groans but nods from the bed, and while the image is a bizarre one, more blood flows to my cock at the thought. But I don't want to do that to her—I don't need to do that to her.

Fox must see what I'm thinking on my face because he places a hand on my shoulder, his cheek twitching in a smile that's not really a smile—a feature of his I've come to know.

"Use her, Nathan. Or if you'd rather, I can tie you up, and you can join her."

The way he says the threat almost joyfully has my body heat rising ten degrees, and I can't deny I'm interested. I've already imagined myself at his mercy. Fuck, I've been at his mercy and came in my pants because of it. I've tasted a little bit of the humiliation that comes from being used, and I liked it, which is why I shouldn't question why Morgan likes it.

But I don't want to be tied up right now—I want to accept what Fox and Morgan are offering.

I take a couple of steps toward the edge of the bed, stopping at the mouth of Morgan's open legs. Her head is partially raised from the position she's locked in, and I stop myself from getting a pillow to make the strain easier on her. Fox hooked her up this way for a reason, and she hasn't used her clicker, so instead, I study her up close.

Her body is flushed, and there's a light sheen of sweat accumulating on her skin from her exertion. Spit drips down her mouth and chin, and her cheeks are wet from tears as her throat works around the gag.

My gaze drags from her tight pierced nipples down the soft rolls of her stomach to the plush mound of her pussy. The way she's spread open, I don't need Fox to show me how her vaginal muscles contract or how turned on she is because her arousal is dripping down her thighs, the fire making it shimmer.

I can also see the jewel from the butt plug that covers her tight back hole. It's shaped like a red heart, and it's still buzzing inside her, keeping her on the brink of orgasm. It's a lot to take in, but I can't deny it turns me on.

I yelp from a swat to my ass, and I turn to find Fox close behind me. That cheek twitches again, and I take the hint, ignoring how much I like the sting his strike left behind. With my eyes still on his, I put my hands in the waistband of my sweats and tug them down.

When I step out of them, my cock bobs in the warm air, and I wrap my fist around it as Fox observes me. I pump once, twice. The feeling of my fist is nothing like Morgan's warm mouth, but it takes the edge off for a second, and it keeps Fox's attention on me like I want.

The man on my mind licks his lips, and my eyes drop to his

lower half. His cock is hard in his sweats, and while I know we're both dominating Morgan—and I understand he's still in charge—I remember what he said about my wolf. His head tilts to the side in question, and I decide then that I need to own what I'm feeling. I'm in a safe place to explore with two people who clearly want me. I need to stop holding back.

"You take her mouth; I get her pussy," I say with a coy smirk.

Morgan moans as Fox takes a step toward me. "Make it good," he taunts playfully. "I want my wife to scream your name while her mouth is stuffed with my cock."

Fox drops his pants to the floor, and, without another word, he proceeds to the bed. He grabs Morgan under her armpits and drags her so she's sideways, giving me enough room to get on the mattress and prepare to fuck her. This also drapes her head over the edge so Fox can use her mouth.

Fuck, this is really happening. It's like my vision from earlier, except I get to watch Fox take her throat as I fuck her pussy.

I jack my fist up and down my cock again, already imagining what it's going to feel like when her hot, silken cunt is milking me and the plug inside her ass vibrates against my shaft. My skin tightens with need, and I crawl on the bed, my focus turning to Fox as he cradles Morgan's head.

He carefully undoes the buckles on the gag, pulling the dildo from her mouth. Morgan sucks in a breath, more saliva coating her face as she takes down air.

"That's it, lamb," Fox soothes. "Breathe while you can." The softness of his tone is a funny match to the words he's speaking, but Morgan obeys, taking in another breath.

"Our little wolf is going to fuck you, did you hear?"

"Yes, Sir."

My pulse quickens at my new nickname, and I observe their interaction with more interest now. New feelings swirl low in my stomach.

Fox hums, licking a tear that's come out from under her blindfold. "Do you think you deserve it?"

"No, Sir."

My movements still—I wasn't expecting her to say that.

"What would make you deserve it?" Fox looks up at me as he asks, his thumb tracing the outline of her swollen lips.

"Only if I pleased you both."

He hums again, the sound rich. "You please me by wanting to, lamb." His hand trails from her mouth, and I become lost in a trance as he reaches her nipple. He thumbs the piercing and then tugs on it, doing the same to the other, only stopping once they're red and Morgan's gasping.

My cock twitches in my palm, and I swallow, wetting my dry mouth.

"What about you, wolf? Has my wife pleased you?"

Sparks light at the base of my spine, and I place my cock at her entrance, notching the tip in. She throws her head back.

"Does that answer your question, Morgan?"

"Yes, Nate." She moans.

I move my cock in a small circle, her opening fluttering around my swollen crown. I manage to hold back a curse and still my hips, placing my hands on the spreader bar that's locking her legs open.

"Morgan," I say, my tone harsher now. "Do not come until I give you permission, yes?" The words feel foreign on my tongue, but I like them all the same.

"Yes, Nate."

I roll my shoulders back and sink my cock inside her another inch, my eyes rolling in the back of my head as I do. Fox chuckles, and my gaze snaps to his as he stands upright.

I stare into his darkening blue eyes with questions in mine, and he dares a gentle smile at me. It's still not a full smile, but it's one he hasn't given me before.

"What is it?" I ask.

"Glad to see our wolf is showing his fangs."

I flash him a playful smile that shows my teeth, then finally act on what I've been imagining since I saw Morgan in this very bedroom.

CHAPTER THIRTY-ONE

Fox

WATCHING THE ECSTASY ON Nathan's face as he slides into my wife's pussy is a moment I wish I'd photographed. His hands white-knuckle the spreader bar as his dick disappears inside her slick cunt, his head dropping back as if he's praying at her altar.

I know the feeling, and it's why I've never understood why people say sex with the same person can get old. Sex with Morgan, sinking my cock inside her warmth, will never not feel like the first time every time.

And watching Nathan now, I want to tell him what a privilege it is to be inside my wife. Morgan trusts him, and especially after what happened with Gabe, that means a lot—not just to her, but to me. I also realize he's giving us the privilege of him. He's being vulnerable and open, and he's pushing himself more than most people are willing to. It's admirable, and I have a lot of respect for him now. A respect that only continues to grow the more he lets himself go.

It's making me wonder if I need to take a page from his book. I know I've gotten more uptight in the last year since Gabe left, if that's possible. Morgan's tried to help me see it, to help me relax and let go a little bit, but I haven't been able to.

But then along comes Nathan, a man we found on his way to death in a fucking snowbank, and I feel as if he's shifting something in me. I've never met someone so open and willing in the same way he is, which is saying a lot given what I've seen and done in my life. He's so sweet and accepting yet has a bark and a bite to him. He reminds me of someone I could've been had I not been born into my life.

Nathan groans, and I study his face. His brow is pinched, and his chest muscles are shining with a bit of sweat. His hair flops against his forehead as he thrusts his hips forward, and then he pulls back out before doing it again. He's beautiful, and part of me thinks he doesn't even know it.

"Oh my god," Morgan chants.

I turn my attention toward her, throwing myself back into the moment.

"Tell me how he feels, baby," I request as I fist my hard length.

"He's big." She cries as he thrusts again, and this time, it's brutal enough that her large breasts almost smack her chin. "Long." Nathan thrusts again, even more forceful now. "I can feel him everywhere."

Nathan lifts his hips, and Morgan's body shifts upward with his, off the bed, as he circles his pelvis.

"Oh fuck!" she cries.

"He's rearranging your insides, little lamb. Fucking you inside out."

"Christ," Nathan says under his breath. "You're so dirty."

"This is nothing," I retort. Nathan's eyes flash to mine, probably surprised by my flirting. But if he's trying to let go, so will I.

"Then show me," he challenges.

I run my tongue over the top of my teeth, considering it. He's seen bits and pieces of what Morgan and I do together. The dildo gag was a bit of a test to see how he'd react, and he'd been fine. Turned on by it more than I could've hoped, in fact.

"Should we show him how dirty we can be, little lamb?" Nathan thrusts into her hard as I ask the question.

"Fuck!" She exhales in a harsh breath.

"That's not an answer," I volley back.

"Yes, Sir. *Please.* Use me," she chants again and again.

I reach down and grab her cheeks, squeezing them together with some force. "You're going to be a good whore, and you're going to show our wolf exactly how well you can take two cocks. Understood?"

"Yes, Sir."

"Take a breath, Morgan."

I release her cheeks, and she does as I ask. I rip off her blindfold so I can see her eyes, which allows her to drop her clicker. She blinks, adjusting to the dim light as she looks back at me with those watery hazel orbs.

"Open that pretty mouth of yours."

She parts her lips wide, and I praise her.

"Now, stick out your tongue."

Once she does, I spit on it.

"Holy shit." Nathan exhales.

I ignore him, my focus on Morgan. I grip her head between my palms, tilting it back so she's now at the right angle for me to slide in. Her jaw opens wider on instinct, and I wrap one hand around my cock, resting the head of it on her tongue.

I slide it back and forth, teasing her so she doesn't know when I'm going to plunge all the way in. My gaze moves to Nathan, who's circling his hips again, his attention zeroed in on what I'm about to do. I dip my cock in further, the head of it touching the back of Morgan's throat. She swallows, the muscles closing around me.

"That's it," I say, pulling out, then pushing back in again. "Keep this wet hole of yours nice and open for me, baby."

Morgan whines but then visibly makes herself relax.

I slide back in again, my piercing running over the roof of her mouth before I force her head up at the same time I thrust down. Morgan's body tenses at her predicament as she tries to breathe around the dick that's stuffing her full and cutting off her air supply.

"Holy shit." Nathan grunts. "She's practically choking my cock with her pussy."

"Such a good little whore," I commend, "using both her mouth and cunt to please us."

Nathan curses again, dragging his length almost all the way out of Morgan at the same time I do. Our eyes make contact, and I nod at him. We punch our hips forward at the same time, Nathan deep inside her pussy and my dick working down her throat.

Morgan expels a choking moan, and I keep a close eye on her to make sure she's okay. She's stuffed full, but she can handle a lot. I've seen her take more than this and walk away with a smile that could rival someone who'd just won the lottery.

I remove my hands from her head and place the clicker back in her hand. Then I take her tits in my palms and squeeze them hard, my hips driving down as I use her throat just as I would use her cunt.

Nathan watches with a sort of awe on his face as I drive into her. Morgan takes it all like I've trained her to do, her gagging sounds only adding to the wet noises of Nathan's cock plunging in and out of her dripping pussy.

"Fuck." Nathan grunts, his hands on the spreader bar pulling Morgan farther down his cock so she bounces like a rag doll with each of his thrusts. I push my cock down her throat again and again in time with him, watching his dick exit her pussy, covered in her arousal.

I push off her chest and slap her tits, sliding my length from her lips. Morgan gasps for air, her face a mess of her own saliva.

"Rub her clit, Nathan."

".Yes, Sir."

I smirk as soon as the words leave his mouth. He's so in the moment, he doesn't realize what he's called me. Maybe I'll have to reward him for that later.

"Oh god!" Morgan calls in a hoarse whisper, her throat raw from my brutal fucking.

"You like it when he touches you, lamb?"

"Yes, Sir."

"Do you want to come?"

"Yes, Sir," she whimpers.

"Can she come yet, Nathan?"

He thrusts into her hard as he pinches her clit. "Not yet."

I expel a dark chuckle, bringing my lips to Morgan's ear so only she can hear. "Told you he was a wolf in sheep's clothing."

Her eyes smile, but this time, she's smart and doesn't say anything. I stand fully again, slapping my cock against her cheek. She opens for me, and then I'm sliding down her used throat, watching my thick cock bulge the skin and the vine tattoo on her neck move as if it's alive and growing.

"Fuck, that's hot," Nathan says. "Please keep doing that, Sir."

My lip twitches. "Because you said please."

Nathan grins, and I direct my cock down my wife's throat as far as it will go, my balls smothering her nose and making her toes curl as I cut off her breath. I hold it there for a good while, watching her struggle and her throat constrict around my length.

"She's squeezing me again." Nathan moans. "I'm going to come soon."

I pull back, my messy erection falling from Morgan's lips as she takes in another gulping breath. She lifts her head up, and her soft belly contracts as she stares at Nathan, who's circling her clit slowly.

"Please, Nathan, *please*, may I come?"

He looks at me, and I shrug. "Up to you."

"Are you almost there?" he asks me.

"I can be."

He gives me a quizzical look, and I make a show of taking my cock in my hands. I use Morgan's saliva to pump myself, running my palm over my piercing and playing with it. The base of my spine begins to tingle, and I work myself harder. I could go longer if he wanted, but Nathan is close, and my pretty little lamb is about to unravel.

"Squeeze me, Morgan," he commands then. "Use that tight little pussy of yours, and make me come."

Morgan's head drops back, and then I hear Nathan grunt. He thrusts into her harder, her breasts bouncing as her body is forced backward from the sheer force of his punishing pace.

Impressed, I place my hands on Morgan's head so she has nowhere to go.

"Push up your tits," I command her.

Nathan watches closely as she follows my order, then I take saliva from her mouth and coat my cock with it before I spit between her breasts. I slide my length in the valley of them, pushing the soft skin around me before thrusting back and forth, fucking them.

"Wow," Nathan says almost comically. "I—" His body stills. "Fuck, baby, I'm going to come."

The way he calls Morgan "baby" incentivizes me to thrust a little harder, molding her breasts tighter around me until my balls are drawing up. "I love your tits, Wife. So fucking big and soft." I grunt. "So fucking mine."

She keens loudly as both Nathan and I continue to use her body, his hand on her clit circling faster as his sounds of pleasure fill the air.

"Please, Nathan, please, I—"

"Come, Morgan," he roars, and my wife shatters.

Nathan's brow pinches, and every muscle in his body tenses before he falls forward, leaning on the bar as his thrusts turn shallow and he empties his cum into her.

The sight of them, along with Morgan's cries and Nathan's ecstasy, sends me falling over the edge with them. With a grunt, I stand up as I come, my fist pumping my cock as I paint Morgan's chest and soft belly with white ropes.

When all is said and done, the room goes quiet. Only our heavy pants and the sound of the dying fire serve as background noise.

Nathan slips his cock from Morgan and sits back on his

haunches to admire the view. His gaze starts on my cum paint-ing her torso before he drags it down, stopping to watch her still-pulsing cunt. And while I can't see it from this angle, I know he's mesmerized by the sight of his release spilling out of her used pussy.

When his eyes finally meet mine, I see a reverence in them that I've only seen from myself. It's a look that tells me how proud he is of Morgan, how he understands that what she allowed him to do was a show of trust.

He takes another breath, then hops off the bed, standing at the edge of the mattress. He looks at me with a slow smile before bending down to Morgan. He cradles her face in his hands and wipes away the wetness from her cheeks before gen-tly kissing her swollen lips. "Are you okay?"

She blinks at him for a moment, realizing it's him checking in with her instead of me. She smiles warmly at him, her eyes shining with gratitude. "I'm perfect," she whispers.

He kisses her lips once more, then her forehead, before stand-ing and stepping up to me. For a second, I wonder what he's going to say, but instead of speaking, he presses his lips to mine in a short kiss.

"Thank you," he says.

"For what?"

"For showing me that it's not wrong."

CHAPTER THIRTY-TWO

Nathan

SOMETHING HEAVY IS ON my waist, and I feel like I'm roasting in a toaster oven. I try to shift, but it's as if I'm being weighed down by bricks.

I crack my eyes open, a soft snore reaching my ears. It's still dark in here, but by the light leaking through the corners of the blackout curtains, I know it's morning—if not midmorning.

My eyes track to the source of the heat and snoring. A heavily tattooed arm is draped over my waist, and Morgan is wedged between myself and Fox. She's curled into his chest, clinging to him like a koala bear. That leaves Fox's face mere inches from mine.

Another soft snore departs from his lips, and I smile a bit. In sleep, Fox doesn't look half as menacing as he does awake. With his features relaxed, I can see he's just a regular man in his thirties. There are no tattoos or piercings on his face, just his well-trimmed beard and minor age lines from a life hard-lived—one I got a glimpse into while we spoke in the kitchen.

My eyes sting as I think of what he told me. I felt honored that he shared even that small bit with me, but I'd be lying if I didn't want to know more about his injury. I sensed a story behind it, and I wonder if it's what led me to finding him in the kitchen in the first place, if his past keeps him up at night.

This couple's history is another thing that's a mystery to me. I know now that Fox joined the army at eighteen, that he and Morgan have been together since they were teenagers, and that they started their business together, but that's about it. Well, and that they're polyamorous and kinky as hell.

Images of what we did together before we fell asleep come rushing back to me. My body is a little sore from all the exertion but in a nice way, one that I'd gladly live with daily if given the opportunity.

The idea stuns me, and in the darkness of the room with Morgan and Fox sleeping beside me, I indulge in the vision of what a life like this would be like.

I don't know much about their business, but I'm not opposed to physical work or using my body. It's one of the reasons I enjoy surfing and working out. But I suppose if they needed help marketing or with social media, I could be of use there. I'm also good at math and working with people who do not have the name Kathy.

If I lived in Starlight Haven, I could wake up, have breakfast with Fox and Morgan, work, and then go into town for dinner with my family. Then there's the sex and intimacy I could have with them, the things I know they'd open me up to beyond what I've already experienced.

I reach up and softly brush a lock of Fox's hair from his face, making sure the action doesn't wake him. Never in my life did I think I'd be waking up next to a man, much less a man and a woman married to each other. But I'd be lying through my teeth if I said I hated it. The way they are with me and how I feel when I'm around them make me realize that maybe what I thought was missing never actually was—that I simply hadn't discovered this side of myself yet.

And now that I have, I don't know if I could ever go back. The idea of driving away from here and pretending as if this weekend never happened physically pains me. And while I don't know what Fox and Morgan see for us beyond our time snowed-in together, I know I can't go back to who I was before, regardless of whether they're in my life or not.

I can't be the man who sits on his hands and plays nice

anymore. The man who goes to work and comes home at night alone with his takeout or climbs into bed with a woman who I know would be great for someone else. The man who chose to settle for that woman out of some guilty conscience to get married and start a family to fulfill my own family's dreams. Especially not after this.

"Stop thinking so goddamn loud," Fox grumbles.

My eyes focus, and I find Fox staring at me. He moves his arm from my waist and rubs his eyes, yawning.

"Sorry," I say quietly.

"You don't have to whisper," Morgan adds, her voice raspier than usual from sleep and how much Fox and I used her mouth yesterday.

Now free from the weight of his arm, I reach for the glass of water on the bedside table. Fox brought it over for her last night after we cleaned her up and took care of her.

"Drink this," I say.

Her eyes peel open, but she ignores me, burrowing herself into Fox's chest.

"She's stubborn in the mornings," Fox says.

"Just the mornings?" I retort.

That makes him chuckle, and Morgan flips over so she can give me a death glare and a middle finger. If she weren't so sleepy and cute, I'd turn her over and spank her cheeky ass. But I refrain. Not only because we used her plenty last night but also because I'm still adjusting to the fact that spanking her is where my thoughts went. How it made the morning wood between my legs harder.

How I'm not judging it this time.

With a disgruntled noise, she snatches the water and chugs it before handing the empty glass back to me. "Happy?" she asks.

"Very."

Once I set the glass down, I turn back to see Morgan cuddling into Fox again, draping herself over him as if she can't get close enough. It's cute and a little weird, but that fits Morgan to a tee. Once they settle, I shift my gaze to meet Fox's. His usual cool blues are warm, and if I had to guess, I'd say there's approval in his eyes at the care I showed for Morgan, even though it seems silly since it was just a glass of water.

Yet in a way, I understand. Their relationship and lifestyle may be out of the norm, but they take care of each other in the way that works best for them.

"Nate," Morgan says.

"Yeah?"

"Why are you thinking so loud and not completing our puppy pile?"

I chuckle, and Fox's cheek twitches as he lifts the blanket up so I can scoot closer, permission from him to join in. A tiny voice in the back of my brain says I should hesitate, but I don't.

I plaster my chest to Morgan's back and wrap my arm around both their bodies. Morgan tangles her legs with mine, and my head rests in the space between Fox's shoulder and neck. Morgan doesn't make a funny comment about my cock being hard, and Fox remains quiet, his arm folding the comforter over us and trapping us in a warm cocoon.

When we're settled with his strong arms around us, I let out a contented sigh, and sleep overtakes me easily.

CHAPTER THIRTY-THREE

Morgan

"WHICH COLOR?" I ASK, holding up both green and white nail polish bottles to Nathan. He's sitting on the other end of the couch with his feet propped up on the coffee table in the freshly washed clothes he wore yesterday, reading a romance novel I gave him.

He looks up from the book and studies them. "Green."

"Perfect. That's the one I wanted."

He chuckles. "Why'd you ask me, then?"

"Because I wanted your opinion." I smirk.

Nathan squeezes one of the feet I have planted on his lap then turns his attention back to the book. He made fun of me when I said he'd like a dirty book about two male wolf shifters and their mate, but it's not as if we have much else to do up here while we're stuck, especially while my mouth and pussy are recovering from my middle-of-the-night funishment. Not that I couldn't go again, or that I don't want to, but it's been nice to just sit and relax.

Fox and I have been so busy with work that we've hardly had time to do whatever we want for days at a time—and my husband is not good at relaxing, anyway. So after we woke up, showered, and ate a Christmas Eve brunch of pancakes and bacon, Fox went to the office. He's been there since, claiming he needed to radio the city and see if they had a timeline for the power to be back on and the roads to be cleared. But that shouldn't have taken this long, which leads me to think he's up to something. I just don't know what.

Nathan asked if we should check on him a few times, which made my heart flutter in my chest, but I assured him that this is how Fox is. It's better to let him do what he needs to do, and he'll join us when he wants. Plus, it's been nice to spend time with Nathan, even if we've just been sitting together by the fire and drinking hot chocolate as he laughs and shares his thoughts on the book he's reading.

I unscrew the cap of the nail polish and get to work painting my nails. As I finish the nails on my left hand, Nathan lays the open book over my ankles. "What's primal?" he asks.

I bite my lip to stop myself from smiling. "Just keep reading; you'll find out."

His eyes meet mine. "I'm still trying to figure out the whole breeding kink thing. Isn't that just human nature?"

I snort. God, he's so cute. "It's not exactly the same, but I can see how that would be confusing. The breeding kink itself is more about being aroused by the idea of having sex without a condom that could result in a pregnancy. It's more nuanced and layered than you would think."

Nathan stares at me, and his mouth parts. After a few tries, he squeezes my foot again, his eyes serious. "I didn't use a condom."

"We didn't." My thighs squeeze together reflexively as if I can still feel his cum dripping out of me. "But I'm on birth control, so no need to worry about little mini versions of us running around."

He nods, but I can see his mind is racing in a million different directions. I pull my legs off his lap and sit up on the couch, holding out the nail polish to him. He eyes it, confused.

"Paint my right hand for me?"

"You want me to paint your nails?"

"Why not?"

"I've never painted nails before."

"I guess I'll be your first," I say playfully.

Nathan huffs a laugh, his features lightening a bit as he takes the polish from me. "If this is ugly, you can't complain."

"I trust you."

His gaze turns warm at my words, laced with deeper meaning.

After some adjusting, my hand is resting on my crossed knee. Nathan sits in a mirrored position so he can focus on his task. He takes my pointer finger in his, and like a man painting the Sistine Chapel, he bends over and goes to work. His lips are pursed and brow furrowed as he paints a delicate line down the middle of my nail.

He exhales a cute little breath. After he's determined he hasn't screwed up, he does another line. When he's finished, the nail is done perfectly. He didn't even get any on my skin.

"A natural," I praise.

He smirks. "I like to be good at things."

"You don't say."

Nathan looks up at me and takes a hold of my middle finger. "I didn't hear you complaining about how good at things I am last night."

I bark a laugh. "Okay, Mister Confidence, keep painting."

With the look of a proud man who fucked my brains out early this morning, Nathan goes back to painting. After the nail is finished, he asks, "Do you want kids?" He doesn't look up at me as he says it, his concentration on my nails.

"That's a loaded question."

He dips his chin as if he understands, and I'm sure he does. When people are in their prime years and single *or* married with no kids, society tends to push its ideals on them.

"You don't have to answer if you don't want to."

"Fox and I have spoken about it. We're both thirty-five now, but we discussed it a few years back. Maybe one day, if our business slows down and it feels right for us, but there's another factor…"

Nathan lifts his head up, his gaze gleaming with an intense

curiosity, but he doesn't ask a question. I study his face, hoping what I'm about to say doesn't go too far for him, though after everything we've done together, I think we need to talk about it.

"If we have another partner, they have to want it, too—and be okay with raising them with three parents." The words linger in the air like a soft echo of the final note of a song.

Nathan sits straighter and screws the cap on the polish. It's then that I see he's finished all five fingers. They're all perfect, even better than my practiced hand.

"Do you want kids?" I ask quietly.

Nathan lifts my hand, his eyes still locked on mine as he gently blows on the polish. I should tell him it's a quick-dry polish, but I'm too enraptured by his action.

His warm breath skitters over my knuckles, and goose bumps erupt down my arms. When he's finished, he continues to hold it, resting our joined hands on his knee. "I don't know. I thought I did, but…I've begun to wonder if it's just another thing I thought I should have because I was told it was part of the plan."

"I can relate to that."

Nathan's eyebrows rise, but before I answer, I take the polish from him.

"Give me your hand."

He studies me suspiciously, but all I do is smile and make grabby hands at him. He chuckles, finally relenting and placing his warm hand in mine. After I finish painting one of his nails, I move on to the next.

"Fox and I grew up in a small town a few hours from here. But unlike him, I had a very typical family and upbringing. Believe it or not, I was a sweet and innocent girl-next-door type."

I glance up at Nathan to see he's grinning. "You know, I can see it."

I huff a laugh. "Despite that, I always had a rebellious streak in me. I pierced my ears with a sewing needle the first time my parents left me alone in the house."

"That doesn't surprise me, either. I haven't known you for very long, but you're adventurous."

"That's one way to put it." I snicker. "Anyway, my mom wanted me to get married to a sweet boy, have kids, and be a stay-at-home mom like she was. And don't get me wrong. There is nothing wrong with that. I have so much respect for what she did for me and for dealing with my teenage years."

I study Nathan's finished right hand and hold it up to blow on it. He watches me intently, the air charging with a different kind of energy now. "What happened?"

"I happened."

We both look up to see Fox coming down the hallway, a couple of wrapped packages in his hands. Nathan and I both smile at him, and a zap of electricity hits me straight in the gut at the sight of him. He's in dark sweats and a white T-shirt that makes the black and gray tattoos on his body more vibrant, and his hair is up in the bun I love so much. Even though I've been with him before I even understood what love was, the feelings I have for him never dull; they only get stronger. Because no matter who or what comes into our lives, he's always there. My unwavering strength and support.

Fox walks over to the fireplace, and Nathan and I watch him put the small packages on the mantel. I think they're presents, which reminds me we don't have our tree yet, and the decorations are still sitting in the boxes—something I hope to remedy tonight, if Nathan is willing.

Fox turns around and looks down at us, his lip twitching when he sees what we're doing. "It suits you," he says to Nathan.

Nathan looks down at his green-painted nails and then back to Fox, his cheeks flushing and the tips of his ears turning pink as if the popular boy in school just told him he's cute. "Thanks," he says quietly as Fox goes to tend to the fire.

Nathan and I both watch as he does it, as the muscles of his back flex deliciously. It's a small moment, one someone might think insignificant, but it's not to me. This is a moment I didn't know would happen after the sauna yesterday, but now I can't help thinking how right this feels. Nathan, despite his newness to everything, fits with us. He's a soothing balm and light that lends itself to the intensity Fox and I share.

I squeeze Nathan's hand, and he turns to me, the flush deeper on his cheeks.

"Other hand," I say.

Nathan gives it willingly as Fox moves to sit on the recliner. "You should sit with us."

Fox stops mid-squat, his gaze on Nathan before his eyes dart to mine. A gentle smile ghosts over my lips at this development, proving once more that what Fox felt about him before we even knew him and everything I've come to feel for Nathan in such a short time is right.

Fox stands upright, not saying a word as he takes the few steps toward the couch. Before I can adjust so Fox can sit behind me, Nathan does it instead. I should say I'm surprised, but I should've known this is what Nathan was after. His soul almost seems too sweet for Fox and me. He cares about my husband already, and it's clear he wants him to feel included, despite the newness of everything for him.

Fox tips his chin in thanks, then wedges himself on the couch behind Nathan, spreading his legs wide and throwing an arm over the back of the couch and the other down the arm. Once he's settled, Nathan leans back so he is resting against Fox's thigh, then looks up at me casually, as if he didn't just do something that meant so much—not just for us but for him as well.

"So what happened then?"

I swallow the sappy emotion in my throat, glancing quickly at my husband, who looks almost as shocked as I feel. "Fox came to our high school at the end of sophomore year, and he rocked my world," I say, a playful lilt to my tone as I watch Fox with a silly grin.

Nathan looks over his shoulder. "Were you a bad boy?"

Fox's eyes darken. "My wife can tell you that."

I laugh. "He wasn't, actually." Fox snorts, and I keep myself from rolling my eyes. "Okay, he was a little bit." Fox snorts again, and I shake my head, taking the hand I just finished and blowing on the polish even though I don't have to.

"Something tells me it was more than a little," Nathan says.

I set his hand down and then put the closed nail polish on the coffee table. "He wasn't so much a bad boy as misunderstood," I say, focusing on Fox again. He nods, giving me permission to continue the story. "He was in the foster care system and was acting out. When we met, I was a fourteen-year-old girl trying to understand myself and all the hormones coursing through my body. Then in comes this boy, and everyone told me to stay away from him. But that only made me want to get closer to him."

"She's leaving out the part where she kneed a kid in the balls because he made fun of me for having no parents."

I expect Nathan to be surprised at that, but instead, he smirks happily. "Good."

I chuckle. "He deserved it. Long story short, we started dating, fell in love, and my parents were scandalized. As soon as Fox and I turned eighteen, we got married, and then he was off to the army and deployed six months later. Needless to say, we understand what it's like to go against the expected—or just not be what people expect in the first place."

Nathan reaches out and squeezes my hand. "You've been through a lot."

"We have, but we turned out okay. More than okay. We've worked hard to have this life, and we'd rather be free to be ourselves than fit in with what people think is normal. If people don't like us, that's a *them* problem."

Nathan studies me before he slides back on the couch so he

can see both me and Fox. "I admire you both. I've never had that courage."

"I beg to differ." Nathan eyes me, so I continue. "You said you quit your job. You made a change. And do I have to remind you that you've been open with us, that you went outside your comfort zone even when you didn't have to? You have balls, Nathan. Big ones."

That makes him laugh, which was my goal. "Thank you, Morgan."

My chest lightens, and I'm glad to see Nathan smile. This conversation has gotten too heavy—it's Christmas Eve, for goodness' sake.

I stand and hold out my hand to Nathan and then to Fox, who stare at my open palms in question. "Come on, boys. Let's make this cabin look like Christmas threw up all over it."

CHAPTER THIRTY-FOUR

Nathan

I PULL MORGAN INTO me as Christmas music blares from the speakers. When I grind my hips against hers, she lets out a sweet giggle. Fox is off in the kitchen grabbing more spiked eggnog, but we're all feeling good and a little buzzed after decorating the living room for the past couple of hours.

"Are you trying to dirty dance with me, Wolfie?" She giggles again.

I chuckle at the nickname, but I'm not going to deny that I like it. I liked it when they called me "wolf" last night, and I like it now. It makes me feel powerful. And I like that they saw that part of me before I could even see it myself.

"Wrap your arms around my neck," I say, my tone laced with command.

"Yes, Wolfie," she purrs.

I shake my head as she loops her strong arms around me. Since we're almost the same height, our bodies meld together perfectly, and my half-hard cock presses harder into the heat between her legs.

"Hmm, someone's excited."

"And someone's got loose lips."

She scoffs playfully, but before she can respond, I dip her down and move her body in a half circle before bringing her back up. Her breasts press against my chest, and she laughs again. "You know how to dance?"

I shrug. "Not really. I just always liked *Dirty Dancing* and wanted to do that."

"Color me surprised."

I circle my hips into hers and move us to the beat of the music as Fox comes back, watching us with hungry eyes. He moves to sit, but I turn us so Morgan's next to him.

"Dance with us, baby," she says.

While Fox doesn't look like someone who would dance, I've quickly learned he also can't deny Morgan anything. He may dominate her, but he'll always give her what she wants in the end.

Fox places the drinks on the coffee table, then stands behind Morgan. I expect him to be awkward, but instead, he moves in close, his arms wrapping around her. At first I think he's going to place his hands on Morgan's hips, but they land on mine. He tugs us in toward him, and hell if my cock doesn't get harder at the possessive nature of it.

"Hmm, Fox-and-wolf sandwich equals one happy lamb," Morgan chirps before licking over my pulse.

I shudder, my cock jerking against her as Fox's fingers dig into my hips. "You're ridiculous," Fox grumbles, but then he smiles. Not just a cheek or lip twitch, either—a genuine smile.

My mouth goes dry at the sight of it, but I don't have time to relish it because he starts to move us, and it disappears. His hands skate over my hips, then to my waist before moving back down again, pulling me impossibly closer as Morgan grinds her pussy against my now-hard erection and her ass against Fox.

On an exhale, I allow myself to get lost in the ridiculous holiday music we're dancing to and the feeling of both Fox and Morgan touching me. When the song ends and another begins, Fox's lips travel down Morgan's neck, biting and sucking as he shifts his hips against her and his fingers dig into my ass.

Fuck, this is hot, and all I can think is that I wish we were naked doing this instead. My mind is already imagining what we'd look like, dancing and grinding on each other with the glow of the multicolored Christmas lights on our skin.

Which gives me an idea.

Morgan tips her head back and stares at me with hooded eyes as Fox continues to suck on her neck. "What is it?" she asks, tugging the hairs near the base of my skull.

"You said I interrupted your tradition to get a Christmas tree."

She traps her bottom lip between her teeth, and Fox looks up at me from where he's still kissing Morgan's neck.

"If you don't mind me joining, let's go get one," I say.

Our dancing stops, yet we remain plastered together.

Morgan's eyes glimmer with mischief, and her hand tightens in my hair. "Are you sure?"

I shift on my feet. "I know it's going to be cold and wet, but the storm has stopped now." It actually warmed up today, too, so the snow has melted more than expected, but that's California weather for you. Fox also mentioned earlier that the sheriff's station said they may be able to plow the roads tomorrow, if not the day after. I'm excited about the prospect of getting to see my family on Christmas Day, but I'm not going to lie and say there isn't a part of me that forgot for a moment that reality exists outside this cabin, that I'm not their boyfriend or partner. That I'm just a man who happens to be snowed in with them.

I clear the thoughts from my head and force a smile on my face. "You should have your Christmas tree," I continue. "And if you don't want me to join in, I can help you decorate it when you get back."

Morgan presses her mouth to mine, and my body warms from the heat of her lips. "Don't be silly, Nathan; we want you to join us," she says.

My gaze bounces to Fox. "Then why do I sense hesitation? Do you not want the tree?"

"It's less about the tree for us and more about the game." Morgan grins.

"Game?"

"That book you read—remember you asked about primal?"

I pinch my brow. I'd started to get into the book Morgan gave me, but I have not read the scene in full yet. "That has something to do with your Christmas tree?"

"Every year, Fox hunts me in the woods. I run, and when he inevitably catches me, he claims me for his prize. The tree that's closest to us we cut down and decorate, a little reminder of the evening."

"A trophy," Fox says darkly.

I know I should be shocked by this information, but after last night, this seems tame. "That's twisted," I say anyway. "Jesus would be scandalized."

Fox unleashes a sly smirk, and Morgan chuckles.

"Would I be chasing, too?" I ask, wondering how it all works.

Morgan's hands flex on the back of my neck. "No."

My skin tingles as I look up to meet Fox's gaze. A sly grin is still planted on his lips, and he looks starved as if he's imagining taking me, claiming me for his own.

Fuck. I can't deny that my dick is painfully hard just thinking about it.

I love adrenaline, and the idea of Fox chasing me, pinning me to the cold ground, and taking me sends a shiver of both fear and desire through me. Even though I've never been with a man like that before, I know I want this—I need to experience it before I leave this cabin. And I want Fox to be my first. I want to fully surrender to everything Fox and Morgan are offering me.

My eyes remain on Fox as I run my hands down Morgan's body until I've placed them over Fox's. "Count me in."

Fox lifts an eyebrow in challenge. "Are you sure, little wolf?"

I hold back a groan at how fucking good that nickname

sounds on his lips, but I also feel my blood heat from the challenge and almost mocking tone in which he delivered it. He wants to rile me up, to see if I'll change my mind and say no.

"Let's see if you can catch me first, *Foxie*."

Morgan chuckles, an "oh fuck" whispering under her breath as Fox's nails dig into my hips almost painfully. "Go get ready, Morgan," he barks. "And prepare Nathan for me, you understand?"

"Yes, Sir."

My hackles rise when Fox shoots me one final dark look, a look that says I'm in for it. Then he stalks off toward the mudroom, leaving me with a grinning Morgan.

Chapter Thirty-Five

Fox

I stand at the open mouth of the garage, staring out into the dark. It's only just after six in the evening, but the winter night is black and cold, the slightly melted snow perfect for what we're about to do.

I tuck the padded pouch of my survival pocket chainsaw into my waterproof pants and remove my coat, leaving me in a long-sleeved shirt as Morgan and Nathan enter the garage. My sky-blue beanie is on his head, and his cheeks are already flushed, which I know is because of the plug currently seated in his ass. I didn't have to tell Morgan what I meant when I told her to prepare him.

Beyond having her give him an outline of the rules and what exactly our little game entails, he needs to be ready for me. Because while I like to inflict consensual pain on my partners, he needs to be prepped and stretched to take my cock, especially for his first time.

"You have a ten-minute head start." I walk forward and tuck a flare into Nathan's pocket. "If we haven't found you and you need the game to stop, send the flare up."

"We?"

I smirk, and Morgan steps next to me. "Surprise, Wolfie," she chirps like the smart-mouthed woman she is.

Nathan's jaw hangs slack, and I step dangerously close to him, pushing his chin back up to close his mouth. "We only need one Christmas tree, Nathan."

He swallows hard, the bit of sass he had before leaving his body.

I chuckle, a sound from low in my belly. "Let's see if this strong body of yours can outrun us."

He blinks, the shock of our surprise evaporating from his eyes. He dares to smile in defiance, and I can't say I don't enjoy it. I like when my prey has some fight in them.

I drop my hand and step away from him until I'm flush with Morgan. "Well, what are you waiting for, Nathan? *Run.*"

Chapter Thirty-Six

Nathan

My body feels as if it's been possessed by something other than myself. The winter winds whip against my cheeks and freeze, making my eyes water. It's hard to see in the woods, and I have no idea where I'm going, but it only adds to the excitement I feel at being hunted. Not just by Fox, but by Morgan, too.

The little minx. I should say I can't believe she made me think we'd both be the ones hunted, but it tracks with her.

I smile to myself as I continue to run. With every step on the ground, not only do I feel the fullness of the plug seated in my ass, but my feet sink into the snow, making it hard to run very fast. But that doesn't stop me from putting one foot in front of the other.

After what has to be ten minutes, I come to a fork in what I'm assuming is a trail. I slow to a stop and look to the left and right. Both directions look the same, but I make a flash decision to go right. My arms pump, and sweat trickles down the side of my face as I try to avoid trees and branches.

There's so much snow, and since some of it has melted, it's a bit icy. The most annoying part of it all is that there's no way to mask the crunching of the fluff beneath my feet and the sounds of my labored breath. The only comfort I have is that I'll be able to hear Fox and Morgan coming.

After I run for another few minutes, I stop again. The sky is dark, and while the moon is out, the clouds cover most of it. But even in the minimal light, I see a large tree branch covered in pine on the ground. I pick it up, an idea sparking in my mind.

I begin to walk again, brushing my footprints away in the snow. While it's not completely perfect, if they're tracking my steps like I know they are, it could fool them for a second, giving me more time to figure out where to go next.

When I'm satisfied enough with what I've erased, I throw the branch and begin to run again. A few minutes go by, and when I look up, a smile lights up my face when I see the outline of what looks to be a small hunting cabin. Hiding there may be obvious, but maybe that will work for me. They may think I wouldn't be stupid enough to go there.

Decision made, I run toward it, sucking in frigid air that burns my lungs as I go. When I reach the door, I pause, the hair on my neck prickling.

I turn around, searching into the darkness. There are no tracks except for mine, and it's eerily quiet, the snow dampening the sounds of Mother Nature so all I hear is my pants. I wonder for another minute if this is smart, but I have to commit. I wipe some sweat from my upper lip, turn back around, and reach to grab the door handle. My hand wraps over the cold metal, and then I'm pulled back, falling into the powdery snow.

I don't look to see who it is, because I *know*. I scramble, my feet kicking out as I try to get up off the snow. But just as I get on my knees, a hand wraps around my ankle and pulls me down. I fall, belly on the snow as I feel a boot press into my back. "Where do you think you're going?"

Morgan's playful voice reaches my ears, and I squirm against the pressure of her foot, my cheek pressing into the cold snow.

I don't answer, instead maneuvering quickly. I flip and grab for her ankle, pulling just hard enough that she loses her balance and falls on her butt into the soft snow.

Her musical laugh echoes around me. "He does have fangs, baby."

I scramble again, crawling away, feeling my cock heavy between my legs at how turned on I am by this. I get only a foot before Fox's boot presses between my shoulder blades, the weight of his large body sinking me into the wintery ground again. "Get off," I grunt, still fighting.

Fox barks a laugh. "I fully intend to."

The crunch of snow signals Morgan's approach, and I continue to struggle against the weight of Fox's boot.

"That tree," she says. I hear the sounds of them kissing, and then I'm being flipped over by strong hands before Fox's boot inches down to my sternum, stealing my breath. My hands move to his ankle, but then Morgan is there, pinning my arms above my head. She stares down at me, her cheeks pink and her smile broad. "Gotcha." She winks.

I try to get away again by bucking my hips. "Let me go!"

They both laugh, and heat flushes my already-red cheeks.

"Don't be embarrassed, Nate," Morgan coos. "Maybe next time, you won't do the obvious."

Next time.

Fox removes his boot from my chest, ending my thoughts as he drops to the ground. In a flash, his hands tug down my pants and briefs, my bare ass hitting the cold snow. I barely have time to register the stinging bite before wet lips wrap around the head of my cock and suck.

"Holy fuck!" I cry. My hips shoot up, and my eyes drop down. Fox's puffy lips are around my cock, his bearded cheeks suctioning as he takes half of me down. If we weren't playing this game, and the snow wasn't a factor, I'd want him to keep doing this so I could absorb the moment, the first time a man has ever put his lips on me.

And fuck if I'm not glad it's Fox, not only because I've come to trust him but also because he's so fucking beautiful it hurts.

I cry out another time as his hand fondles my balls and he swirls his tongue around my swollen crown.

"If I let go of your wrists, are you going to be a good wolfie and stay put?" Morgan asks me.

I manage to look up at her and nod. Even if I wanted to move, I don't think I could. Fox's mouth is just too damn good. The way his beard tickles the sensitive skin of my shaft, it's—

"Yes, fuck yes!" I grunt as he takes me farther down and suctions. My pelvis thrusts up, and as my eyes look down again, he slides his mouth from me. I groan as the night air freezes his saliva, but then he's playing with the plug in my ass, and I forget the sting of the cold.

He taps the toy, then bears down on it until I'm writhing in the snow. I've never felt anything like it. It's full, overwhelming, and I have no idea how I'm going to take his cock.

"Put your coat under him," Fox says.

Morgan peels off the coat she has on and has me lift my hips. The reprieve from the cold on my ass is a welcome one, but I'm so aroused, it really doesn't matter. My body is scorching, and I need to be touched. I need to come.

"Such a little slut, our wolf is," Morgan taunts playfully. "Had I known he was like this, I would've suggested our tradition sooner."

Fox pushes against the plug again before removing it almost all the way and shoving it back in. My cock pulses when it hits what I think is my prostate, and I almost come right there.

"Better hurry, baby. He's not going to last long," Morgan observes.

Fox's hand grips my shaft hard, and my head flies up as I grit my teeth from the jolt of discomfort. "You come when I tell you," he barks.

"Yes, Sir."

Satisfied, Fox relaxes his fist at the same time he pulls out the plug. I groan at the empty sensation, but it doesn't last long.

His thick fingers enter me, probing and stretching. "Such a tight little asshole," Fox admires. "I'm going to stretch you so good, little wolf."

I bite my cheek and try to think of anything that will help me not to come.

"Touch him, but don't make him come yet," he commands Morgan.

Morgan's hand wraps around my cock, and she pumps my hard length, the coolness of her skin giving me a brief reprieve from feeling as if I may explode. A moment later, I feel something warm and realize it's lube one of them must have been carrying. It drips down my shaft as she works me, her fingers swiping over the sensitive crown before she rubs her thumb across the slit.

"Does that feel good, Nathan?"

I nod. "Yes. God, yes."

"Are you ready for my husband's cock?"

I nod vigorously, not caring that this whole thing is bizarre as hell. I feel as if I'm flying high in a kinky winter wonderland, but hell if I want to leave it.

Fox's fingers return to my entrance, his digits slippery. The lube must be the kind that warms, because it leaves a pleasant sensation everywhere it touches, and I don't feel cold at all.

After a few more strokes, Fox stops, and I watch through hooded eyes as he opens the zipper of his pants and pulls his cock out. The cool moonlight glints off his piercing, and I realize I totally forgot about that. Fuck, he's going to split me in half.

"Do you want to stop?" he asks, mischief lacing his words.

"No." Fox lifts an eyebrow. "No, Sir," I correct myself.

"Good boy." If the praise didn't make my dick harder, the sight of Fox stroking himself while kneeling between my legs would. Morgan's hand wraps around my erection now, and she languidly strokes me while Fox grabs under my knees. He spreads my legs wide, my ass still on the jacket as he lifts me up.

"May I?" Morgan asks, her gaze on Fox. I don't know what she's asking, but he nods.

Morgan reaches with her free hand, taking Fox's cock in hers. She strokes him a few times until precum leaks from the tip. He expels a sound of pleasure before she removes her other hand from me and takes something from Fox. I hear a crinkle, and then she slides a condom over his length. Once she's done, she drizzles the warming lube over his sheathed cock and places the head of it against my tight ring of muscles, feeding just the tip of him inside me.

I curse, my head falling back at the intrusion.

"Breathe in," Fox orders, his palms stroking my knees. I do as he says, then follow his command to exhale. As soon as I relax, Morgan guides more of him in. The burn and stretch draws a groan of pleasure from my lips, but I like the ache of pain. It heats my body, and I feel alive.

"That's it, breathe again for me. Halfway there."

"Fuck me," I groan, and Fox chuckles but continues to stroke my knees and thighs, making sure my skin has circulation and warmth.

I exhale another time, and he uses his grip on me to sink in while Morgan's hand moves away to give him space before she wraps it around my length again. I swallow hard and attempt to keep breathing as I feel the piercing on the underside of his cock sliding in me deeper and deeper, as if Fox is branding himself inside me inch by inch. When his pelvis is finally flush against mine and his balls hit my sensitive skin, I cry in relief. But at the same time, I want more.

"Fuck, you feel good," Fox grunts.

"You do, too. You both do," I say, looking from Fox to Morgan.

She smiles, and her hand squeezes my cock, jacking me up and down in different pressures while Fox swirls his hips slowly. Stars start to form behind my eyelids as I become completely aware of every sensation in my body, most of them new.

"I'm going to move now," Fox says.

"Please," I whimper.

Fox pulls out, and I claw at the snowy ground. I think he's going to ease back in slowly, but then he thrusts hard enough I swear I feel it in my throat.

I arch off the ground, and Morgan grips my cock like a vise, my lower stomach clenching and my balls drawing up tight. I don't have time to recover, though, because Fox moves out again, his pace quicker this time.

"You two look amazing together," Morgan hums, her lips near my ear while she pumps my cock. I turn my head toward hers, and knowing what I want, she gives in to me, our lips meeting before she sucks my tongue into her mouth. We groan together, and Fox hurries his pace, gripping my knees and slapping my body against his until it echoes among the trees.

His length slides into me deeply, filling spaces I didn't even know existed, but I surrender to it, accepting his thrusts and enjoying everything he gives me. "That's it, little wolf. Take my cock."

His words dig into my chest, wrapping around my heart. Fuck, I'm never going to be able to come back from this. The only thing that would be better is if my dick were buried inside Morgan at the same time.

I break away from Morgan's lips, the image almost too much. "Fuck, I'm going to come."

Fox speeds up, his balls slapping against my skin as his pierced shaft hits my prostate again and again. "Pump him harder, Morgan—I want to see him come all over your hand."

Morgan makes a sound of pleasure, pulsing her hand up and down my cock.

"Fox," I cry breathlessly. "Please."

He grunts, shifting his body forward and changing the angle, going even deeper now—which I didn't think was possible.

"Oh, fuck. Please, I can't hold it."

Fox drops the hand with the tattoo that says *mine* from my knee and leans forward, gripping the column of my throat. He squeezes tight, his blue eyes staring directly into mine as he ruts, fucking me into the snow like a feral fox as Morgan continues to stroke me. "Come," he growls.

Fireworks explode behind my eyes as I moan wildly into the night, the sounds stifled by Fox's grip on my throat. He comes, too, his thrusts turning choppy as his own cries of pleasure join with mine in the cold night.

When I finally feel able, I open my eyes to Fox's sated stare, his chest heaving and his arms shaking. I inhale a harsh breath, unsure of what to say or do. That was the most intense thing I've ever experienced, but it's not like I should say thank you, even if that seems like something I want and need to say.

Fox exhales and releases his grip on my throat. He still stares at me as I reach up with a shaky hand and play with the strands of his beard. When he doesn't speak, I lift my head, my abs contracting as I gently kiss his chin, the masculine scent of him filling my nose. When I pull back, his eyes are soft, and a look I can't quite place is on his face. But one thing I can't miss is the small smile that teases at his lips.

Then he's pulling back. "Come on," he says quietly. "We need to get you both warm."

"What about the tree?" I ask, turning my head to look at the closest one. It's big and covered in lots of snow.

Morgan giggles softly, and I gaze up at her, her pink tongue darting out to clean the mess of me from her fingers. "Don't worry; we'll get the tree."

CHAPTER THIRTY-SEVEN

Fox

MORGAN PLACES THE STAR on top of the Coulter Pine, adjusting it until it's just right. This type of pine is not the best to decorate, and a lot of its needles are missing from the storm, but it does the job.

When I plant her back on her feet, she wraps an arm around my middle and squeezes, taking in the full image of the tree decorated with multicolored lights and green and red ornaments we got years back at a flea market.

"It's perfect," Morgan says. "Good pick, Nate."

Nathan flushes, and I stifle a laugh. "I don't know if you can say I picked it."

She cackles, pulling him to her so he's standing with us, her arm around his waist now, too. All three of us look at our handiwork, basking in it for a moment.

"Now it feels like Christmas," Morgan chirps.

She's right, it does. Our cabin went from looking like it does most days out of the year to looking like Santa threw up with the tree and all the lights and baubles we put up earlier. A lot of them Morgan and I haven't seen since we bought them, opting to go for only a tree and stockings most years. Even when Gabe was here, we didn't do much. It's just not something we cared to do. But it makes Nathan happy, and given how Morgan's eyes are shining and her skin is practically glowing, it makes her happy, too. Though I know a lot of that has to do with Nathan himself.

I study his profile while he looks at the tree, skin reflecting the rainbow lights on his now scruffy face. I left him a razor in the bathroom, but I'll admit, I'm glad he didn't use it. The shadow of facial hair on his handsome features suits him. If I hadn't seen his transformation for myself, I wouldn't even believe this to be the same man we met two nights ago. His shoulders are relaxed, his eyes are brighter, and his spirit is lighter, as if being here took a large weight off his shoulders. The thought stirs something inside me, a feeling of pride and happiness, because I think Morgan and I are partially responsible for that.

His face turns, and our eyes meet. Color rushes from the collar of his shirt up his neck, and his lip twitches into a smile. I abandon my usual non-smile and lift the corners of my mouth until I feel my cheeks pinch.

Nathan's eyes widen a bit, but then he's smiling, his straight white teeth making an appearance. "You're beautiful when you smile," he says.

Morgan turns to look at me, and my heart stops in my chest. She sees my smile before I school my features back to my normal neutrality. Her grip around my waist tightens, and I know she's trying to encourage me to smile like that again, but I won't.

After my accident in the army, the day I lost my friend and the man I considered a brother, I no longer allowed myself to give my happiness, my smile, to anyone other than Morgan. It may seem silly, but it's not to me.

I know Morgan wishes I'd allow myself to express my emotions the way she and Nathan can. But I learned back then, when I was still naive and cocky enough to believe that life was done throwing me horrible curveballs, that smiling, allowing myself to feel deeply, didn't change the outcome—it just made me vulnerable.

It was one of the issues Gabriel had with me, the reason he ultimately left so abruptly. He'd asked why I couldn't let myself surrender to him, to my feelings. He wanted to know why I couldn't give myself to him like I could Morgan.

But my wife is different. Morgan long ago buried herself so deep in my heart, in my very being, that even if I wanted to, I wouldn't let her go, couldn't let her go, even if someone tried to carve her out of me. Not only is she marked on my skin, but she's marked on my soul.

Which makes this moment confusing, because I smiled for Nathan. That gut feeling about him being a partner for us was right, and I know what I'm feeling for him goes deeper than anything Gabe could have ever been. I feel like an idiot for not considering what feeling this way could mean for me and my emotions—especially with someone we just met.

"Sorry," Nathan says quietly. "I didn't mean to embarrass you."

I swallow the thickness in my throat, and Morgan's grip tightens almost suffocatingly around my waist as if she knows every thought racing through my mind and can see the fear now flickering in my eyes. It's a fear I have no right to feel, considering I was the one who urged her to give Nathan a chance. But now, as reality closes in, I'm questioning whether I made the right choice. Even if I've allowed myself to care for Nathan as deeply as I do for Morgan, I'm a lot to handle—and not just my moods, either, but me as a person.

I know Morgan can handle me, but can Nathan? He's shown he can handle me physically, but what about when I'm at my worst? When my PTSD flares up and all I do is bark orders and push people away, can he handle that, too?

Can he do what only Morgan has been able to do and handle me outside the bedroom?

"You didn't," Morgan says, forcing a bright smile to her face. "He's not used to being called beautiful. More like rugged, handsome, and scary," she teases, her arm giving me a reassuring squeeze.

Nathan laughs softly, but I'm not sure he buys it. The

comment, however, serves its purpose, and the tension in the room breaks. I embrace Morgan back in thanks as I inhale a soft breath, willing myself to relax. It was only a smile, a fucking *smile*, and I need to get it together and not spiral. I need to control myself, so I do, taking in another breath and willing my shoulders to relax. Now is not the time to think these things, especially when Nathan could be leaving as soon as tomorrow—a thought that stabs painfully at me even if I don't want to admit it.

"Sorry, you're a very handsome and scary lumberjack," he amends. "Please forgive me?"

"Logger," Morgan corrects.

"Sorry, a very handsome and scary logger. *Now* will you forgive me?" Nathan teases. His eyes meet mine, and while they're still unsure, they're gleaming again.

My muscles relax a little more. "I'll think about it."

"Just think?" Nathan's head is cocked, his lips pulled up in a playful grin.

His sass brings me back to myself, and I feel the emotional walls I've carefully built up reinforce themselves and keep the dam from breaking. I give my full attention to Nathan's now teasing stare and do what I do best: divert to things I *can* control.

"I could be persuaded to forgive you," I say, my tone laced with its easy dominance, one I know will shift the energy in the room.

"Oh?" Nathan's gaze darts to my lips and then back up to my eyes.

"Careful, Wolfie," Morgan teases with her new nickname. "My husband is not easily persuaded."

"Depends on the method of persuasion." I shoot Nathan a look of challenge, daring him to give me his best offering.

His gaze drops to my lips once more, and I know he's thinking about our encounter in the woods because he shifts on his feet and his skin flushes before he meets my eyes again. "Fox," he says after a moment.

"Yes?" I say slyly.

"That contraption you have, the one in your room from the other night, can Morgan lie face up on it?"

Morgan freezes against my side, and I'm no longer ruminating over any of the thoughts I was moments ago. Mission accomplished. "Yes, why?" I ask.

"I have something I'd like to try, but I need your help."

I stare at Nathan with heat in my eyes. "I'm curious as to how this will earn you my forgiveness."

His smile is coy as he says, "Because you get to help me make your wife come."

I chuckle at his brazen statement. The man we met two nights ago would have never said those words out loud, but I can't say I don't like it.

"Plus, I don't want her to feel left out after our little adventure."

Heat curls in my low belly as I shift my attention to Morgan, who's already turned on. I can tell by how her nipples have pebbled under her thin sweater and how her arm grips my waist tighter.

"Were you feeling left out tonight, lamb?"

She shakes her head. "No."

Feeling more like my usual self again, I step in front of her and drag my hand down her sternum, then over the plush curves of her, belly until I'm cupping her hot cunt beneath her leggings. "Does that mean you don't want to come, then?"

"If you're offering." She grins.

I chuckle, rocking the heel of my palm against her sex so the fabric rubs her clit, forcing her to moan. "Your Wolfie is offering. Do you want him to take care of you?"

She eyes Nathan, bratty grin still on her lips. "If you're offering."

Nathan steps forward and takes her chin between his fingers. I watch them carefully, the way she looks at him with adoration and a little bit of awe, how Nathan's eyes overflow with lust and infatuation.

Nathan smiles. "I'm offering."

"Then yes."

Chapter Thirty-Eight

Morgan

While I expected to be getting some action tonight—it *is* Christmas Eve, after all—I didn't expect to be strapped to the special stockade Fox ordered for me and laid out like a sacrificial lamb for Jolly Old Saint Nick in front of the Christmas tree. But here we are—and I'm not complaining.

Nathan kneels between my spread and bound legs, admiring my body as he runs his hands up and down my thighs. My head is angled up by the face cradle so I can see whatever he's about to do to me, and my arms are bound in the stocks above my head. I'm once again completely at the mercy of two insatiable men, and my pussy is dripping almost embarrassingly for them.

Fox approaches fully dressed, a curious look in his eyes. I was anxious about his reaction to Nathan calling his smile beautiful, and truthfully, I still am. But as he gazes down at me with love, I push those thoughts aside. Now isn't the time to have a deep conversation, and I doubt my husband would appreciate a heart-to-heart while I'm in this position.

Or maybe he would, but I hold back, knowing we'll talk later and hoping he'll work through whatever's on his mind. Because no matter what he thinks, he deserves happiness. We all do.

Fox brushes his fingers down my cheek. "Everything feeling okay, lamb?"

"Yes, Sir."

He nods, tracing my lips with the pad of his thumb. "You don't have to be formal tonight. It's Christmas, after all."

I blink at him, my chest warming. "Is it midnight?"

"Just after."

"Merry Christmas to me, then."

Fox chuckles, slipping the tip of his thumb between my lips. I suck on it, and he slides his finger farther in, pressing down on the pad of my tongue. My mouth starts to water just as he pulls back, and he puts his lips to my ear to whisper, "Later."

My inner walls clench at his promise, and Nathan groans.

We look over at him together, his hands still stroking my thighs as he watches us. He's taken off his shirt, and the fire is making his skin glow and the corded muscles of his arms more prominent.

"Someday, I'd love to watch you two together."

"Again?" I tease.

Nathan's hand comes down on my clit in a light slap, and I jump in surprise. "So bold to be teasing me when you're tied up."

My head turns to Fox, who looks like he's biting his cheek to keep from laughing. Despite the predicament I'm in and the fact that he's trying not to laugh, I'm glad my husband is letting himself go a bit, even though I know it's hard for him. Especially after all the things he's gone through and everything he does for me and our business.

"Do it again—I dare you." I smile cheekily at Nathan.

He smirks and lifts his hand up, smacking my clit again— not once or even twice, but three times.

"We created a monster," Fox mutters against my ear.

"I think it's your fault," I groan.

Fox's lip twitches before he stands, making his way toward where Nathan is kneeling. He grabs something off the table behind him before pulling over a wooden chair so he has a direct view of my pussy and Nathan. Only then does my brain register what Nathan said: *Someday, I'd love to watch you two together.*

My chest grows heavy, and butterflies fill my stomach at the prospect of it. He fits in with us so well, he's almost too perfect. But he's perfect for us.

Nathan smiles up at me, then uses his green-painted thumb to trace broad circles around my clit without ever actually touching it.

I lick my lips. "What are you going to do?"

He continues his ministrations. "Fox is going to teach me how to do something I imagined doing yesterday."

My interest piques. "Is that so?"

He nods, his thumb still drawing a circle around my clit, gathering wetness from my pussy with each swipe.

"You'll like it, baby," he says, a reminder that the same endearment slipped from his lips while he was inside me. It sounds good coming from him, and I'll admit, I could get used to it. Which is a little scary. But at the same time, I've come to realize that what we had with Gabe—or any other partner, for that matter—was never going to work. Not because I don't think they could ever truly understand who Fox is and our dynamic together, though that was largely true, but because they weren't Nathan.

Another little slap to my clit has my eyes refocusing on the man between my thighs. I press my head back into the padded cradle as Nathan strokes around my stinging sex.

"She will like it," Fox assures cockily.

My eyes flit to my husband's as he takes what's in his hand and gives it to Nathan. A bottle of lube.

"Make her come; get her nice and relaxed," Fox tells him.

"Yes, Sir."

I don't miss the way Fox's lip twitches at his reply, and the image of them together in the woods comes to mind. I still don't know if I'll recover from watching that.

Nathan flips open the cap of the lube and dribbles the thick liquid over my pussy lips. He catches it with his fingers, handing the bottle back to Fox as he rubs it over my clit. My eyes roll back slightly, and I wiggle against my restraints.

"You're so needy," Nathan says. "I think I could tease you for hours."

"Please don't," I groan, causing both men to chuckle.

"Always such a little whore, Wife," Fox says.

I nod, my body itching for more touch. More feeling. More anything. I just need more than the small touches Nathan is giving me.

"She's being so good. Give her two fingers; start stretching her."

My gaze fixes between my legs again, and I see Nathan's thumb still working my clit while his other hand moves to my opening. When he dips his two fingers inside, my hips grind into the air, already seeking more.

"That's it," Fox says. "Use your mouth; make her come."

Nathan doesn't hesitate. He leans forward, his lips sucking over my sensitive bundle of nerves. I cry out his name, my hips thrusting up off the table. Fox shifts so he can lay his palm flat on my belly, adding pressure that heightens everything happening inside me.

"Yes!" Nathan's fingers turn and hook, brushing against my G-spot as he flicks his tongue over my clit.

"She's close already," Fox says. "Add a third finger. Fuck her harder."

Nathan's third finger enters me, and I can't take my eyes off him. He's staring up at me, a smile in his eyes as he licks and sucks me, the veins in his arm protruding as he fucks me hard and fast.

Fox adds more pressure to my belly, and I know what he's trying to do.

"Let it happen, lamb. Make a mess."

I press my head into the cradle of the stockade, my hands fisting as Nathan moves his fingers harder and faster, hitting my G-spot again and again. The sound of my pussy being fucked, the noise of my wetness, is perverted and wild, and I love everything about it.

"Let go, Morgan. Nathan wants to taste that sweet cum."

At another press against my stomach, I feel my release take over my body. Wetness coats my thighs and Nathan's hand as I squirt and pulse around his fingers, falling hard and fast.

"Nathan!" I cry. He doesn't let up; instead, he adds a fourth finger. I don't know if Fox told him to do that, but my head is fuzzy, and my vision is spotting.

"Holy fuck, that was amazing." Nathan groans. "You taste so good, baby." His tongue laps over the wetness on my quaking thighs, and his fingers continue to move inside me, riding me through my orgasm and prolonging it.

When I feel more lube dripping down my heated pussy, I peel my eyes open and look at the two deviants with complete and utter control over me.

Fox draws circles over my belly and then trails his hand down my thigh. "That was one, lamb."

My chest heaves, and I take a short inhale as a bead of sweat drips down my forehead. "More?"

Nathan's fingers move in a circle inside, and my entire body twitches. "I still haven't completed my mission," he says.

I drop my head back down and cry out again as his four fingers flex inside me. When he starts to rub my clit once more, working his fingers deeper, it clicks. "Nathan," I whine.

"Yeah, Morgan?"

"Make it good."

CHAPTER THIRTY-NINE

Nathan

"Do you want me to gag her?" Fox asks from my side.

I study Morgan, tied up and bound again at our mercy. It's a sight I don't think I could ever tire of. "No, I like hearing her cries."

"Hmm, she is pretty when she screams."

I stare at Fox. He's not smiling like he did for me earlier, but he's beautiful, nonetheless.

Beautiful. He's beautiful.

The thought is almost a natural one now, even if it's still a little shocking. But after what we shared in the woods, I can't *not* admit I find him attractive and that I like him. And, if given the chance, I'll do everything in my power to get him to smile again.

"How's she feel?" Fox asks, his attention on my hand, the one that's almost fully inside his wife.

"Like heaven."

That has his lip twitching. "I know that. I meant, is she ready to take your whole hand?"

My cheeks flush. Everything we've done has been dirty, but this—this feels sinful. Especially in this innocent setting near the tree, surrounded by Christmas decorations. Even if said tree is a reminder of our previous activity—which was also not so innocent.

Morgan writhes as I sink my fingers deeper, spreading and moving them until her inner walls stretch and flutter around me. Shit, she's so wet. She may have made a mess on the couch yesterday—and when I fucked her—but I've never seen a woman squirt quite like that before. If I can make her do that every time she comes, I will. I can only hope I'll have more opportunities after tonight.

"Keep rubbing her clit, and when you add your thumb, make your hand smaller, like this." He holds up his hand, showing how it's collapsed to look like a duck bill.

"Got it," I say. My eyes meet Morgan's. Her body is relaxed, but I can see the anticipation in the way her nipples are tight and her hips wiggle. "You ready, baby?"

"Please, Nathan. I need you."

I shift, my cock twitching in my pants as I pull my hand almost all the way out, a little smile on my lips when I see the green polish on my nails from earlier.

I take a moment to indulge in sliding my hand in and out, my painted fingernails disappearing into and then reappearing out of her wet pussy. I never thought I'd ever have painted nails, but I like it. Maybe I'll have Morgan paint them for every holiday.

"Enjoying yourself?" Fox teases.

"Immensely."

Morgan shifts, but since her body is tied, she can't get far.

"Impatient?" I ask her.

"Please, Nate," she begs. "Fuck me."

"I'll take care of you, baby," I say, thumbing her clit as I do what Fox showed me. When my fingers move past the first knuckle easily, I keep going, the tip of my thumb disappearing. "Fuck, you're so amazing, Morgan."

She keens as I work my hand in, Fox and I both praising her as I go deeper. My thumb is almost all the way in now.

"That's it," Fox says. "Nice and easy."

As I slowly work my hand in deeper, Morgan's body opens for me like a flower, and I twist my hand to sink in even further.

Morgan's hips tip up at the same time my entire hand slides in. "Nathan!" she cries wildly.

"Goddamn, baby," I say in awe. "My fucking hand is inside you."

Morgan moans again, and I move it slightly deeper, the heat of her indescribable as her pussy clenches around my hand and my wrist. Holy fucking shit.

"Are you okay?" I ask.

"Yes—fuck—oh my god." She throws her head back as Fox strokes her thigh.

"You're doing so good, lamb. Can you see his hand inside you?"

Morgan's chin lowers, and her eyes open, looking down at her round stomach, which clearly shows my hand moving inside her. With her gaze on me, I gently thrust it up and down for her, and she keens, her inner muscles fluttering.

"Longer strokes, Nathan," Fox commands. "Bring your fingers down slowly into a fist, and start fucking her."

My cock jumps at his words, reminding me how turned on I am by this entire thing. I look down at my hand and still can't believe I'm doing this. When I was fingering her earlier, it crossed my mind, but I didn't think it was possible—yet Fox assured me it was.

I slowly bring my fingers down, my hand turning into a full fist. Her vagina clenches, and her body tightens at the size of me.

"Relax, baby," I soothe. "You're doing so well."

"Nathan," she moans. "Please."

"Do it, Nathan," Fox barks. "She can take it."

With my hand still in a fist, I begin to move, Morgan's hips lifting and writhing. I thumb her clit harder, circling it the way I've figured out she likes. When her body relaxes, I move deeper and circle, playing with movement and the location of my fingers until I figure out a pace she likes.

"I'm going to come again." Morgan whimpers. "Please, more."

"Told you," Fox whispers against my ear. "Fuck her, *Wolfie*."

That makes me chuckle as I fuck her harder with my fist and keep pressure on her clit.

"Nate." Her back arches. "Oh my god!"

"That's it, pretty girl. You're so fucking beautiful."

Morgan cries out again, and Fox's hand returns to her stomach. He pushes down so even I can feel the pressure of his hand, and Morgan curses. I think she calls him a bastard, which makes Fox smirk a little.

I twist my hand and fuck her deeper, hitting every single spot inside that makes her pull against her restraints. "I'm going to…I'm going…" She gasps.

Morgan can't get the words completely out, and it makes me feel like the fucking king of the world. "Come, Morgan. Fucking soak my hand."

Fox adds pressure to her abdomen, and I pinch her clit at the same time I drag my fist down. Morgan screams, her eyes squeezing shut as she shakes and convulses. Fox holds her in place to keep her safe, praising her and soothing her because of the sheer intensity of it.

My hand is soaked like I wanted, her release dripping down onto the floor as her orgasm squeezes the life out of me.

"She's sucking my hand in," I breathe out.

Morgan moans and strains against her bindings, delirious with pleasure. I ride her through it, allowing her to take what she needs. It takes her a while to come down, and I use every moment to memorize this, burning this experience into my core memories—another first.

But, God, I fucking hope not the last.

CHAPTER FORTY

Morgan

MY EYES POP OPEN, and my stomach swirls. It's dark in the bedroom, the fire having died out hours ago now, as I blink sleep from my eyes. My body is heavy with exhaustion from our activities, and a dull ache throbs between my legs.

As I sluggishly blink awake, I try to figure out why I woke up feeling like something was wrong. Nathan's warm breath puffs against my forehead, and his hand rests on my waist, but as the brain fog clears, I know what's missing: Fox.

I gently remove Nathan's hand, shifting backward into the empty space of the bed that's gone cold—a sign Fox has been up for a while. When I'm free, I grab my robe and quietly make my way to where I know I'll find him.

He hears me approach, his head lifting from his mug of tea to meet my eyes. The light of the kitchen glows overhead, and his shoulders look as if they bear the weight of the world. I know my husband—how can I not after how long we've been together and how much we've been through?—and I know that whatever he's thinking is not good.

I pad softly to the table, pulling out the chair at the head of it and moving it until we're close enough that I can place my hand on his shoulder after I sit. His muscles relax momentarily at my touch, and his gaze meets mine in the soft light.

"Hey, baby," I say quietly. "Did you have a nightmare?"

He shakes his head. "I didn't fall asleep."

I inhale a breath through my nose and rub my hand gently down his back. "How long have you been out here?"

Fox shrugs. "This is my second cup."

"Do you want to talk about it?"

He doesn't break eye contact as he says, "Not it. Nathan."

My stomach flips, and I drop my hand, placing it in my lap. I understand now; him being out here and not in our bed relates to whatever was going through his head earlier. But I was right about one thing: Whatever he's thinking is not good.

"Fox." His name comes out in a faint plea. "Tell me what you mean."

His chin drops, and he stares at his mug of tea. "We need to be realistic."

"Realistic how?" There's an edge to my tone, one that surprises both of us given the flash in his eye.

"I don't know if he's right for us, Morgan."

"Bullshit."

"Morgan—"

"No, you're sabotaging it before it has even had time to grow because you're scared."

"That's not it," he argues. "I'm trying to protect us."

"No," I spit, my voice coming out louder than I intended. "That's bullshit, Fox."

"Weren't you the one who was hesitant just yesterday?"

I fist my hands. "No, you don't get to turn this around on me, especially when you were the one who convinced me to give him a shot, remember?"

Fox remains silent, so I continue.

"And as much as I hate admitting you were right, I'm glad you were. Because Nathan is incredible. You see and feel it, too. That's why we're even having this conversation. But I'm not going to let your fear of letting him in do this to us, Fox. Not this time."

His fingers flex around his mug. "What are you saying?"

"I don't need to tell you why Gabe left so suddenly; he told us."

"So it's all my fault?"

I shake my head vehemently. "We've been over this. He had his reasons for leaving, but at the end of the day, we are both at fault. You couldn't fully let him in, and I didn't push you on it."

"I tried, Morgan."

I blow out a soft exhale. "I know you did, and I'm not blaming you. In the end, it didn't work out because it wasn't meant to. There were problems with jealousy even before that, so it was never going to work. Plus, he's not Nathan."

I place my hand on Fox's forearm. The muscle flexes under my touch, and I wait for him to look at me again. When he does, my heart contracts at the fear I see in my husband's eyes. He doesn't want to react like this or push Nathan away. I saw the way he is with him, and I know he's been taking care of Nathan in ways that many people wouldn't even notice. Leaving clothes out for him, making sure he eats regularly and drinks enough water. I even caught Fox pulling the covers over him before I fell asleep. He cares for Nathan already.

Regardless, I should've been more observant, noticed that Fox needed my assurance and help. But he'd seemed so sure in his advances toward Nathan. I think I was caught up in my own fear of starting something with him, of opening my heart again and being rejected, that I didn't see how hard and fast Fox was truly falling, at least until his smile earlier. A smile may seem like something so small, but a smile from my husband means something. It means a lot of somethings.

"What are you afraid of, baby?" I ask, breaking the silence. "Let's talk about this instead of making a rash decision."

Fox's jaw tenses, and for the first time in a long time, I see emotion well in his eyes. It's fleeting, but it's there. "I don't want you to get hurt, Morgan," he says, though I can hear what he's not saying. *I don't want* us *to get hurt.*

"I love you, Fox, but you can't always protect my heart—or yours, to be honest—no matter how hard you try. We chose to live this way; we want to live this way. That means we have to be vulnerable, and we have to communicate. It's been our flaw, and if we want this to go any further with Nathan, we need to talk about this, and we need to talk about this with him. We told him in the beginning this could be whatever we wanted it to be. Now we have to see where his head is at and if he wants to go further with us."

"And if he does?"

"Tell me you wouldn't want that," I say. "You said you felt like he could be the one, that he could be ours. Do you only feel differently now because you're starting to have real feelings for him?"

"He doesn't belong here, Morgan."

"Fox—"

The floor creaks, and we both look up to see a half-asleep Nathan looking both sad and confused. My stomach sinks as I stand up from my seat.

"Nathan, what are you doing up?" The words feel so silly leaving my mouth, but I'm unsure of how much he heard or what to say.

His gaze darts from me to Fox, his hands flexing at his sides. "I couldn't sleep."

"Why don't you sit down? I'll make you some tea."

He shakes his head. "It's fine; I'll go back to the guest room." *The guest room.* He's not going to go back to our bed.

"Please sit," I plead, knowing that if he goes back to his room, this is most likely over.

"It's all right. I'll see you in the morning."

"Nate." I take a step forward, but he backs away, my heart splintering. "Please stay."

"I'll see you in the morning."

His footsteps fade away, and when I hear the click of the door on the spare room closing, I turn to Fox. His hands are clenched so hard around his mug, I'm surprised it hasn't shattered.

"You didn't really mean that," I tell Fox.

"Even if I didn't, it's better this way, Morgan," he says quietly.

My eyes shine with tears, and despite being upset with Fox for being hot and cold, for trying to throw away something good because he's scared to be vulnerable and give himself fully to another person besides me, I take a deep breath. I know he doesn't want to be this way, and I know this is hard for him.

I walk back to him, leaning down to place a gentle kiss on his forehead. I feel him exhale, but his body remains tense.

"I love you, baby. I love you so fucking much, and you know I'll do anything for you. But please, don't let Nathan walk out of this cabin thinking that you don't want him here." I turn Fox's face until he's looking me in the eye. "Because I know you do."

After a moment, he brings one of his hands up to grasp my face. "I don't know how to really let him in. I thought I could, but then…What if it's too much, Morgan? What if we're too much?"

My chest grows heavy at his admission. I'm thrown back to when we were teenagers. He was so different then—rebellious, angry, and just looking for someone to love him, to tell him he was wanted. In so many ways, he's different now, but at the same time, that teenage boy I met is still inside him. Only now, he keeps people at arm's length under the guise of protecting me. But I know he's just trying to protect his own heart. And in his own way, he's trying to protect Nathan's, too.

I sit back down in my chair and take Fox's hand in mine, interlacing our fingers so our *yours* and *mine* tattoos become intertwined.

"Do you remember when that cheerleader, Jessica, told me I was 'too much' in front of the entire senior class?"

Despite our serious conversation, Fox's lip twitches. "How could I forget?"

I smirk. "Do you remember what you told me then?"

Fox looks down at our intertwined fingers, studying our tattoos before he looks up again. "That Jessica could go fuck herself."

A puff of laughter leaves my lips. "Yes, that. But what else?"

"That someone's too much is someone else's just right. That I'm your just right."

I bring our hands to my lips, kissing the heart tattoo on his wrist.

"We're just right, Fox. And what if Nathan is, too?"

Fox sighs. "But what if—"

I stop him with a short kiss. "He should be the one to decide that. Not us. Don't make decisions for other people."

Fox chuffs, and I smirk.

"I know you like to, but this is his *life*, Fox. It's our life. Do you really want to throw away something that could be amazing because you're afraid? That's not the Fox I know and love."

"You give me too much credit."

I shake my head. "You had a gut feeling about Nathan—listen to that. Nathan deserves a chance. We do, too."

Fox leans forward, our hands still linked as he rests his forehead to mine. "I love you, Morgan."

"I love you, too, baby." I gently kiss his lips. "Now, go talk to him."

CHAPTER FORTY-ONE

Nathan

He doesn't belong here, Morgan.

Fox's words ring over and over again in my ears. Now I'm questioning if any of what I've felt and experienced over the last two days was real or if Fox and Morgan just used me.

Thinking that feels wrong, though, because I know it's untrue. We may have just met, but with what we've shared, I can't think that poorly of them. Even if I'm hurt.

I sit up in bed, knowing I'm not going to get any sleep in this room. It's also cold in here since the fire hasn't been lit and the bed hasn't been used, making the loneliness I'm suddenly feeling even worse. My body craves the warmth of Fox and Morgan, remembers how it felt to have them both near me as I slept. Fox's large arm on my waist and Morgan's soft legs tangled between mine. It was a feeling I could get used to, that I wanted to get used to. I guess they didn't feel the same.

I flip on the side table lamp, my eyes adjusting to the light. The clock on the wall says it's after four in the morning. I wish I had a sleeping pill, because maybe I could sleep in late. Then, if the sheriff was right, I could leave here without needing to interact with them again. I could eat Christmas dinner with my family before having to figure out how to get my car back and everything that comes after that.

The idea of leaving this place, Starlight Haven, and driving back down the mountain to my real life is something I haven't really thought about since I started this thing with Fox and

Morgan. We've been in this little bubble, and it's been easy to pretend that reality doesn't exist.

My eyes focus on the artwork above the fireplace that I saw when I first woke up what seems like ages ago. After everything, the fox-and-lamb motif makes sense. Fox is sly, cunning, and a predator. I'd even argue, he's playful. Morgan is his lamb. Sweet and docile but also social, intelligent, and emotional.

When I look closer at the river scene, I remember I saw something else that I couldn't make out before. I study it closer, my eyes drawn up the river and to the woods. My throat becomes thick when I see it, and I honestly don't know what to think.

I blink to make sure I'm not making it up, but it's staring right at me: the two yellow eyes of a wolf on the prowl among the trees. He's there, waiting, watching, considering his next move.

I rub my hands over my jaw, which needs a shave. God, I'm so confused. It's not like they planned for me to crash, and I'm not living some weird kinky fairy tale. Maybe Morgan's right that fate brought me here. Because even if they don't want me, I'm leaving here a changed man. I can no longer go back to a job I hate and work for another Kathy. My teeth have been sharpened, and I'd eat someone like her alive.

Knock, knock!

My back stiffens when I hear the soft rapping on my door. I don't have to open it to know who it is. That knock was too sharp for it to be Morgan. And from what I've learned about her so far, she'd send Fox here to speak with me. He may dominate Morgan most of the time, but it's clear she has him wrapped around her tattooed finger. That she, too, is a wolf in sheep's clothing—or rather, a lamb's.

Another two soft knocks, and I know I have to let him open the door. My light is on, and while I don't want to talk to him or have him comfort me with words he doesn't mean, I don't want to cower before him, either. "Come in."

The door opens, and Fox's muscular form fills the doorway. His sharp blue eyes stare at me, but he doesn't take a step forward.

"Do you need something?" I ask. I intended for my tone to come out clipped, but instead, I sound tired.

"Can I talk to you?" he asks, though it's not a question.

I want to say something sassy, to make him feel how I felt, but I go with the mature route. "What is it?"

Fox steps into the room, leaving the door open. In two strides, he's looming over me, his blond hair a mess from what looks like his fingers threading through it, probably from nerves. And now that he's closer, I see a frown marred in his brow and an unsure look in his eye. It's weird to see him like this, such a contrast to the grumpy, domineering side he usually displays. "Can I sit?" he asks.

I tip my chin to the space in front of me on the bed, and he sits without pause.

A minute or so passes before he releases a tense breath and turns his head to mine. "I didn't mean for you to hear that."

I frown. "I figured that, Fox. Is that really what you came to tell me? Because if so, please leave."

A sound like a small growl expels from his chest, and he rubs a hand over his face. "I—" He pauses. "I'm not good at shit like this, Nathan."

"What, talking? Yeah, I know."

Fox's eyes narrow at me, and I know I'm pissing him off. He likes being in charge, and he doesn't like pushback, but that's too bad for him right now. I knew that his words hurt, but until he sat down in front of me, I don't think I quite realized how much.

"Yes. I'm not good at it. Especially feelings and apologies."

My breathing slows. "If it's only an apology, I don't need

it. We're strangers who got trapped together and had sex. It doesn't need to be more than that."

Fox's jaw ticks. "Is that all this is to you?"

I blink at him. "If you need a reminder, *you're* the one who said I don't belong here."

"You caught me at a weak moment."

"Words mean things, Fox. You said it."

He's quiet for a minute before he says, "I can only give so much, Nathan."

I cock an eyebrow at him. "I don't know what that means."

"It means I need you to understand that if you're in a relationship with us, I'm not always going to be able to express myself the way Morgan can. I'll piss you off, and you'll probably piss me off. I need you to give me time and some grace. My past has been difficult, and I don't always say the right thing... or anything at all. I know that's not an excuse, but it's who I am."

I blink at Fox, my brain trying to register all the words he just spoke—the most he's said to me at once. And did he say relationship?

My mind reels, and I feel as if I have whiplash. "I still don't understand what you're saying."

Fox inhales a breath and shifts on the bed. Then he reaches for my hand, taking it in his. His calloused fingers are rough against my skin, and the fire that had been doused reignites. He rubs his thumb over my knuckles, his eyes watching the movement. "Morgan and I had a relationship before this, one that didn't work out for a few reasons, but the biggest was that I couldn't let myself be what he needed. I have a lot of hang-ups from my past, and again, it's not an excuse, especially for being an asshole. But I said you didn't belong with us not because I don't want you here, but because I'm worried if you stay, you'll leave when you figure out I can't be what you need. Just like our last partner did and others have before him."

My chest smarts from his vulnerability, and I find myself squeezing his hand. "And what is it you think I need?"

His eyes look up, a deep pain and sadness visible in them. "A stable partner, one who won't make you want to leave."

I swallow the large lump in my throat and place my other hand over our joined ones. "I don't know your entire past, Fox. I can figure out a lot of what you've been through from what you've shared, and I'm not asking for you to tell me right now. But please, don't assume what you think I need."

Fox's gaze doesn't move from mine. "What is it you need?"

"I want to be wanted, respected."

"We *do* want you, Nathan. We *do* respect you. And I'm sorry if I've made you feel otherwise. I shouldn't have said what I did, and I'm sorry you overheard it. It's on me, and I regret saying it."

I contemplate his words as I look down at my hand in his. It looks so much smaller and more delicate against his tattooed skin, something I never thought I'd say about my own hand. "Are you saying you think I do belong here, then?"

My eyes shift back to his, and he swallows, his jaw tense. "I am."

I can tell he's speaking the truth, but my heart still feels shattered. We may have just met, but what I've experienced here has changed me, and his words cut me deep. "I think I need time."

Fox stares into my eyes, his gaze searching. "Time for what?"

I almost laugh at his gruff question. It's so... *Fox.*

"To figure out if this is right for me." And that's the truth, because even if I didn't overhear Fox, I would've had to speak with them about our future and whether we had one. I would've needed time to know if this was plausible long-term and what that meant for my life.

After a long moment, he nods, though his facial expression looks sad at my answer. "I can understand that."

"Are you and Morgan okay with that?"

"Of course we are," Morgan says.

Fox and I both look to the doorway, and my gaze meets her serious one. She smiles gently as she steps into the room wearing only her thin red robe. She sits on the other side of me on the bed, the mattress sinking under her weight as she places her tattooed hand over the top of the one I have resting over Fox's.

"Take all the time you need. We want you, Nathan, and we'll wait for you."

My stomach flips at the seriousness of her words and the truth she's placed into them. "How can you know that's what you want so soon?"

A small smile tugs at the corner of her lips. "Maybe it's fate, maybe it's a gut feeling, or maybe it's your fist." She smirks, and I blush. Leave it to Morgan to break the tension. "But I like you, Nathan, and so does Fox."

My eyes connect with his cool blue ones, and he nods. "I do."

The words send a shiver up my spine, and Morgan brushes a piece of hair behind my ear. "You are wanted, Nathan."

I glance between the two of them—two people I never would have imagined befriending let alone sharing what we've shared. Yet now I can't imagine my life without them. It makes me want to say I want them back, but I know I need to take the time I asked for and think things through. Given everything I've learned about Fox and Morgan, I don't want to rush into this and give Fox the satisfaction of a self-fulfilling prophecy, even if he seems intent on making it happen—or at least, he did.

"I really am sorry," Fox says, his eyes never leaving mine.

I squeeze both their hands. "It's okay, Fox. I forgive you."

Chapter Forty-Two

Fox

Our conversation ended with the decision we'd keep sex off the table for the rest of Nathan's stay here. That's how we all ended up moving to the living room to sit in the glow of the Christmas tree. Nobody spoke, and eventually, Nathan fell asleep with Morgan's head in his lap. When her eyes closed, too, I allowed mine to shut for a bit. Now, I'm wide awake with the sun, and all I can do is stare at the two people on the couch.

"Quit thinking so loud," Nathan's sleep-husky voice says, echoing my words to him from yesterday morning.

Our gazes meet, and his lips move into a soft smile.

"What time is it?" he asks quietly after seeing Morgan asleep on his lap.

"Just after eight," I whisper.

"Merry Christmas."

"Merry Christmas," I echo.

Nathan's eyes move to the tree, and I don't miss the way the morning light highlights the flush of his cheeks.

"How do you feel?" I ask tentatively. "I know that was a lot."

"A little frostbitten."

My brow knits with concern until I see Nathan's chest shake with quiet laughter. "I'm fine, Fox. I liked it."

"I know."

Nathan shakes his head at me, but before he can respond, Morgan groans. "Too early," she whines, burying her face in

Nathan's crotch. His head drops back on the couch, and his eyes shut tight.

"Lamb," I say. "You're not on a pillow."

She doesn't say anything. Instead, she rubs her cheek against Nathan's growing wood like it's a magic lamp.

"Morgan," he says huskily. "Don't tempt me."

I see her pout, but then she shifts off his lap. When her eyes fall on the packages on the mantel, she brightens, suddenly awake and perky like a child is on Christmas morning.

"I think we should open presents." Morgan stands and takes the packages from the mantel, keeping one for herself and then dropping one in Nathan's lap. I didn't expect to have one to open, at least not traditionally. Morgan knows I don't like receiving gifts unless they're practical or in the form of sex. Knowing my wife, she'll surprise me with one of those two things later.

Nathan shifts uncomfortably, and he looks between the two of us, his brow adorably wrinkled. "Why do I have a gift?"

"It's from Santa." Morgan smiles, and I tug her to me. She wiggles her ass on my crotch as she settles on my lap. "Right, Santa?"

I shake my head at her antics but glance back at Nathan. "Open it."

He stares at the package for a long moment before he says, "You first, Morgan."

"You don't have to tell me twice," she chirps. While Morgan and I don't celebrate this holiday as much as some, my wife likes gifts, and I like giving them to her—and I know she'll like this one.

Nathan watches Morgan with a broad smile on his face, one that bites into my chest and makes me wish I could erase everything that happened in the last few hours. When she pulls back the paper and pops open the small box, he looks just as excited as she is. Images of every holiday being like this appear in my mind, and I'll admit that while it's a little scary, it's nice.

We'd be like this, together. A family. I wonder if Nathan's family would join us, too.

Morgan rips open the box and pulls out a small piece of paper folded in half. She flips it open, and I think her jaw hits the floor. "Are you serious?" she asks me.

"I wouldn't give that to you if I wasn't."

She holds the paper to her chest, and a devilish smile appears on her face.

"What is it?" Nathan asks curiously.

"Can I show him?"

I nod, and Morgan smiles wider, handing the paper to Nathan. We both watch him read it, his nostrils flaring and his throat bobbing as he gives it back to Morgan.

"I didn't know you'd do that," he says.

"Rarely. Let's just say someone new came into our lives the other night, and I felt compelled," I say.

Time stops as the three of us look at each other. So many things being said, so many things left unsaid.

Eventually, I clear my throat, looking down at the package in Nathan's hands. "Open it."

"All right," he says quietly. "But I don't have anything for you."

My lip twitches at his thoughtfulness. "I wouldn't expect you to. Just open it."

He expels a small breath, then tears open the brown paper before taking out the small box and popping the top open. When he looks inside, my heart races while I wait for him to take out his gift.

He swallows. "You made this?" He holds up the small wooden figure of a wolf. The wolf I carved for him.

"I did."

"Is that why you took so long in the office the other day?" Morgan asks.

"I wanted both of you to have something to open on Christmas," I say simply.

Nathan clears his throat, his eyes fluttering rapidly as he runs his fingers over the lines of the carving with reverence. "Thank you. It's beautiful."

I open my mouth to respond when a loud noise draws our attention outside the cabin. We freeze as if a bomb has gone off. The reality that we're no longer snowed in settles among us when we see the headlights of the plow clearing part of the driveway. A moment later, the slam of a car door makes Nathan and Morgan flinch.

"I guess that's my ride," he says quietly.

My hand tightens around Morgan's waist, knowing she needs the extra comfort.

While we knew this was coming, and Nathan asked for time, I think part of her hoped we could change his mind before he left. That we could erase my stupid words completely and go back to the way things were before I changed everything. But now our time is up, and we have to let him walk away.

The doorbell rings a moment later, and Nathan stands, the wolf gripped tightly in his hands.

"I should get my things."

Morgan and I stand with him, and then we're all staring at each other, unsure of what to say. Eventually, Morgan steps forward and throws her arms around him, hugging him tightly and kissing his cheek. "I'll get your clothes for you." Then she darts toward the mudroom, leaving Nathan and me alone.

"Will she be okay?" he asks after a brief heavy pause.

"My wife is a strong woman."

"She is," he says wistfully.

Another ring to the doorbell, and Nathan glances over his shoulder.

"I'll get it. You go get ready," I say.

As I move to step around him, Nathan grabs my arm. Before I have time to react, he kisses me. It's not a gentle kiss but a hard one, one that's searing, claiming. One that catches me off guard and stuns me, not allowing me to take over.

"Thank you for helping me see that there's nothing wrong with me." He reiterates the words he's said before, his tone so somber it makes my heart ache. I want to say more, to take him in my arms and tell him to stay, that he can take the time he needs with us, but I know that's not what he wants. He needs to process this weekend, and maybe Morgan and I do, too.

Nathan takes a step away, but this time, I'm the one grabbing him. "We'll wait for you, Nathan," I say with conviction. "We're on your time."

He clenches his jaw and blinks back the tears I see in his eyes. I squeeze his biceps one final time and drop my hand reluctantly.

As he walks away, I think I hear him whisper, "I hope so."

But I could've imagined it.

CHAPTER FORTY-THREE

Nathan

"KAS IS PASSED OUT," I tell Lindsey as I walk into her living room. Her tree casts white lights across the small space, and even though hers looks nothing like the one at Fox and Morgan's, my heart still aches because it makes me think of them.

"Mom is, too." She smirks.

"I'm surprised she made it till nine."

"Honestly, I don't know how I'm awake. Last New Year's, I went to bed at eight with Kas. Mom actually stayed up past when I did."

I chuckle, joining her on the couch as she hands me a flute of champagne.

"So…" she says. "You gonna tell me what happened to you?"

"What do you mean?" I ask.

"Cut the crap, little brother. You're different."

"I did quit my job."

She takes a sip of her champagne. "Yeah, that's not why."

"Care to share your thoughts?" Lindsey shoots me an annoyed-big-sister look, the kind that says, *Are you really going to make me say it?*

I down half the champagne before I place it on the coffee table. "Something happened at the cabin."

Her brown eyes glimmer as she frowns. "I figured as much, but I need you to elaborate."

"I—" I try to think of how to phrase it. "Are you sure you want to know this?"

She quirks an eyebrow. "Oh, that kind of something?"

I flush and nod.

Her eyes narrow. "Wait. Didn't you say they're the married couple who owns Starlight Lumber & Logging?"

I think I turn the color of a tomato. "Yep, that's them."

"Wait, wait, wait. Are you saying you slept with his wife?" Shock and horror crosses her face. Her ex cheated on her, and she'd disown me if I slept with someone's spouse.

"Yes and no."

Her face goes from anger back to shock, then to confusion, then back to shock again. "Nathan, are you…?" *Gay, queer, bi?* she wants to ask.

"Bi, I think." Though what I don't say is that while I've thought a lot about it in the last few days, nothing fits. I just know that I want Fox and Morgan. I don't want anyone else. I even tried to watch a little porn, but it all felt wrong. The only time I was able to come was in the shower, thinking of all the time we spent together and what it was like being tangled up with them in bed.

Fuck. It's only been six days, and I miss them.

"Um, wow. I was not expecting that. I mean, I thought the nail polish was odd, but you said you got bored in the cabin."

I snort. "A man wearing nail polish doesn't mean he's queer."

She cringes. "Sorry, you're right. That was wrong of me to say—I'm just in shock. I never thought…You never…" She struggles for words.

"I know. I didn't ever allow myself to explore."

"But now you have?"

"I have."

Lindsey takes another sip of her drink before continuing. "I'll admit, I don't really understand what happened, and I'm not sure I want to. You're my brother, after all, but are they polyamorous or…?"

"They're Fox and Morgan," I say, as if she'll understand

what I mean. Just like how I struggle to put a label on myself, I don't think any label will fit them. They're just them.

"Nathan," she says quietly, "you know I love you. Whatever happened there, that's your personal life. I just want you to be happy."

"Even if that's with a married couple?"

She laughs awkwardly. "Again, I don't know if I'll ever understand it. But I do understand love. And just like I teach Kas, love comes in all different kinds of forms. You don't have to have a mom and a dad to be loved. You don't have to have a grandpa and a grandma. Or a sibling. You don't have to love one person or someone of a different gender. Love is love."

My chest tightens at her words. "I wouldn't say this is love. We just met—and it's complicated."

"Does it have to be complicated?"

I think of the conversation Fox had with me before I left. He wanted to complicate it because not only is it hard for him to feel vulnerable and open with someone who isn't Morgan, but he also wanted to protect her heart—and of course, his.

But in the end, does it have to be complicated? Because while we had some speed bumps in the beginning, a lot of it felt easy, like how surfing feels. Hard to catch the wave, but once you catch it, it's often a smooth and beautiful ride if you find your balance.

"What about Mom?"

"What about her?"

"You think she's just going to be chill with me dating a married couple who live in the woods?"

Lindsey giggles. "She'll be shocked at first, and it'll probably take her a bit to get used to it. Maybe she'll cry a little, but she'll get over it. I think she's more accepting than you think."

"Are we talking about the same mom? The very same person who asks me almost daily when I'm going to get married and give her grandchildren? I thought you'd be more upset with how much you pester me about it, too."

Lindsey purses her lips. "I'm sorry, Nathan. I didn't know that upset you. We just don't want you to be alone. We want you to be happy."

"And Dad?"

She sighs. "I love Dad, but he's not here anymore. Would he have liked it? Probably not. But that doesn't matter. He's still proud of you; we all are. You've done and accomplished a lot. I know you stayed at that shitty job because you thought it made everyone proud. Maybe it's time you do whatever it is your heart wants you to do instead of trying to make other people happy."

I stare wide-eyed at my sister, a little shocked at her insightfulness and that I didn't realize she knew all that.

"I pay attention, Nathan. I'm your big sister, after all. And I really am sorry if you felt pressured by me. I love you, and I want the best for you. That's all."

"Even if I'm jobless and confused?"

She shakes her head. "Even then. But what are you confused about?"

"My life has flipped upside down in less than two weeks. I think I'm bi, and I like a couple who's been together since they were fourteen."

"Fourteen?"

"Yep."

"Wow."

"I know."

Lindsey pats my thigh. "I guess that's a little complicated."

My chest rumbles with laughter. "I asked them to give me time."

"To what?"

"To figure out if I wanted what they were offering. But the more I think about it, the more I don't really know what they're offering long-term. Fox mentioned a relationship, but I don't know how it would all work."

"Have you spoken with them?"

"I sent Morgan a text when I got my new phone and they got reception back, but that's it. I think she's giving me space."

"But you don't want space?"

I rest my head against the couch and blow out a long breath. "I just don't know what to do, Lindsey. I quit my job. I have an apartment, a home; I like the beach, surfing. I have friends where I live. What am I supposed to do—move up here if they'll have me and ask them if I can be a freeloader?"

A small smile tugs on her lips. "I think you're thinking too much, Nathan. People do long-distance relationships all the time. And you'll figure out the job—but in the meantime, you have savings, right?"

"Yeah."

"And you like them?"

"I do." I think of Morgan's smile and Fox's lip twitch, the way they made me feel as if I'd found the "something more" to life I'd been looking for.

"Then why are you sitting here with me?"

My stomach flips, and I sit up a little straighter. "I told you; I needed time."

"You've had time, and I've never seen you look how you did just now. Were you thinking about them?" I nod. "And have you stopped thinking about them since you left?" I shake my head. "Then go to them. You should be spending the New Year with them."

"You're serious?"

She laughs and pushes my shoulder. "I love you, Nathan. But for the love of all that's holy, go do what your heart is telling you to do."

I lean across the couch and pull Lindsey into my arms. We hug for a few moments before I pull back, my decision made. "Can I borrow your car?"

She smirks. "Yes. Just don't crash into a snowbank. We don't need two cars out of commission."

"Ha ha."

Chapter Forty-Four

Morgan

"You smell like cedar," I murmur into Fox's neck as he sways me around the living room, Etta James's "At Last" playing over the speakers.

"Only because that New Year's Eve blowjob in the sauna you gave me lasted so long."

"And whose fault is that?"

Fox nips at my ear. "You're the one who keeps giving me sass. I had to shut you up somehow."

I pull back from him, my arms still looped around his waist as I glare at him. "Do I need to cash in on my Christmas gift?"

Fox groans. "I should've thought about that harder, maybe put a time limit on it."

"It's been six days." As soon as the words leave my mouth, I regret them. Six days since he gave me my little gift, but more importantly, six days since Nathan walked out of our cabin.

Fox tucks a hair behind my ear. "What are you thinking?"

"That I miss him."

"I do, too." Fox tugs me back into him, placing his chin on top of my head.

We sway to the next slow song as I try to fight the tears that sting my eyes. Nathan asked for time, so we're giving it to him. I understood why he needed it, especially after overhearing part of my conversation with Fox. But I wish he could've stayed. When he stood in the doorway, back in his corporate clothes, it felt so wrong. But I kissed him goodbye, and then he left.

I've texted him to make sure he was okay, but that's been it. And with every day that passes, I can't help but feel as if we've made a huge mistake in letting him walk out the door. Because unlike our last relationship, where we knew it was time to let go, Nathan is different. He was different from the moment we met him.

Our wolf.

Fox brushes his hand down my hair. "I'm sorry, Morgan."

I stop dancing and pull back, looking up into the blue eyes of my beautiful husband who's afraid to fully give his heart to someone new. "What for, baby?"

"Had I just listened to you in the first place, none of this would've happened. You wouldn't be hurting."

I want to say he's hurting, too, but I know that won't help anything. "Had you listened to me in the first place, we wouldn't have had the weekend we did with Nathan. You were right to follow your gut, Fox. And you did listen to me; you let him set the pace. Everything we did was because we all wanted it. Because it felt right."

"But had I not fucked it up—"

"Fox," I interrupt him. "I won't have you beating yourself up. You told him why you said what you said, and he asked for time."

"And what if, during that time, he figures out he doesn't want us?"

"Then we have each other."

He leans down and rests his forehead against mine while my hands grip his biceps. He kisses my nose and then my lips, so gentle for a man who looks anything but.

When he pulls back, I see the worry in his eyes and how they miss the spark both of us had when Nathan was here. Yes, we have each other, and yes, that would be enough, but having Nathan? He completes us. He makes us whole. Or at least, that's what I hope.

"We should go to him," Fox says suddenly.

"What?"

He tugs my hand toward the mudroom, and I let out a huff of laughter.

"Maybe he'll turn us down, but we should show him that this is what we want. That he does belong here."

I stare, stunned at Fox's words while he puts my coat on for me before grabbing his. I feel like I'm in a dream, because never once has he wanted to chase someone who walked away. And now I see I haven't ever wanted to, either. But for Nathan?

"Are you sure?" I ask.

"As sure as I am in my love for you."

My heart expands like the Grinch's—three whole sizes—and I get up on my toes to kiss his lips. Just as we part, the doorbell rings, and we're back to staring at each other.

"You don't think...?" I ask.

Fox smiles, the same smile that Nathan called beautiful. My lips tip up, and Fox takes my hand, my coat still on as we hurry toward the door. I suck in a breath as he opens it, afraid that it won't be who we want on the other side.

But when my eyes meet earthy brown ones, my stomach fills with butterflies.

Nathan looks me up and down. "Were you leaving?"

I let out a happy laugh. "We were coming to get you!"

"You were?" He pushes some of his floppy hair off his forehead, his boyish smile wider.

He's shaved since he left, the angles of his jaw more prominent without the scuff he'd been building up. While I kind of miss it, I also like this. It's the Nathan we first found in the snowbank, sans his work clothes. Instead, he wears jeans and his coat with a pair of boots.

"Let him in, Morgan."

Nathan's eyes connect with Fox at his command, and their stares hold. I let them have their moment, two men who are so different yet have found a likeness in each other. It's something

I don't think I'll ever fully understand, but I'm okay with that. Just like someone could never fully understand the history Fox and I share.

"Please, come in," I say.

Nathan's gaze falls back to mine, and then he comes in from the cold evening. When the door closes, Fox steps forward, and Nathan looks up at him. While I expect him to look unsure or ask Fox what he's doing, he doesn't say anything.

"May I?" Fox asks as he lifts his hands toward Nathan's coat zipper.

The air in the room tenses like a tightrope, and Nathan licks his lips before nodding. I stand there as Fox's inked hands gently lower the zipper. The sound of the teeth clicking downward, followed by the swoosh of material lowering, fills the space. I take the bag from Nathan's hand and set it on the ground so Fox can fully remove his coat before putting it on the hook next to us. Then he does the same for me—removing my coat before giving his attention back to Nathan.

"Hi," Nathan says. His voice is husky and hoarse, as if Fox's gentle action made him emotional.

Fox smiles in response, the smile that Nathan needed to see.

Time around us freezes as Nathan's eyes widen, and slowly, a smile to match my husband's tips at his lips. Then he lifts a tentative hand and delicately runs his fingers over Fox's beard.

"You're beautiful when you smile," he says.

Fox leans into his touch, and his eyes close. Tears sting my own as I observe them, a moment I know I'll remember forever. My husband, my home, letting himself find solace in someone the way he does me, even if only for a moment. I know our relationship is going to take time. It's new, we're going to have hiccups, and we still don't know what Nathan wants from this.

"Morgan."

I blink my teary eyes as Nathan's free hand reaches for mine. I grip his palm, his hands still cool from the winter evening.

"Are you okay?" he asks.

"You're here" is all I can say.

"I'm here, baby."

My stomach flips at his endearment, and then he surprises Fox by moving his palm from my husband's cheek to take his hand. I can't remember the last time Fox held anyone's hand but mine. But after a moment, Fox relaxes into it, his gaze shifting between me and Nathan as we stand there, all connected.

Nathan brings my knuckles to his lips and gently kisses them. "You were both going to come get me," he states with a grin. "What happened to giving me time?"

"Time was up," Fox quips, his eyes now clear and his shoulders broad.

Both Nathan and I smile at each other, and he squeezes my hand.

"What Fox means is that we wanted you to know that we missed you. That something's missing without you. That the cabin hasn't felt right since you left."

Nathan sucks in a breath. "You mean that?"

"We do," Fox says.

"We definitely do," I reiterate.

Nathan's eyes bounce between the two of us, and he grips our hands. "Good to know."

I bark out a laugh at the cheekiness of it, then throw my arms around him. It catches Nathan off guard, and he almost stumbles back, but Fox keeps him steady, Nathan's hand still in his.

"Does this mean you want to try this with us?" I ask against his ear.

He rubs my back, his body relaxing into mine. "If you'll have me."

"You know the answer is yes."

"We have a lot to talk about, and we need to figure out how this will all work. I don't even live here—"

I cut him off with a kiss, one that's steady and sure. "We'll figure it out. Let's take it day by day."

Nathan tucks a strand of hair behind my ear and nods. "Okay." He pulls back just a bit so we can look at Fox. "Fox, I—"

Fox steps forward and cuts him off with his own lips. The kiss is demanding, devouring, one that makes my knees weak. A shiver runs down my spine, and I'm not even the one being kissed. But I know that kiss, and I know what it means for Fox. He's giving Nathan his all if he'll accept it.

When he finally pulls back, they're both panting, and Nathan is squeezing my hand so tightly I think the circulation is being cut off.

"You belong here, Nathan," Fox states, brooking no argument.

"Are you—"

"Don't ask me if I'm sure, little wolf. You already know the answer."

Nathan's spine straightens, and color blooms on his cheeks, though there's still a bit of hesitancy in his eyes. I understand why, but I want to show him that he can trust us. He can trust that Fox and I want to try this with him.

An idea sparks in my mind, and I tug on Fox's hand. When his attention is on me, I get up on my toes and put my lips to his ear, whispering what I want, what I think we all need.

His shoulders stiffen, but after a long breath, he relaxes, pulling back with vulnerability but agreement in his blue gaze. "I'm yours," he says.

Then my husband drops to his knees.

"And yours, Nathan."

Chapter Forty-Five

Nathan

"What are you doing?" I whisper as I stare down at Fox on his knees.

"I'm cashing in on my Christmas gift," Morgan says.

My eyes dart between her and the man on his knees before us, his head bowed like Morgan's had been that afternoon in the living room. It's a sight to see, and I'd be lying if I said I didn't like it, even if it feels almost wrong to see him this way.

"An act of submission," I say quietly, remembering the paper she showed me from inside her gift box. "You want to share this with me?"

Morgan steps next to me and draws my lips to hers, kissing me softly. "We're all in, Nate; let us show you."

My heart flutters at the meaningfulness of this moment. The man who hates to be vulnerable is at our feet, offering himself to us both. And the woman at my side wants to share her gift with me, share herself with me.

"Okay," I say. "I'll follow your lead."

A wicked grin appears on her face, and she shakes her head. "We'll lead together." She pecks my lips again before she snaps her fingers. "Come, pet," she commands.

It takes me a second to realize she's speaking to Fox, but then he goes to his hands and knees, following Morgan into the living room.

Fuck. Fox is crawling. Literally crawling.

Morgan glances over her shoulder with a demure grin, clearly in her element. "Are you going to join?"

I smirk back at her. Her smile is infectious, so I nod, quickly slipping off my boots and joining her near the Christmas tree. The tree that Fox cut down after he fucked me in front of it. My entire body heats, and my cock grows behind the placket of my jeans. While I'd love to order him to do that again, I have something else in mind.

"How should we use him, Wolfie?"

I smirk at her nickname for me as I glance down at the top of Fox's blond head. His hair hangs loosely around his shoulders. "Look at me, Fox."

Fox's eyes snap up to meet mine. I expected them to be hard, to show resistance, but all I see is his acceptance, his desire to please. It stuns me, and I swear my heart stops in my chest.

"Take my cock out," I demand.

Morgan chuckles and nips at my ear. "Fox knew you were a natural at this. I'm glad he gets a taste of it now."

I kiss her forehead and watch as Fox opens the button of my jeans and pulls the zipper down, his eyes never leaving mine as he does.

"Good boy." I smirk when I see his lip twitch and bite the inside of my cheek. It was a glimmer of the Fox hiding underneath, reminding me that this is something he doesn't do, which makes me even more grateful that he's giving himself to us in this way.

"Hmm, I like this," Morgan says as Fox pulls my cock free through the front flap of my briefs.

I chuckle and stroke Fox's head. "Jack me. I want to see your inked hands around my cock."

Fox doesn't hesitate, wrapping one of his fists around my length. I hiss at the contact, then become enthralled as his rough hand moves up and down my filling shaft in slow but evenly pressured strokes.

"Don't be shy, baby. Get it nice and wet," Morgan commands.

Fox spits, his fingers gathering the wetness and working it

over my heated skin. I lean my head back in pleasure as Morgan nips at my neck.

"Fuck, that feels good," I groan.

"You want his mouth on you, Nate?" Morgan purrs.

"What about you?"

"Don't worry; I'll get mine."

"Then yes."

"You heard him, pet."

The moment Fox's soft lips close around the head of my cock, I practically weep. Memories of the cold snow and wind biting at me as he did this in the woods come back to me. His lips move farther down, and one of his hands cups my sac before he hollows his cheeks and sucks.

"Goddamn." I moan. "You're good at sucking dick."

"He looks so good doing it, too." Morgan runs her hand over my chest and then into Fox's hair, weaving the tresses between her fingers. "Let's see how good he looks choking on it."

Morgan drives Fox's head forward, and his tongue flattens as he takes me all the way into his wet mouth. Like he was with her, she doesn't go easy on him—Fox's nose is now flat against the fabric of my open jeans. He chokes, but Morgan doesn't let up.

"Breathe through your nose, baby."

He does, his eyes tearing up as the back of his throat closes around my cock.

"Such a good fucking boy," I praise.

Morgan pulls him up by his hair, then pushes him back down again. "That's it, pet. Such a beautiful hole you are. Maybe you should be on your knees more often."

Fox's eyes narrow despite his predicament, and Morgan chuckles, driving his head further until he gags.

"Don't try to top me from the bottom; that's not part of my gift," Morgan scolds.

Fox sucks me harder, and I know that's his way of toying with me, too.

I grunt and bring my hand to the back of his skull, pulling him off. He gasps for breath as I tug on the roots, and Morgan drops her hand.

"Naughty," I say. "Trying to make me come, were you?"

Fox's swollen lip twitches. "Isn't that what you wanted, *Sir*?"

Fuuuck. I like the sound of that on his lips. I grab his face with my other hand, my wet cock bobbing near his cheek. "Such a sassy mouth you have. Maybe Morgan can put it to good use."

Beside me, Morgan pulls her white sweater from her body, revealing the large tits I love so much, the barbells driving through her hardened nipples.

"Fucking beautiful," I say under my breath, making her smile.

Morgan continues undressing before she comes over to me. I nod in permission, and she removes my clothes, leaving Fox the only one dressed.

"On your back with your head near the couch," Morgan barks.

Fox follows her orders, the hard outline of his cock now fully visible under his pants. "I'm going to sit on your face, pet. You ready for me?"

He licks his lips. "Yes, ma'am."

I chuckle at his eagerness, knowing I would be the same way if it were me. Morgan wastes no time squatting over him and using the couch cushion for leverage.

"Take a breath," she commands. I faintly hear one before Morgan seats herself with confidence over her husband's face till all I can see is his beard.

"Oh god, yes!" Her hands grip the couch, and her delicious ass flexes.

I fist my cock as I watch the pair. "Grab her ass." I gently nudge Fox's foot. "Drown yourself in her sweet cunt."

"Jesus, Nate," Morgan exhales, her hips working, her pussy sliding over his face as Fox's hands dig into the round globes of her ass.

"Fucking hot." I step closer, and Morgan turns her head before she reaches out one of her hands toward my erection.

"May I?"

I shake my head, and she pouts. "I have a better idea."

Her eyebrow rises, and I leave the room, quickly grabbing what I need from their bedroom toy chest before returning. I stop to watch the show for a moment, watch Morgan fucking Fox's face, his hands gripping her ass so hard he's going to leave bruises. His fully clothed body writhes under her as he pleases his wife. I don't think I'll ever get sick of seeing it; nor can I be jealous of it. They're too fucking perfect together.

"Oh, fuck, I'm coming. Right fucking there." Morgan reaches her hand down and grabs the back of Fox's head, holding him to her clit and riding his face with reckless abandon before she screams out his name, her orgasm ripping through her body.

"Such a good little Fox," Morgan hums. "So fucking good when you submit to me."

I observe them for another moment, enjoying the show as Morgan comes down. Eventually, she releases his head and maneuvers herself until she's sitting on his chest, most likely soaking his long-sleeved shirt. "You okay, pet?"

"Yes, ma'am."

She smirks down at him adoringly, and then I clear my throat. Fox's blown-out pupils turn to mine, beard glistening with Morgan's cum as he sees what's in my hand.

"How do you feel about double penetration, baby?" I ask, lifting my gaze to Morgan.

Her smirk is wild as her eyes connect with mine. "I feel great about it."

"Then get on your husband's dick and offer me that pretty ass of yours."

Morgan bites her lip as her cheeks flush. "Yes, Sir."

My dick twitches, and I stroke myself as Morgan slides off Fox's body. They make eye contact with each other as she pulls down his pants. His proud pierced cock stands erect and ready, and I order her to keep his shirt on. While I'd love to see his tattooed chest, there is indeed a wet spot from Morgan's pussy on his shirt. I like that he'll wear it like a badge of honor while we fuck his wife, our little lamb, into oblivion.

"Such a beautiful cock," Morgan says. She wraps her hand around his length and then tugs on his piercing. Fox groans, and I pump my own cock harder. "Someday, we'll have Wolfie spend an entire twenty-four hours worshipping it. Would you like that?" Morgan asks him.

"Yes." Fox groans, and Morgan squeezes his shaft so hard he gasps. "Fuck! Yes, ma'am."

Morgan chuckles her satisfaction before releasing his cock. Fox exhales a breath but then groans again as Morgan straddles him, sliding her wet folds over his length. I step closer to the couple, and Morgan and I make eye contact as I drop to the floor. She grins coyly at me before she presses her hands to Fox's chest and lifts. "Be a good wolfie, and put my husband's cock inside me."

"My pleasure," I purr.

Morgan raises her hips, and my hand wraps around Fox's wet shaft. I squeeze the base for good measure, and he groans loudly as I place the head of his broad crown against Morgan's wet opening.

She slowly slides down, and I watch as the piercing disappears inside her pussy, her body clamping around him. She moans and drops down another inch, then another until I'm forced to move my hand away so she can fully seat herself on his dick.

Fox's hands are clenched at his sides, and he grunts as Morgan shifts back and forth in small movements, adjusting to the cock inside her and letting out small mewls of pleasure.

"Fuck, that was hot," I say, picking up the lube and snapping it open.

"Quick, Nathan," Morgan says breathlessly. "I need you both inside me."

I swallow hard and get to my knees, squirting the lube over my cock.

"Grab her hips, Fox," I bark. I swear Fox groans in relief as his fingers dig into Morgan's flesh. Morgan lets out her own sigh of pleasure, and then she flattens herself against Fox's chest, presenting her ass to me like a gift.

Morgan kisses her husband, and I move closer, my eyes dropping to the sight of Fox's length inside Morgan, his balls drawn tight and his thick thighs flexing. I thought seeing them together was hot before, but like this, so up close—holy fuck.

"Nathan," Morgan pleads. "Please."

I lick my lips and drip lube between her seam, setting down the bottle and running my fingers over the tight ring of muscle. "You're sure you can take us both?"

Two breathy chuckles reach my ears.

"I can take it, Nathan. Now please, fuck me."

Fox spreads his thighs without asking, and I position myself between his legs and behind Morgan, rubbing the slippery head of my cock over her hole. She pushes back, and I smack her ass playfully. "Such a greedy lamb."

"Oh, fuck." Morgan moans. "Call me that again."

I press the tip of my cock inside just a bit until I feel her tight ring of muscles pulse around me. "I love this ass, little lamb." I press my length farther in and smack one of her ass cheeks, once more watching a red mark appear on her skin and the flesh jiggle.

"Yes!" She shifts back on Fox's cock so he groans, and my shaft pushes farther inside. "Do it, Nathan. Fuck, I need to feel you both."

I inch myself even farther in, my cock disappearing. "Holy shit," I exhale, my eyes fluttering shut at the sensation.

Fox groans, and Morgan whimpers, one of her hands reaching back to grip my thigh. I think she's telling me to stop, but then she shakes her head. "Fuck me, Nathan."

I snap at her command and punch my hips all the way in, my pelvis hitting her ass. My brain tries to catch up to all the things I'm feeling, but it's so much. Morgan's ass gripping my cock, her hand on my thigh, and— "Holy shit! I can feel his dick inside you."

"Put your hands on my shoulders, Nathan," Morgan says breathlessly.

I lean forward, the new position sinking me impossibly deeper. We all groan, and Morgan shimmies her hips, fucking herself on both our cocks. My fingers flex as my gaze drops to Fox. His blue eyes are blown out in pleasure, and his brow is tight as if he's trying to stop himself from coming.

"You two are so fucking big. I love it." Morgan writhes. "Grab my tits, pet."

Fox follows her command, and he grips the flesh with his inked hands. My own brow furrows as sweat coats my forehead.

"Move, Nathan."

My fingers flex on her shoulders, and I pull out, then thrust back in. The three of us collectively cry out at the action, and then it feels like something clicks. I start to thrust my hips while Morgan fucks herself on Fox's cock. I feel every movement, and I swear I can feel Fox's piercing from inside Morgan every time I thrust.

"Yes! Harder, Nathan."

I grunt and let myself go, thrusting my hips almost wildly.

"Just like that," Morgan chants.

Time seems to slow, and Morgan turns her head. I kiss her sloppily until she breaks the kiss so she can kiss Fox.

This goes on for another minute, but then I feel myself unable to hold back any longer. "I'm going to come," I announce.

"Me, too." Morgan moans before she clamps her inner muscles around us, and Fox and I both swear. "Give it to me, pet," she pleads. Fox pistons his hips up from the ground, and the hard movement against my cock while Morgan clamps down sends me spiraling over the edge. We all lose ourselves in sensations and limbs, our actions becoming slow and choppy as stars spark behind my eyes. I have to stop myself from falling on top of Morgan.

Her body shakes with pleasure beneath me, and we all ride through it, her every muscle bearing down and trembling as she takes her pleasure. Fox takes his as well, his eyes clamped shut and his hands now gripping Morgan's low back.

When I finally catch my breath, I pull myself from her heat, my cum leaking from her ass. It drips down onto Fox's shaft where he's still inside his wife, his own cum leaking out. I groan and take a mental picture, wanting to do this again but with our positions reversed: me in the middle with Fox behind me while I sink into her perfect pink cunt.

I drop to the ground, my chest heaving. After a second, Morgan joins me, wedging her sweaty and sated body between Fox and me. We all stare up at the ceiling for a while, our breaths ragged as the fire crackles.

Eventually, Morgan shifts, placing her hand over my heart. "You okay?"

I turn my head to meet her hazel gaze, then look up at Fox behind her. His eyes aren't hard or guarded; instead, they're soft and, dare I say, loving?

My chest twinges, and I swallow. "Shouldn't I be asking you two that?"

"I'm fucking fantastic." Morgan sighs with a sated grin.

Fox smiles, the beautiful smile I know I want to see every day if he'll let me. Then he nods while playing with Morgan's wild hair. "I'm good."

For a brief time, I feel as if I should say something more. There is a lot left unspoken between us, things we need to talk about and emotions that need to be sorted, but after this, after seeing Fox be vulnerable and given the way we just shared Morgan…I can't explain it, but I know everything is going to be okay.

I smile at the couple, a goofy grin now on my face. "Then what do you say about going for round two?"

Morgan laughs, shifting to look back at Fox. "You hear that, baby? I think we've created a monster."

"No," Fox says slyly, his eyes staring directly into mine. "A wolf."

Epilogue

FOX

"Stop squirming, or we're going to strap you down," I bark.

"That won't make me stop squirming." Nathan waggles his eyebrows behind his blindfold. He's currently on Morgan's massage table, my wife bent over his arm as she works on his Christmas present.

"He's not lying." Morgan chuckles. "But seriously, stop squirming, or I'll fuck it up."

"Fine," Nathan says through a clenched jaw. A jaw that's been covered in dark scruff for almost a year now, making him look like a true man of the woods. Or a "lumbersnack" as Morgan likes to call him.

The term is ridiculous, and one she'd never dare call me, but Nathan's face lights up every time she calls him by it, so the endearment has stuck. Especially since he moved up here this past summer to help with one of our reforestation efforts and be closer to his family—a family that has come to accept Morgan and me as their own.

It's funny in a way. Nathan, once a man who claimed to hate being landlocked, the cold, and just about anything to do with a mountain town, has transformed into the outdoorsman he claims he "didn't know he was meant to be."

He also decided not to go back into marketing. Instead, he's not only helped us with the physical aspect of our work but the business side of things. We've almost doubled our revenue in the past year and helped with reforestation efforts in the southern part of the state, something Morgan had always dreamed of doing.

"Quit thinking so loud," Nathan says from the table, squeezing my hand he's been holding.

"I'm not. And you can't even see me. You're blindfolded."

"I don't need to see you to know you're thinking—ouch!" Nathan grunts.

My chest tightens at his words, but I chuckle. "You can take my hand on your ass, but you can't take a little needle?"

Nathan yelps again. "She's pushing harder than she has to."

Morgan grins. "I am not. You're just a baby."

"You two suck."

I dig my nails into Nathan's free hand as a warning. "Careful, little wolf, or I'll have her give you an entire back piece while my cock is buried so deep in that cute ass of yours, you'll feel it in your throat."

"That's not a threat."

Morgan cackles. "You're asking for it, Nate. Don't let him bait you. You know what happened the last time I fell for that."

My gaze moves to Morgan's, and my eyes narrow. "Naughty lambs get punished."

Her eyes glimmer, and she shifts in her chair. I know her pussy just flooded thinking about that night. "I had bark burn for weeks," she groans.

My cock twitches in my pants. "We could do a repeat, if you want. But this time, instead of you tied to a tree, it will be Nathan."

"Hey! It's freezing out."

"You like being fucked in the snow," I counter, thinking of our Christmas tradition last year. One we have yet to complete this Christmas, but we plan on doing so tonight.

"For brief periods of time," he retorts. "Preferably after I've been running to heat up my blood. I'd rather not be tied up and fucked against one until I can't remember my name.

Though, I'm not opposed to being in a bed if you want to do it there."

Morgan and I both shake our heads. Sometimes it's hard to believe that this is the same man who tried to run out of the cabin after seeing Morgan and me fuck last year. Not only has he turned into a wolf, but he's voracious. Morgan teased that we'll need to buy stock in Viagra so I can keep up with him, a comment that got her a good edging session. Not that she complained.

I grip Nathan's hand and lean down to run my nose over the shell of his ear. "Bad wolves don't get beds. They sleep in the doghouse."

Nathan shivers, and I watch in pleasure as his cock hardens beneath his pants.

"*Oooh*, someone likes that idea." Morgan smirks. "Maybe we should get him a cage."

"A birthday present, maybe," I purr against his ear. "I bet you'd look good with a collar and a leash." Nathan licks his lips and squirms.

"You're not helping here, baby," Morgan chides. "Keep him still."

I use both hands to pin down his arms, my lips hovering over his.

"I'll agree to that," Nathan says huskily after a moment. "Only if you let me use it on you, too."

I chuckle darkly. "Never."

Nathan grins, and I know that, under his blindfold, his eyes are smiling, too. "Never say never, Foxie. You loved being on your knees for me last New Year."

I growl, gripping his biceps harder. "Says who?"

"Your cock."

Morgan laughs like she can't believe he just said that. But we both know this is just who Nathan is. He likes to push. He likes to play. He's a wolf yet a puppy wrapped in one. And we love him for it. Even if it annoys me a lot of the time.

"I can't believe that, out of all the people in the world, I got stuck with two switchy little brats," I snipe.

A full-blown smile appears on Nathan's lips. "You know you love us."

My fingers flex on his biceps, and my features soften. I lean forward and press a short kiss to his lips. The rough hair of his beard scrapes against my lips, and I almost give in to him when he seeks more contact, but I pull back before we can go any further. "Needy," I whisper.

"For you and Morgan"—he inhales—"always."

"All right, done!" Morgan chirps. She puts her tattoo gun down and rolls her chair back. "Sit him up slowly."

I pull back and help Nathan sit up until his feet are planted on the floor. Once he's situated, Morgan stands next to me, and she looks up at me with excitement but also nervousness. I grip her hand and gently kiss her forehead in reassurance.

"Can I take my blindfold off now?" Nathan asks.

"Yes," Morgan says, her hand gripping mine tighter.

Nathan takes his right arm—the one that wasn't tattooed—and pulls the black silk off. He blinks a few times, his eyes adjusting to the light of the room before he looks down at his left hand. The fire crackles in the background, and music plays softly, only echoing Nathan's silence as he stares wide-eyed at my wife's work.

Morgan rocks on the balls of her toes, growing more nervous the longer he doesn't speak. Eventually, his brown eyes look up at us, glassy and shimmering in the light. "You—you both—you want…?"

My gaze meets Morgan's, tears now in her eyes as we both get down on our knees and kneel in front of Nathan. His eyes turn into saucers as I take his newly tattooed hand in mine. Morgan not only inked the word "OURS" over four of his fingers, but she's created a woodland scene cuffing his wrist and just up his forearm. She's incorporated a fox, a wolf, and a lamb into the scene, much like the painting in the guest room.

But none of that is what he's referring to. It's a thin line around his ring finger, one that matches a newly inked one Morgan put on mine earlier today while Nathan was visiting his family in town and one that I inked on Morgan right after.

"If you'll have us," I say clearly. "We love you, and we want you to be a part of our family. Officially."

His mouth parts as we stare into each other's eyes. A wordless conversation passes between us, one that promises a life full of joy, acceptance, love, and maybe even a baby someday if the three of us decide that's the route we want to take.

Morgan grabs his right hand, and he focuses on her, that same silent conversation passing through their eyes. The love and devotion they have for each other is so palpable, it makes my chest tighten and my skin heat. "Marry us, Wolfie," she says with conviction.

Nathan's lip twitches at the nickname; then he looks down at the matching tattoo rings on our hands before wiggling his ring finger.

"A little presumptuous, don't you think?" He quirks an eyebrow.

"I can change it to something else if you want." Morgan smirks, jumping up and moving as if she's going back for the tattoo gun.

"Don't you fucking dare." Nathan reaches for her, tugging her close. "Yes, I'll marry both of you." He looks down at me still on my knees, and a coy grin slides onto his lips. "I told you that you loved to be on your knees for me."

"That does it." I stand with them, broadening my shoulders and darkening my gaze. "Wrap his tattoo, Morgan."

My wife turns to me, startled. But then she sees the look on my face and chuckles, quickly wrapping up his new artwork.

"Hope you've been getting your cardio in, Wolfie," she says as she finishes up.

Nathan meets my eyes and smirks. "An hour a day."

I take Morgan's hand in mine and kiss the back of it. "Think our soon-to-be husband stands a chance?"

She taps her chin thoughtfully, her eyes happy and smiling. "No."

"Hey!" Nathan shouts. "Aren't you supposed to be a supportive wife and all that stuff?"

She shrugs. "Not married yet, just engaged."

He shakes his head at her, and I grip the back of his neck, turning his focus on me. "You have ten minutes, little wolf." I smile.

His eyes widen, and his nostrils flare. "I'm not wearing the proper clothes."

"Then I suggest you hurry."

Nathan's eyes dart between us, and then he scrambles off the table toward the mudroom. Morgan giggles as she watches him, and I grab her neck.

Her eyes widen, and I lean in until my lips brush her ear. "You, too, Wife."

"What?"

"I've got two to catch tonight."

"But—"

"Run, little lamb. Run as fast as you can."

The Wedding Night

MORGAN

When Fox and I got married at eighteen it wasn't a normal wedding. Our ceremony was in a courthouse before he started basic training. I wore an off-white, knee-length dress I found at a thrift store that hardly fit me, and he wore a blue suit from the seventies that had ruffles on the collar. We both looked ridiculous, but it didn't matter. We had each other, we made our vows, and we fucked afterward like it was our last day on earth.

Today looked different. There was no courthouse, instead a beautiful space we decorated in the woods with a proper officiant at the end of the aisle and the people we love watching on. Fox bought a fancy tailored suit, and the dress I chose to wear is beautiful, sexy, and cost a lot more than ten dollars. The white lace material hugs my curves, the back open and the train pooling behind me. I opted for no veil when I walked down the aisle. Instead, a crown of flowering dogwood adorned my head, still pinned in place with several bobby pins despite all the dancing I've done. Nathan's sister, Lindsey, said I look like a bride straight off a Pinterest board, and I agree. This look, our wedding, it's everything I never thought to imagine, because I never thought I'd have a second wedding

That is, until Nathan Clark came along and changed everything.

"Morgan?"

Speak of the devil.

Nathan appears to my left where I'm standing on the deck of our cabin, looking out at the now-empty dance floor we rented, a bright smile on his bearded face. He looks exactly like the man we first met that snowy Christmas nearly three years ago now, and yet nothing like him. He still has the same optimistic attitude, beautiful brown eyes and dark brown hair, but instead of a buttoned-up, unsure businessman, he's the picture of what he likes to call "a lumbersnack." A very hot and confident one. Well, minus the flannel and an axe.

Today he traded his in like Fox did, wearing a black two-piece tux in a modern cut, form-fitted to his body with a bow tie while Fox opted for a regular tie. It's undone now and hanging on his neck, his suit jacket unbuttoned as well. He tugs me to him, my back to his front, and places a kiss on my neck.

"What are you doing out here?"

The last of our guests left our reception not too long ago. Fox went to make sure no food was left out to attract animals while Nathan used the restroom. I had followed him into the house to change, but something drew me back outside. To the quiet of our property and the decorations hanging in the trees. String lights and lanterns that glow a yellow color, illuminating the portable wooden dance floor littered with a few random pieces of trash. All things that will be gone tomorrow when the rental place returns to pick everything back up.

"Just thinking," I say, placing my hands over his on my stomach.

"About?" His warm breath tickles my ear.

"How this was the best day of my life."

Nathan's heart beats wildly against my back, and he presses a kiss to the side of my head, his cheek bumping against the flower crown.

"It was the best day of my life, too."

"I third that."

My cunning and stealthy Fox walks from the shadows and climbs up the stairs. The light of the porch illuminates his golden hair, which was pulled into a well-styled half ponytail that's now mussed from the summer heat and dancing. In his time looking around the property, he discarded his suit jacket and tie. He's only in his slacks and button up white shirt, which he's rolled to his forearms exposing his thick muscles and tattoos.

Nathan's cock, which was becoming hard against my ass, gets harder, and I can't say that I blame him. Our man—our husband—is attractive. Like a Norse god that you only see illustrated in books of lore.

Fox takes us both into his large arms, huddling us against the railing so we're all looking out at where our reception took place. The echoes of celebration and toasts still ring in my ears. I'll never forget dancing with them both on that floor and kissing them under the moonlight while our friends and family watched on, celebrating what most call an unusual type of love. But one I couldn't imagine my life without. Marrying Fox was the best decision I've ever made, and Fox and I asking Nathan to marry us, was an even better one. The only one.

I rest my head on Nathan's shoulder, and Fox takes my hand, giving it a squeeze, like he knew what I was thinking and had to agree. We stand there locked together and touching, enjoying the quiet of the late evening and our thoughts. My gaze drifts up to the full moon in the sky, and a wolf howls in the distance. Perfect timing.

"I think that was a sign," Nathan says, his voice an octave lower than usual. Goose bumps pebble over my skin, and my nipples tighten.

"For?" I smirk, lifting my head so I can see his eyes. I know what he's thinking, but I want to hear him say it.

He turns against Fox's body so he can see us both. "For our wedding night to begin."

Fox grips the back of Nathan's neck in a dominant embrace,

the energy of the air charging with the promise of what's to come…literally.

I play with the new wedding band my new husbands surprised me with during the ceremony. It fits perfectly against the princess-cut diamond I already have from Fox, the stones set with three different colored gems alternating around the entire ring. Blue for Fox, pink for me, and green for Nathan. On the inside of the band, they had engraved "Fox, Wolf, and Lamb" with the date of our wedding. It's perfect, and I nearly lost it when they slid it on my finger.

"Inside or here?" Fox asks.

Nathan wets his lips. "Anywhere."

Fox grips his neck a little harder and looks at me. "I think our new husband should decide, don't you think, wife?"

My lip twitches up. God, I love that we can call him our husband now. We already have been, to be honest, but I like that it's official. It may not be real in the eyes of the state, but it's real in every way possible that we could make happen. We've been meeting with lawyers for over a year to add Nathan to all our property deeds and anything else we could think of. He was ours before, but now he's completely ours, just like we're his and always will be.

"I think so, husband," I reply as my eyes fall to Nathan.

His boyish grin appears on his face, and instead of answering with words, he starts to unbutton his shirt.

"I take it that means here?" I tease.

"I want to have you both now."

Fox releases his neck so he can tug off his nice shirt and undone bow tie, dropping them to the deck.

"I'll go get the lube," I say.

Nathan's hand reaches out and takes mine, tugging me back to him. He puts his hand in the pocket of his slacks and pulls out a little travel bottle of lube.

"Our little wolf was prepared," Fox rumbles. "Are you still wearing your plug?"

"Yes, Sir."

Arousal shoots through my body. "Were you wearing one all day, Nate?"

He flushes under the low light, the skin beneath his beard turning pink.

"Since the middle of the reception."

Fox picks my hand up and kisses my ring, his blue eyes simmering. "I bent him over in the woods and slipped it in."

My clit pulses at the image he just gave me.

"I would have invited you to watch, little lamb, but I wanted the plug to be a surprise."

"Oh?"

Fox snaps his fingers, and Nathan knows what he wants. He removes his shoes and drops his pants, black briefs included, stepping out of them. His half-hard cock, which is getting harder by the second, hangs heavy between his muscled thighs.

"Grip the railing and bend over."

The Nate we first met would have been shy about the request, but not anymore. Our wolf loves being told what to do and degraded, nearly as much as I do. His hunger for it only grows the longer we're together. Not to say he doesn't enjoy being dominant, because he loves to tag team me with Fox. It just depends on the day.

Nathan presents his perfect ass to us, and Fox gently smacks both cheeks before spreading them so I can see the base of the plug. I can't help the smile that plasters on my face when I read what the top says: Nathan Malone.

"Is that so we don't lose him, baby?" I tease.

Fox plays with the plug, making Nathan groan. "It will go nice with his collar."

I think about the leather collar our wolf got made for Fox's birthday present last year. The one that says "Property of the Malones" on it.

"It will."

Fox smacks Nathan's ass again and asks for a kiss from me.

I give it to him, letting his tongue gently explore mine. When we part, he smiles his smile that's always been just for me and now Nathan too. He's so rugged and handsome, that my heart flutters like butterfly wings in my chest.

"Prep him for me while I get you out of this dress."

"Yes, husband."

Fox grunts in approval and steps away so I can take his place behind a very naked Nathan. He looks over his shoulder at me, features lit with arousal, need, and love. He watches as Fox unzips my dress and helps me out of the arms, the top of the dress pooling on my wide hips. I've got on a white strapless bra, and Fox makes quick work of the snap while I take the small bottle of lube from Nathan that he'd been holding in his hand against the railing.

My nipples turn to hard nubs when the night air drifts over my breasts, and I bite my lip to keep from demanding Fox to touch me. I know he'll give me what I want when he's done undressing me. He won't be able to resist. All night he's been copping a feel of not only my tits but my ass. Both him and Nathan. I almost stole them away for a quickie but knew we'd have all night and the next few days together before we went back to work.

Fox trails his hands down my back, and I focus on the task I was given. I drag my nails over Nathan's ass, mirroring Fox's touch, making him groan and push back into my fingers. I swat his butt which is a bit red from Fox's spanks, with a laugh before I open the lube. The snap of the cap seems loud among the quiet night and only adds to the pulse building in my clit. I find the flat top of the plug, tracing the printed letters.

"Nathan Malone," I say out loud. "I like how it sounds."

Fox grabs my breasts like I knew he would, and he squeezes. I gasp, the sound turning to a groan, when he bites my earlobe.

"I like it too," he says.

I tug on the plug and pull it out slowly. Nathan sucks in a

breath, his thighs trembling from the release of pressure. Fox moves his hands to my waist so he can push down my dress.

"Do you want me to hang it up?" he asks, kissing my thrumming pulse.

God this man. Looking at such a big and grumpy lumberjack you'd never think he'd ask that, but he cares about me. And he knows this dress was expensive. My eyes water, and I blink the tears back.

"Just drape it over the railing for now."

He kisses my neck again before having me step out of the material and doing as I ask. I get back to work sliding the plug in and out of Nathan's tight little asshole, enjoying the whimpers I'm drawing out of him.

"Is our wife torturing you, little wolf?"

Our wife.

"Yes," he groans, his head dropping forward. "But I like it."

"Of course he does," Fox says as he takes his place behind me again. He goes back to my waist, fingering the band of the thin white lace thong I wore to match my dress. "Do you need these?" His question vibrates against my ear.

"No," I say.

Fox rips them from my body with such force I'd fall if he weren't holding me with his other hand. The motion does, however, catch me off guard, and I pull the plug the rest of the way from Nathan's ass, barely holding on to the lube in my other.

"Fuck," Nate groans.

Fox chuckles and drops my ruined panties to the ground, but not before smelling them. His inhale is deep and long, loud enough that Nathan turns to see him do it.

"Jesus," he groans.

I move a touch forward so I can use my tongue to rim Nathan's tight ring of muscle. His body twitches from the sensation, and he cries into the night.

"Beautiful," Fox praises, his hand dipping between my thighs. "Goddamn, you're soaked already."

"I have been since I walked down the aisle," I murmur as I tongue Nathan.

Both men groan, and I move my mouth aside to squirt lube between Nathan's cheeks. Fox circles my clit with his calloused fingers, nipping at my shoulder and sucking on my skin. I dip my fingers into Nate's stretched hole, scissoring them. Fox mimics my action, sliding his digits into my cunt.

Nathan and I both whine. I'm already on the verge of coming, and I don't have to see Nathan's dick to know he is too.

"Fox." I look over my shoulder at him.

"Does my whore need a cock?"

I bite my lip and nod. His fingers leave my channel, and he smacks my ass.

"Use your words."

"Yes, Sir. I need my husbands' cocks."

"Good girl." He swats my ass again. "Switch places with Nathan. I'm going to fuck our new husband into that tight pussy."

I stand to my full height, and Nathan stands too. I give Fox the bottle of lube before Nate pulls me in for a quick kiss and I take my place in front, my hands gripping the railing where he just was.

"Stick out your ass, little lamb. Show Nathan the body that we both own."

I arch my ass and remove my hands, spreading my legs and then pulling my cheeks apart so they can see all of me. The position is open and vulnerable, and a breeze brushes past my thighs and across my heated sex.

"Look at her cunt. It's clamping around nothing," Fox says to Nathan. "Why don't you give it something to milk."

Nathan doesn't need to be told twice. One of his hands grips my hip, and he slides the swollen head of his shaft up and down my crease.

"Please," I plead when he teases for too long. "Give me your big dick, Wolfie."

"Since you asked so nicely." Nathan thrusts into me hard, every part of my body jiggling from the force of it. My cry echoes through the forest, the sound of his balls slapping against my skin making my clit pulse. I love the sounds of sex, the lewder the better.

"Fuck—thrust—Morgan—thrust—Baby." He grips my hips hard, shoving his dick in as deep as he can go. "You feel so fucking good."

The curved tip of his head hits the perfect place inside me, and I white knuckle the railing in my grip.

"You feel good too," I murmur.

Nathan slows his movements to a near stop, and I hear the cap of the lube. I glance over my shoulder, squeezing my inner walls around Nathan's dick so he whimpers. I grin slyly before focusing on the both of them.

Fox drops the lube bottle to the ground and meets my gaze while he guides his cock to Nathan's entrance. He's still wearing his clothes, and I love that he's impatient to be inside him. To fuck our new husband into me with everything he has so I essentially feel them both.

I know the moment he pushes inside because our little wolf's face transforms into pure pleasure. His cock sheathed in me is completely still, but his fingers dig into the flesh of my hips almost painfully.

"Oh fuck, fuck, fuck," Nathan chants.

"That's it," Fox grunts, his hands sliding to Nathan's shoulders. "Your ass is swallowing me up."

"Shit!" he cries as Fox pushes him, so his front is pressed into my back.

I drop my chin to my chest, unable to keep looking back. I give over to the sensations, my stomach digging into the rail causing my breasts to swing in the night air. I gaze out at the lanterns in the trees and the dark forest beyond. I love that Nathan chose to stay out here to consummate our vows—it's fitting. We're among the land that brought him to us years ago now, and I'm looking out at where we just made so many memories together.

"Move with me, Nathan," Fox's low voice commands. "Let's fuck our wife together."

"Yes," he agrees in a low growl. One that tells me his inner wolf is out to play now.

Nathan keeps one hand on my waist while the other slinks around to find my clit. His hips pull back a short amount, and when he slams back in, it's with double the force from Fox's perfectly timed thrust inside him.

The sound of our mixed pleasure fills my ears, and I push my ass back for more. I'm not going to lie. It's a bit painful, but I love it. I want more of it. I want to feel their cocks and touch branded inside me and on my skin for days. I want to not just wear their rings, but their marks. Like the tattoos I have for them on my skin.

"Morgan," Fox growls. "Use your safe word if you need it."

I shake my head. "Harder" is all I can get out.

Fox growls, and they pull back again. They find a perfect rhythm, my breasts swaying with every hit, the slap of Nathan's balls on my pussy and the hit of his pelvis adding to my pleasure. His touch on my clit is sloppy due to his own body being used, and on a big thrust from Fox, he drops his head to my shoulder and bites down hard enough to leave a mark.

"Fuck!" I cry. "I'm going to come."

"Me too," Nathan keens. "You both feel so good. I'm so full. Oh god."

I feel the brush of Fox's fingertips on my side, and I take a hand off the railing, reaching back to grip them.

Fox snaps his hips hard, his sounds of pleasure sending tingles down my spine. Fuck, it feels as if Nathan's cock is in my throat every time Fox fucks him into me.

Their movement abruptly stops, leaving Nathan wedged so hard against me I can barely move.

"Both of you come," Fox growls. "I want to hear your screams while I rut. Until I fill our husband's tight ass with my cum."

Fox pulls back and does as he said. His hips snap back and forward, thrusting Nathan into me repeatedly, my stomach pressing harder into the railing. I keep a grip on Fox's fingers while my other holds on for dear life. Nathan circles my clit, and his cock pulses inside me, the sound of his pleasured scream as he unloads his lust into me ringing through the trees and vibrating against my hair.

White sparks flash behind my eyes before colorful fireworks fill my vision, my orgasm hitting me like a freight train. I tumble over the edge, and my inner walls clamp down on Nathan's dick while I unleash the yell my husband wanted. I think I hear the wolf howl again in the distance, or maybe that was Nathan. My body shakes, not only from my release but from Fox's continued thrusts, fucking Nate's twitching cock and hot cum inside me.

The pounding goes on, drawing my orgasm out until I'm nearly limp. If the railing weren't in front of me, and both my husbands weren't holding me up, I'd be a limp puddle of pleasure on the floor. I think Nathan might be too if Fox weren't behind him.

Another thrust, and the pressure of strong fingers still on my clit has me coming for a second time. A strangled cry escapes from my mouth, and I'm faintly aware of the sounds of Fox coming, the gruff groan of his orgasm signaling the completion of our joining. I drop his fingers and lean fully on the railing, Nathan's sweaty forehead registering on my back.

Fox is the first one to move, and I don't know how Nathan keeps standing but he does. He drops a kiss to my shoulder and supports me by holding my waist.

"I'm going to pull out now," he says.

"Okay," I exhale tiredly. The excitement of the day has left my body, and now all I want to do is take a nap between my husbands before we fuck again.

I hiss as Nathan slides out, his cum dripping down my inner thighs. Fox's hands find me, and then I'm being lifted. I roll my head to his shirt-clad shoulder, smelling his pine scent mixed with sweat.

"You alive, little lamb?"

I open my eyes to meet his caring blue ones. "Barely."

He chuckles, and before I know it, I'm in bed. I drift in pleasure-land for a bit while they both clean me. Then Fox cleans Nathan up and eventually himself. The light turns off, and Nathan lies next to me, facing me and wrapping our legs together. A moment later Fox gets in bed and becomes the big spoon, all our legs and arms becoming a tangled mess.

"Wake me in a few hours, husbands. I want you to fuck your wife in the shower."

They both chuckle, the warm vibrations of their amusement filling me with contentment. I fall asleep with the beat of Fox's heart at my back and Nathan's breath on my cheek. Safe, warm, and thoroughly loved. How I know I'll be for the rest of my life, and beyond.

Turn the page for a sneak peak of Kayla's next novel in the Starlight Haven Lumbersnack's series,

AXE MARKS THE SPOT

@DomInTheWoods
New Upload From @DomInTheWoods

⋮

Did you drink your water today, baby?

I'll take your silence as a no. Such a defiant woman you are.

I know you're sorry, but a sorry doesn't keep you hydrated. I'm only looking out for your well-being, you know that, right?

Hmm, well, I think you want to be punished, don't you? What privilege should I take away from you for disobeying me?

You don't know?

I'm thinking no underwear for a week, your bare p*ssy brushing against your clothes while you work, the rough fabric of your jeans the only touch you'll receive until you can't take it anymore. Until you're begging me to let you touch yourself. Hmm... No, no, that won't do. You'd like that too much, wouldn't you?

You're such a beautiful and naughty little sl*t.

● ● ●

♡

10,222 views
Username #@DomInTheWoods
view all 26 comments
6 DAYS AGO

CHAPTER ONE

Lindsey

You know that limbo between exhausted and horny? That state of being where you want to face-plant into bed but you could really go for a good orgasm...or two?

No? Just me?

"Mom!" my daughter, Kas, yells, scaring the shit out of me to the point I jump, my hand flying over my chest as my heart beats rapidly.

"Goodness, Kasandra. I'm right here."

My eight-year-old rolls her eyes at me from across the picnic table. It's her new favorite way to express her annoyance, one I've tried and failed to nip in the bud.

"I've been calling you for five minutes," she chides.

"You have not been," I assure her.

"She yelled it five times."

I flick my gaze to my brother, Nathan, who's sitting next to Kas. His once clean-shaven but now scruffy features are lit with a smile, but there's concern in his earthy brown eyes as he takes a bite of his funnel cake.

I hold back a sigh and give my attention to Kas, who's shifting on her butt excitedly as if she's ready to take off and run somewhere. Which is odd to me because she hates running.

"I'm sorry." I exhale and put on a smile. "What do you need, honey?"

"Uncle Nate said there's a kids' obstacle course. I was asking if I could go."

"I thought you wanted to watch the speed pole climbing." I check the time on my phone. "It starts in thirty minutes."

"You want to watch that, Mom."

Nathan chuckles, and I bite the inside of my cheek. My kid is becoming sassier and sassier every day, a trait I fear she inherited from both me and my smart-ass brother.

"I'll take her. You can go watch loggers climb poles." He waggles his dark eyebrows at me, and I glare at him.

"Yeah, Mom," Kas adds, Nathan's innuendo thankfully going over her head.

I take a sip of my sweating lemonade, the cold condensation on the cup feeling good against the heated skin of my hand. It's July, and while it's fairly cool in our little mountain town of Starlight Haven during the summers, it's still hot enough that I'm sweating even while wearing a tank and shorts.

"You really don't want to watch?"

Kas shakes her head. "I want to go to the obstacle course."

I look at my bouncing kid, who's had too much sugar today, to my younger brother, who's observing me with interest. I'm still getting used to the fact that he looks like a logger now. The ex–corporate businessman once wore button-up shirts, slacks, and loafers. Now he's in a T-shirt that has the logo of the logging company Morgan and Fox, his partners and soon-to-be husband and wife, own on it and a pair of jeans with red suspenders. His tapered brown hair is still neatly styled, but the beard and laid-back look throw me every time. It's only been a year and a half since he met them, and yet it feels like he's transformed overnight.

"Okay, but you have to promise to stay in your Uncle Nate's line of sight."

"I'm eight," she groans.

Nathan holds in his chuckle, but a bit of a snort breaks through. God, this kid. I should be grateful she inherited my

AN EXCERPT FROM *AXE MARKS THE SPOT* 305

and my brother's cheek over the stick-up-his-ass personality of my ex-husband, Jeremy, but sometimes it's a lot. Especially when I'm tired, overworked, and in desperate need of…well, release.

It's been years now since I've had sex that wasn't with a silicone dick. Two years, to be exact. I feel as if my pussy is gnawing at the bars of my self-imposed chastity.

God, Nathan is right. I do want to watch loggers climb poles. And it would be nice if I were climbing one of their poles, too.

"Sis?"

My cheeks flush, and I snap my eyes to his. I should not be thinking about that right now. What the hell is wrong with me?

You're exhausted and horny, remember?

I push back the thought and reply, "You'll keep your eye on her?"

"You know I will," Nathan assures me.

I turn to my kid and shoot her the classic mom-eyebrow, my head tilted just enough in question. "And you won't try to ditch your uncle?"

She sighs. "I won't, but Starlight Haven is safe. Lowest crime rate in California, remember?"

Nathan tugs on Kas's ponytail and chuckles. "She is right about that."

"Regardless, you stay in sight of your uncle, or you'll lose your video game privileges. Got it, Kas?"

"You wouldn't!"

She's right, I probably wouldn't enforce it with how things have been going for me lately, but I nod and keep my features stern. "I would."

Kas presses her lips together, probably to stop herself from arguing with me. It's no secret she loves her video games and would dramatically "die" without them. Or so she's said before. I often think it makes me a bad mom, letting her play them so young, but I'm doing the best I can.

Especially since my mom moved back to our home city,

Santa Solana, at the beginning of the year. She tried her best but deemed small town life not for her.

All this to say, after a long day of working in the ER, I don't have the energy to argue with Kas or force her to go outside all the time. I guess I should be glad she wants to go to the obstacle course now. Maybe she'll make some new friends while she's there.

"Okay," she says finally.

"You promise?"

"I promise."

"All right then, have fun."

Kas jumps up and cheers. "Let's go, Uncle Nate!"

"Go wash your hands and face and use the bathrooms first—there aren't any over by the course. The portable bathrooms and sinks are right there," Nathan says, pointing to an area behind me in his line of sight.

Kas takes off running without complaint, and I sigh. "I'm glad she listens to you at least."

"She listens to you, too." He smiles softly, polishing off the last bite of his funnel cake and brushing the powdered sugar from his hands over the side of the table into the air.

"Only after arguing with me."

I take another sip of my lemonade as Nathan stares at me. "You okay, Linds?"

"Yep, I'm fine."

"Liar."

I tap the side of my cup and exhale a breath. "I am, really. Just tired is all."

"Tell you what—why don't I watch Kas for the rest of the afternoon. I bet you can meet a lumbersnack to throw you around. Maybe you can even get a nap after." He waggles his eyebrows at me teasingly.

I laugh. "I forgot I told you that."

"You've only been talking about it since you moved here."

"Have I?"

Nathan's brow furrows. "You really must be tired because,

yes, you missed the games last summer because you had to work and talked about it then. Not only that, but you mentioned it a time or two right after you moved here. Truthfully, I think you wanted to come to the games today more than Kas did."

Nathan's right. Kas didn't really want to come to this event at all. I convinced her with the promise of funnel cake and other sugary items. Plus, Fox and Morgan's company, Starlight Lumber & Logging, host the games. The couple doesn't participate in it anymore, but they are a huge part of setting it up and getting sponsors for it.

"Linds?"

"Yeah?"

"Are you really fine?"

I look into my younger brother's eyes. We've always been close—even more so after the death of our dad three years ago from a stroke and then my divorce from Jeremy. In many ways, he's become more than just a brother. He's a friend and a solid male presence in Kas's life. And now that he's officially moved to Starlight Haven to be with his partners, he's a person both Kas and I can count on to be there when we need him.

But though we're close and I've shared "jokingly" about wanting a lumbersnack to throw me around, I'm not going to share with him that I'm not only exhausted but in need of a good lay, too. I'm also not going to tell him that the reason I haven't put myself out there in the past two years is because I'm still dealing with hang-ups from my ex. That's not stuff I want to talk about with Nathan, especially when he has such an amazing relationship with not one but two people. A relationship I can't help but feel jealous of sometimes.

"I really am," I assure him. "Like I said, just tired."

He taps his fingers on the table. "I don't believe you, but if you don't want to be honest with me, I'll deal with it."

"Nate—"

"It's okay. Maybe if I get you liquored up tonight, you'll spill the beans."

"Tonight?"

"Okay, yeah. Definitely not fine."

"What's tonight?"

"Kas has that birthday sleepover at Moira's, and you're going out with Fox, Morgan, and me. All of us need a little social time, and Moose's Bar has that drink special tonight and live music. It took Morgan and me a week to convince Fox to go, and you're going, too. No backing out."

I want to smack my forehead. "I totally forgot."

"Obviously." He chuckles.

"Maybe instead of watching the speed climbing, I'll just go home and nap. I could use the sleep instead. I can pick up Kas's room, too, while she's with you."

"Nope. Not happening. And why are you cleaning Kas's room? She's old enough to do that on her own."

My stomach sours and gurgles, the acidic lemonade turning into heartburn. Nathan's question is valid, and I know it's not meant to be mean, but it only reinforces this idea I have of myself: I'm not a great mom. I probably let Kas get away with too much, but she's been through a lot between her dad and me breaking up and then moving to a small town. I think it also hurt when her grandma left. The two of them had become close.

"I—wait, where is Kas? She should be done by now."

Nathan points behind me. "I've got eyes on her. She's talking to some kids."

I look over my shoulder and see she's chatting with a boy and girl her age. My heart warms at seeing it, and a bit of my stomachache eases. Besides her best friend, Moira, whose birthday I forgot about—which reminds me, I need to get the kid a gift—she doesn't have many friends. She's like me in that way, too. It's not that we aren't friendly. We just tend to absorb ourselves in the things we like. She loves her video games, for example. I, on the other hand, prefer bingeing comfort television shows like my favorite, *Gilmore Girls*.

I turn back to Nathan to find him still staring at me. I know he's not judging me, but at the same time, I feel like he is.

But I don't want to get into why I clean my kid's room, so I divert. "Okay, fine. I'll go to the speed climbing event now and still meet you all at Moose's later. But only if you stop asking if I'm okay."

Nathan looks hesitant at first but eventually nods. "Fine. But the offer to tell me the truth still stands."

The corner of my lip twitches. "You're relentless."

He shrugs. "Runs in the family."

"Uncle Nate!" Kas runs up to the side of the picnic table. Her short auburn hair she inherited from Jeremy swishes around her cherubic face.

"Yeah, kiddo?"

"Tyler and Sara are here for the course, too. Can we go now?"

He glances at the two kids behind me with a smile and stands. "Of course we can."

I stand, too, and move from the table over to Kas, who's bouncing on her feet and looks more than happy about her new afternoon plans. The heartburn intensifies once more as my mind spins with thoughts of how bad of a mom I am. I thought Kas only wanted to play video games and hang with Moira, but maybe that's because I don't get her out enough to be with more kids. I'm just so busy and tired from working three twelve-hour shifts a week and picking up extras.

I wipe off a bit of powdered sugar still on her cheek. "Have fun, and don't get hurt."

"If I do, you'll fix me. You're a nurse."

My heart clenches, and I pull Kas in for a hug. She goes willingly, and I'm glad she hasn't hit that phase yet where she finds me embarrassing. "I'd rather not have to fix you. Now go, have fun." She lets out a little excited noise and runs toward her friends. "But remember what I said, Kas!" I yell after her.

She stops and turns. "Stay in sight of Uncle Nate," she says, shooting me a thumbs-up that has me shaking my head. I turn back to Nathan, who's grinning.

"I'll text you later so we can meet back up," he says.

"You're sure you're good with watching her for the rest of the day?"

"Yep."

"You don't want to watch hot lumbersnacks climb poles?"

Nathan steps up beside me and bumps my shoulder. "I have my own personal hot lumbersnacks who climb my pole, remember? Don't need to watch."

I gag. "I didn't need that image, thanks."

Kas yells for Nathan, and he bumps my shoulder again. "Go have fun, Linds. You deserve it. And you'd better not go home!"

Before I can say anything else, he jogs off to Kas and her friends. I watch them leave, then pick up the empty funnel cake plates and cups from the table, throwing them in the trash while debating if I should defy my brother and go home or stay. I could get some cleaning done, maybe even take a bath instead of having a nap. That sounds nice. More than nice, actually.

But then I remember I need to get a gift for Moira. Ugh, Mom life.

I walk out of the open-sided tent and head toward the parking lot instead of the speed climbing event. There's a toy store not far from here, but I'm not sure they're open today—the downsides of living in a small town is the stores are all open on random days and times, even on Saturdays.

I pull my phone from my purse to look it up and get only two steps before I bump into something.

A startled yelp escapes me as solid weight slams into my body, knocking me off-balance. Gravity yanks at my spine, the ground tilting away beneath me. But before I can fall, strong hands clamp around my biceps. Air rushes past my ears, my stomach flipping with the sudden shift in direction.

In a split second, I'm upright again, my feet planted, my chest flush against a solid and warm chest. I squeeze my eyes shut and inhale a breath, the scent of cedar and spicy vanilla wafting into my nose.

"Are you okay?"

The deep male voice thrums through my body like the vibrations of a guitar string. If my pussy meowed, I think she'd be doing it. I was horny before, but that voice mixed with his warm body and touch has clicked the lock of my self-imposed chastity belt wide open. I don't even know what he looks like, but in a way, I don't think I even need to.

"Miss?"

Did he just call me miss? I think I love him already. People usually call me ma'am now that I'm over thirty.

I take in another breath and open my eyes, but part of me wishes I didn't. If I didn't have thick thighs and he wasn't looking at my face, he'd have seen me squeeze my legs together because holy lumbersnack.

Determined hazel eyes stare into mine. They're a mix of blue and green with flecks of golden brown and a dark-brown ring around the iris. The midday sun above us only adds to their power, drawing me in and making me forget my own name and the fact that I'm pressed against a strange man who I'm staring at like a cut of Wagyu beef.

"Do you need me to get you a doctor?" His light-pink lips, framed by a well-trimmed dark-brown, nearly black beard mixed with silver hairs, say the magic words that finally break me from my spell.

"No, no. I'm fine."

He makes no move to pull away, but I don't, either. His hands on my biceps squeeze gently as he studies me with those beautiful eyes of his. My nipples, which, like my vagina, have a mind of their own all of a sudden, harden against what feels like a very muscular chest. Heat rises to my cheeks, and I step back, forcing him to drop his grip.

"You sure?" his velvet voice rumbles.

"Yeah, I'm sorry. I wasn't looking where I was going." I cross my arms over my tank-top-clad chest and look down at the ground. While I'm curvy everywhere else, my chest is small, so I only wore a thin bralette under my shirt. If I leave my hands down, this insanely attractive man will see my headlights.

"It's okay. I wasn't, either. I'm glad you're okay."

He clears his throat with a sound almost like authority. The tone of it has my gaze snapping to his without thinking. His eyes are partially closed now to block out some of the sun, and to avoid looking at the rest of him or falling into a trance staring at his eyes, I focus on his nose. It's a nice nose. The kind of nose you'd take to a plastic surgeon and say, "I want that nose." Is having a nose fetish a thing?

"Miss?"

"Uh, yeah?" My voice comes out in a weird and squeaky tone that has him chuckling.

"Are you sure you're good?"

I dare a glance at his eyes once more but force myself not to look anywhere else. I think I'm going to find every single body part, down to this man's ankles, attractive. At least I've already seen his eyes, right?

"I'm good. Just tired." I don't know why I told him that—I felt like I had to justify my weird behavior, I guess.

The stranger's hazel pools study me, and after a second, it's almost as if he's staring at me with disapproval. I dip my chin to the ground and drop my arms from my chest, hiking my purse up my shoulder and slipping the phone I'd managed to hold on to into the main pocket.

"Sorry I ran into you again," I mutter. "Have a nice day."

I hear a sound slip from his mouth as if he's about to say something, but I don't wait to hear what it is. I walk off, not looking back.

Acknowledgments

I HAVE TO ADMIT, in my dream of dreams I wasn't sure I'd ever see my spicy plus-size babes on bookshelves, but here we are, my first ever traditionally published book in the hands of people all over the world. Isn't that incredible?

When I hit publish on *Axes & O's* in 2024 I had no idea where it would lead. Thank you, first and foremost, to my readers. Thank you for loving Nathan, Fox, and Morgan. Thank you for shouting your love for them to any and everyone who would listen. Without you, I would not be here. Without you, I would not be able to write smutty books with plus-size babes for a living and put this kind of representation on the shelves. Thank you for reading, loving, and sharing my books. I love you!

This was also made possible by my incredible agent Jill Marr, my editor at Forever, Sabrina Flemming, and of course my family, Linda, Randy, and Tanya, and my amazing friends cheering me on and supporting me every step of the way. Thank you for always championing me and my stories.

I would like to thank the people who kept me going and listened to all my voice notes, rants, and general freak-outs every time I write a new book. Nicole Reeves, M.A. Wardell, Victoria Connolly, Bailey Hannah, and Elliott Rose, I love you more than words can say. Thank you for listening to me blab and for helping me come to terms with the appropriate time for two characters to go from looking to touching to fucking.

Thank you to Kristie (IG/TT: @read_between.the_wines)

for your help during our book plotting session. She gets props because she is the one who came up with the primal Christmas tree tradition between Fox and Morgan. So please, be sure to thank her for that brilliant idea. I loved working with you, Kristie, and I'm so appreciative of your help!

Of course, I must give lots of hugs and kisses to my alpha, beta, and sensitivity readers: Matt, Sophie, Brianna B, Alex, Melissa W, Melissa B, Miya, Julie, Erika, Shakeeta, Aimee, Brianna P, and Cassie. Thank you for helping me make sure Morgan, Fox, and Nathan were the best versions of themselves. I truly love this book, and I'm so grateful for you all helping me make it even better and making sure I handled Nathan's biawakening with love and care.

I've got to give a big shoutout to Brenna Jones, my cover artist who saved my behind, Nicole Reeves, my OG indie formatter, and Mason Frey, my indie editor. I could not have done this without all of you!

Lastly, I can't forget some super important people. I want to give a massive thank-you to my Smut Obsessed and Smut VIP Patrons. Your support allows me to keep creating plus-size babes for the world's enjoyment. You're all amazing!

Thank you for reading *Axes & O's*. I can't wait for you to read the next book in the series, *Axe Marks the Spot*, where we follow Nathan's sister Lindsey, and her lumbersnack Dom.

About the Author

Kayla Grosse, author of the inter-
national bestseller *Trick Shot:
A Spicy Christmas Novella* and
a collection of sweet and spicy
plus-size romances, grew up in
a suburb of Madison, Wiscon-
sin. Though she lived near a big
college town, her backyard was a
cornfield, and her favorite hobby
was riding her horse and imagining herself flying through the
fields with a cape on her back and
a sword in her hand. Her overactive imagination led to writing lots of FanFiction, scripts, and publishing several books.
When not writing, Kayla can often be found riding horses
or drinking fancy espresso. She lives in Los Angeles with her
cockatiel, Fiyero, and Quarter Horse, Atlas.

Want more Nathan and his lumbersnacks?
Get bonus chapters, access to NSFW artwork, and safe for
work artwork at: www.patreon.com/kaylagrosse

Find Kayla:
Website: www.kaylagrosse.com
Instagram: @kaylawriteslife
Facebook: Kaylaholics Facebook Group
TikTok: @kaylagrossewriter

RAISING READERS
Books Build Bright Futures

Thank you for reading this book and for being a reader of books in general. We are so grateful to share being part of a community of readers with you, and we hope you will join us in passing our love of books on to the next generation of readers.

Did you know that reading for enjoyment is the single biggest predictor of a child's future happiness and success?

More than family circumstances, parents' educational background, or income, reading impacts a child's future academic performance, emotional well-being, communication skills, economic security, ambition, and happiness.

Studies show that kids reading for enjoyment in the US is in rapid decline:

- In 2012, 53% of 9-year-olds read almost every day. Just 10 years later, in 2022, the number had fallen to 39%.
- In 2012, 27% of 13-year-olds read for fun daily. By 2023, that number was just 14%.

Together, we can commit to **Raising Readers** and change this trend. How?

- Read to children in your life daily.
- Model reading as a fun activity.
- Reduce screen time.
- Start a family, school, or community book club.
- Visit bookstores and libraries regularly.
- Listen to audiobooks.
- Read the book before you see the movie.
- Encourage your child to read aloud to a pet or stuffed animal.
- Give books as gifts.
- Donate books to families and communities in need.

BOB1217

Books build bright futures, and **Raising Readers** is our shared responsibility.

For more information, visit **JoinRaisingReaders.com**

Sources: National Endowment for the Arts, National Assessment of Educational Progress, WorldBookDay.com, Nielsen BookData's 2023 "Understanding the Children's Book Consumer"